The Search for the Villa Melzi Gardens

... and Other Tales of Mystery, Struggle and Redemption

The Search for the Villa Melzi Gardens

... and Other Tales of Mystery, Struggle and Redemption

JANE LAWLESS

Portions of this book have been previously published in *Absolutes!*, *Bellowing Ark*, *Big Muddy*, *Chicago Quarterly Review*, *The Clothesline Review*, *descant*, *Rosebud* and *Zahir*.

Copyright © 2016 Jane Lawless

All rights reserved.

ISBN-10: 1530664608
ISBN-13: 978-1530664603

ACKNOWLEDGMENTS

Where to begin? A writer owes so much to those who support, teach and offer really great critique! My husband, Rick, always my first reader, offers perspicacious advice and unflagging faith in the value of my writing. My writing-practice partner, Edna Wallace, has cajoled and encouraged and laughed with me as we write our best and worst at Jives Coffee Lounge in Old Colorado City.

My colleagues in Chicago's Monadnock Fiction Workshop and Molly Ramanujan of the University of Chicago helped me get started writing short stories. Syed Haider, founder of *Chicago Quarterly Review,* was the first to publish my work. Brian Skinner pulled me into doing summer writing workshops for at-risk and gifted students in Adams County, Wisconsin.

In Colorado, Dina Hollingsworth-Guevara's support and sharp proof-reading eyes have been a great gift! A common passion for winemaking brought Spring Creek Vineyards' Dave and Karin Fuselier into our lives. In return for editing his own delicious murder mysteries, Dave has edited and formatted this collection for publication. Thanks, Dave, for your help and friendship. And thank you, Karin, for your hospitality and for sharing your husband's time so generously!

For my husband, Richard J. Lawless,
and for my mother,
Kathryn Mary Skeen Brock (1914-2010),
who read to me

CONTENTS

The Search for the Villa Melzi Gardens	1
Why I Failed the Superwoman Stress Test	24
Tree Angel	33
Columba Livia	55
The Trespasser	59
Snakes	73
Hospitality	76
All of It	89
Nova	94
The Hunting Season	110
Secrets	128
The Visitor	154
Moon Path	179
Threes	196

THE SEARCH FOR THE VILLA MELZI GARDENS

"YOU WANT TO GO see those gardens?" Sal asks, not looking at me. It's our last day in Bellagio; tomorrow we leave for Venice. We've seen everything except for the famed Giardini di Villa Melzi, which Birnbaum's says we ought not to miss.

This trip was my sister Rose's idea. "Go away for a few weeks," she said. Her daughter Fara was trying to pull out a handful of my hair and the baby wailed in the next room. "Go to Italy, why don't you," she said, getting up to fetch the baby. "How many years of Italian did you take in high school? Three?" She came out of the baby's room unbuttoning her sweater. "Ouch!" she said, as the baby grabbed her breast. "This kid's got teeth like Dracula already." She sat down again, looking at me in a way that I couldn't bear. I put Fara on the floor among her toys. "Look," Rose said, her voice softening. "I don't know what to tell you, Sis. But it just seems to me like if you went someplace different for a while . . ." She shifted the baby's weight on her arm. I looked at her full breast, its golden olive skin and delicate pattern of blue veins. The ache in my belly started up again, but by now it was so familiar that I hardly noticed it.

"Sure," I tell Sal cheerfully, because it is a cheerful morning. The sky is milky blue, the autumn ivy on the courtyard wall glows like red neon, and on top of it against a background of green-black pines, a white cat grooms itself in the sunshine. It is a perfect scene, the kind of scene people come to Italy to see.

We're sitting on the balcony of our hotel room drinking coffee and eating *panetone*. Across the tiny courtyard, we can hear the soloist singing for the mid-morning mass. She has a sweet, melancholy voice that is just barely audible through the walls of the old basilica. If I had known, I'd have gotten up and gone to church just to listen to her. It's been exactly six months since I attended mass. Sal stirs sugar into his coffee and glowers at the hazy sky.

"You know how to get there?" he asks.

"I think so." I try to sound calm. It is my responsibility to find out where things are and how to get to them. It is also my responsibility to deal with desk clerks, waiters and shop attendants, since I speak some Italian and Sal speaks none. It is exhausting work, all this communicating in a foreign language, but then I have a lot to atone for.

We finish our coffee but we cannot finish the *panetone*, the heavy yeast cake stuffed with nuts and dried fruits that is a regional delicacy. The first time I'd seen them in a *pasticceria*, I grabbed Sal's arm and rushed inside to buy one. We took it back to our room, and when I undid the green ribbon and folded back the white paper in which it was wrapped, its fragrance put me instantly into my grandmother's kitchen and the week preceding Christmas, when I and my cousins would go straight from St. Ann's grade school to Noni's. She would line us up at the kitchen table, yelling at us in Italian to sit still, be quiet, mind our manners, and she would serve us coffee heavily diluted with milk and chunks of hot fresh panetone. Nono sat at the head of the table drinking espresso and smoking a cigarette that he held in a bobby pin while opera records played. His favorite was *Pagliacci*, and sometimes he sang the tragic tenor arias along with Benjamino Gigli. Nono had been a stonecutter in Italy. Then he laid bricks in Manhattan, except for one six-year period when he practiced his old trade on the Cathedral of St. John the Divine.

After Sal and I got married, Noni shocked me one day when she told me, her cheeks hectic and flushed, that during those years, Nono had been like a young man again, and she was afraid she would end up with a change-of-life baby.

Now, wrapping the leftover panetone, I look at Sal's unreadable face and think of my grandparents' long marriage and the little renaissance of passion that warmed their middle years. I put my hand on Sal's arm and move toward him. He embraces me briefly, kisses my hair. We go through the drill of checking our pockets: passports, money, keys; then we're off.

Our *pensione* is at the top of a narrow serpentine street next to the church piazza; all the waterfront hotels are closed for the season. We have to follow a street that runs perpendicular to ours that leads to another piazza where I have seen the sign about the Giardini di Villa Melzi. It's a pretty street, full of little *botegas* and balconies hung with autumn flowers. It is also a very old street, and the buildings in it are old, and I often wonder what it's like to live in a place that has been inhabited for hundreds of years. I wonder if the apartments are imbued with those other lives, if the dead ever instruct the living.

There aren't many people on the street this morning, only a few churchgoers. The shops are shuttered and dark like faces with closed eyes. As we walk, the bell in the basilica begins to toll. It has a deep, resonant voice, full of dignity and pathos.

We come to a place where the street widens, and Sal tugs on my hand to stop. He does this often. European construction fascinates him, especially the ancient structures, their quality and design. He is a building contractor by profession, and his chief frustration in his work is his inability to express his own standards of perfection: materials and labor are too costly, and no one wants to pay the price anymore. So we pause frequently in our wanderings as Sal points out the joining of roofs, the placement of joists and beams, the patina of old wood, the intricate patterns of cast bronze hinges and iron doorplates, chiseled messages in stone lintels. He turns slowly, taking in everything, and I turn with him, trying to see through his eyes.

"What's that?" he asks at last. He stares at a building we've passed several times but never paid attention to. Looking at it now, I see why. It's a modern building, red brick, square and squat and institutional-looking. On the roof is a cross, below that a white-lettered sign. Sal pronounces the words awkwardly. "*Asilo D'Infantile*. What does that mean?"

"*Asilo*—asylum. *Infantile*—babies, children. An orphanage."

We cross over to the high iron fence separating the courtyard from the street. The paving stones of the courtyard are littered with dry leaves, and in the flower bed that runs along the perimeter, the last roses of the season are dropping their petals. Sal stands with his hands in his back pockets, staring through the fence. I try not to notice. He does this a lot the last few months, but he will never tell me what he's thinking. I shift my gaze and walk along the fence. Near the gate, I see one last magnificent rose, about half open, growing at the top of a long stem. Its color is golden pink, like a sunset sky, its petals flawlessly formed, curling away from the tiny closed fist of its center where some final secret waits to be revealed.

I reach through the fence and pull the rose toward me, but I can't bring it close enough to smell. Just as I am about to release it, a door opens and a nun steps into the courtyard. I open my hand and the rose arcs back. A thorn grazes my thumb. I watch the rose dance prettily on its stem and I imagine what the nun sees: a tourist stealing flowers through the fence.

"Signora! Signora!" she calls. I can feel the heat flood my face, and I try to think of the proper words to explain that I wanted only to smell the rose, not steal it. A scarlet drop swells on my thumb. I turn to face the nun.

She hurries toward the fence, her veil flying out behind her like the white wings of a gull. I see immediately from the stiff movement of her limbs that she is an old woman, and I am about to brace myself for a scolding when she suddenly smiles at me. I smile back. I have not been misunderstood after all.

"Buon giorno," I call out as she approaches the edge of the rose bed. Sal moves up beside me.

"Buon giorno, Signora, Signore!" She turns her smile on Sal. Her teeth are bad and she wears thick spectacles that make her eyes look huge and owlish. Over her habit is a gray sweater that is too big for her. The cuffs are frayed and it looks as though it has been chewed by moths. It strikes me suddenly that the vow of poverty is very real for this nun. I wonder if her teeth hurt.

She is still smiling as she begins twisting the stem of the rose. I protest. *"Sorella, no, per favore!"* I protest. But it is too late; she reaches into the folds of her habit and produces a small pair of pruning shears. She cuts the rose off cleanly and starts to hand it through the fence, then hesitates. She's speaking in a soft voice, but it is a dialect of Italian that I don't understand.

"What's she doing?" Sal asks.

"I don't know."

She takes the rose between her fingers at the base of the blossom and brings it close to her eyes. Her face with its bad teeth and thick glasses is drawn into a frown of intense concentration. Carefully, she snips off the thorns, one after the other, working toward the bottom of the stem. When she has finished, she brings the flower to her nose. She closes her eyes and breathes deeply. Then she looks up, smiling again, and presents the rose to me through the bars of the fence.

I smell the rose and its perfume is an autumn fragrance, dark and rich, full of the sweetness of dissolution. *"Bellisima,"* I tell her. *"Grazie."* I pull a paper hanky out of my pocket and wrap it around the stem.

Just then the double front doors of the orphanage swing open and twenty or thirty children erupt into the courtyard, shouting and laughing. The nun gives us a wave of her hand and turns toward the children. A small boy flings his arms around her legs and she bends to stroke his hair. I'm filled with the giddy joy of serendipity and I look up at Sal, but the expression on his face as he sees the children kills my words before I can speak.

"Come on," he says, taking my arm, and we walk up the street, past the end of the fence, back into the narrow lane of shuttered *botegas*.

It's not as though we haven't talked about it. In fact, all we did for the first three months was talk. On the day I left the hospital, my doctor said to us, "I think you two should get some counseling." He handed Sal a card with a name and phone number. "This guy is very good," he said. "He works with a lot of couples in your situation." So we made an appointment, and for three months we talked about how long we had waited for children, how we'd given up and resigned ourselves to childlessness, how I'd eventually gotten pregnant, how labor finally had to be induced early because of fetal cardiac stress, how our little boy lived less than a day. And then we talked about grief and anger until I refused to go anymore, because I simply don't believe all those clichés about the resilience of human relationships. Some knowledge is too heavy for the fragile structure of a marriage; some truths have to be borne, for the rest of one's life, alone.

So we walk along in silence, Sal and I, arms linked deceptively. We've grown patient with our pain. We go through our days trying to be kind to one another, like satellites circling the cold brilliant point of a distant star, waiting to be drawn into the gravity of a nearer orbit. I clutch the rose in my hand, I bring it to my nose again to smell its sweetness, and Sal puts his arm around my shoulders. We stop; he smells the rose.

"It's nice," he says. "That was a nice thing for the sister to do. There are still kind people in the world." He blinks hard a couple of times and looks around, as though emerging from sleep. "Where are we?" he asks.

We've missed a turn somewhere. "I don't know. Shall we turn back?"

"No, let's go that way." Sal points to another street branching off from the one we're on. It seems vaguely to be in the right direction. We pass a cinema and stop to look at the posters, Arnold Schwarzenegger as *The Terminator,* dubbed in Italian. Sal asks, only half-jokingly, if I'd like to go later tonight to see it.

I think of the previous week when we were driving through the mountains. We'd been marooned in a small, isolated hotel by a freak blizzard, and had spent an entire afternoon watching *Gone with the Wind* broadcast from Munich on the TV in the bar. Hearing Scarlet, Mammy, Rhett, Ashley and Melanie speaking their lines in harsh German gutturals had struck us both as hilarious, but we hadn't dared show it.

We weren't relaxed travelers, Sal and I. We had watched other Americans totally at ease summoning waiters in sidewalk cafes, strolling through the markets and cathedrals, all of them looking prosperous and confident and unworried.

They were expensively dressed; they emerged from expensive hotels, expensive shops, expensive restaurants. After the first few days in Europe, Sal and I looked for cheap restaurants and unobtrusive hotels, telling ourselves that the food and atmosphere were more authentic, which was true. But the deeper truth is that we are the daughter and son of a bricklayer and a landscaper. So we sat watching *Gone with the Wind* in silence among the other stranded travelers, mostly Italians and Swiss. We drank our Campari and soda and bit our lips, ashamed of our amusement, knowing what it indicated about us.

I look at Arnold Schwarzenegger again, the shining biceps, the wraparound sunglasses that give him the look of a carnivorous insect. "No," I tell Sal, "I don't want to see it."

Sal starts to say something, then stops himself. We begin to walk again, and the street becomes an avenue of chestnut and persimmon trees. The persimmons are ripe, big and brilliant as oranges, glowing like jewels among the deep greenery of the branches.

"Where the hell are we?" Sal says suddenly, and the edge in his voice makes me flinch. It's a new sound, this tone of his, and I never know when it's coming.

Sal and I were married a year after I got out of high

school. We were going to wait until he graduated from college but he quit after his second year because he was doing so well at his remodeling business. He started working with his Uncle Rocco right after high school to earn college tuition. His goal was a degree in chemistry. He made good money that summer, and the next summer he did better.

Uncle Rocco started referring people to him to build screened porches, garages, then additions. At the end of the third summer, when the new term was about to begin, he said to me one night, "I can't start classes. I've got too much work. I'll go back in January."

When December arrived, he was involved in a renovation project, an old Victorian on the Upper East Side. He hired Nono to redo the fireplaces, which meant matching marble and searching out antique tile; his Uncle Vinnie hand-carved rope-twisted balusters to replace the ones that were missing from the staircases; the plumbing and electrical went to my cousins. Between our families, we had nearly all the craftsmen necessary to complete the restoration. "I'm making good money at this, and I like it," he said just before Christmas. "Maybe I'll go back some day and get my degree, but not now. Let's get married."

Everyone in both families agreed—everyone except my cousin, Theresa. Theresa and I were the same age, had grown up across the street from one another, gone to the same schools. From childhood we were inseparable. She was valedictorian of our graduating class, a straight-A student, so focused and single-minded that she frightened her parents. Without a moment's hesitation, she cancelled her date for the senior prom to take advantage of a free ride to Harvard to check out their astronomy department. She was home from Harvard on Christmas break when I told her the news. "He's dropping out?" she said, as though I'd announced that Sal stole from the elderly.

"He's good at what he's doing," I said. "He can make better money renovating old houses than he can teaching chemistry."

Theresa cut me off. "That's the trouble, don't you see? The attitude that the only purpose of education is to make money. The goddamned Guinea mentality! That's the difference between us and the Jews. That's why they're running the country and all we're running is the Mafia!"

Theresa and I had planned our weddings from childhood—we would be one another's maid or matron of honor. Now Theresa said, "I'm never getting married. I'm not going to waste my life washing socks and making manicotti on Sunday for some guy whose greatest aspiration is to own a flat-screen TV and grow tomatoes in the back yard."

Rose stood up for me. Theresa came to the wedding, though. She brought her new boyfriend, a graduate student named Steve Rabinowitz who had wild black hair and a beard. He was a poet; they were both heavily involved in left-wing politics. I had the feeling that Theresa was showing us off to him, as though we were zoo animals, amusing perhaps, but an inferior species.

"I thought you knew how to get there," Sal says.

"I asked you back at the movie theater if you wanted to turn back." My voice is tightly controlled. It amazes me, how close to the surface my anger is these days. I hold it in because I am so afraid of a scene. "Please, Sal," I say, aware that I'm begging. "Please, let's not fight. I thought I knew the way. I guess I don't, I'm sorry. Let's go back to the hotel."

Sal stands apart from me, his hands jammed in his

pockets again, his shoulders rigid. After a moment or so, he looks at me. "No," he says. "Let's just keep walking. The town's not that big. We'll run across it sooner or later. C'mon, don't be upset." He takes my hand. "Let's walk."

On our right, beyond the high wall that borders the street, the land rises in a hill. There is a break in the wall; a narrower street—so steep that it is all steps—winds up the hill, also walled on both sides. These ever-present walls fill me with frustration. I want to see behind them, but doors and gates remain invariably closed, houses shuttered at sunset so that traveling through Italian towns at night, one would think they were deserted: not even light escapes the shutters.

Earlier in our trip, we drove one evening through the wine-growing country in the north. The grape harvest was on and everywhere farmers were hauling huge flatbed wagons full of grapes. For a while, we had crept along behind one such wagon; the road was too narrow to pass. We had come finally into a little village. It was high-walled and dark, not even a street lamp was lit, and I had been aware suddenly of an eerie sense of expectancy. The air was hazy and sweet with the smoke of wood fires. Except for the clatter of the tractor pulling the wagon, I would have thought we'd stepped into another century. When Sal reached over to take my hand, I knew he felt it too. At last the wagon slowed to a stop. Sal drummed his fingers impatiently on the steering wheel. Suddenly the blackness on our right blazed with light; a big double gate in the wall swung open as though a curtain were being raised in a theater. "Oh, Sal, look!"

Inside the gate was a huge courtyard frantic with light and activity. Men and women were unloading tubs of grapes from another wagon; I could see horses, dogs, children, agricultural equipment, a golden cascade of hay spilling from a loft. Slowly, the wagon turned and entered the courtyard. There were shouts and laughter. It was an old village, laid out in the medieval pattern, and every feature of the courtyard bore the unmistakable stamp of centuries. As we watched, a woman began pushing the gate shut behind the wagon. Sal eased the car into gear and we edged forward, so that I was only a yard or so away from her as we passed.

For a moment our eyes met, and I felt a small shock of what I later realized was recognition. She was about my age and she had my coloring: black hair and eyes and fair skin. She wore a kerchief over her head, a shapeless dress and work boots. Despite the coolness of the evening, her sleeves were rolled high, and her forearms were black with grape juice. She paused, her hand on the gate; a man was pushing the other half closed, coming quickly up behind her. Her gaze was calm, direct. *"Buona sera,"* I said as our car slid past. She gave me a little wave. *"'Sera,"* she replied. I turned to wave at her and she stepped back into the courtyard silhouetted against the light as the gate closed.

"They must work eighteen hours a day this time of year," Sal said as we drove again through the open countryside.

"Yes, I suppose so."

"Don't grapes have to be picked between frost and the first hard freeze?"

"I'm not sure."

I thought of the woman, her straight back, the tilt of her head, the self-contained way she had looked into my eyes. Was this how people were when they worked the same land, lived in the same village, among the same neighbors, century after century? I asked Sal what he thought.

"I don't know," he said after a while. "I wonder what it's like?"

The next morning over coffee, looking at the map, I realized that we were only fifty or so kilometers from Noni's home town, Santa Lucia. There had been intermittent correspondence with some elderly spinster cousins up until my childhood, but it had stopped. I had gone to Noni's house after school one day and found her sitting under the grape arbor, weeping. In her lap was an odd yellowish envelope filled with strange stamps. The letter, hand-written in Italian, was as indecipherable to me as Martian. *"A tutti partito,"* Noni had said, shaking her head. Tears slid down her cheeks. *All gone now.*

Sal asked if I wanted to drive to Santa Lucia and take pictures. Perhaps if Noni were still alive I'd have said yes. I thought of the woman from the night before, how she had stood framed in the light from the courtyard, how the gate had swung shut, leaving the street featureless and empty. "No," I said. "What would be the point?"

We turn up the street that is all steps. It's a fairly steep climb, and midway we stop to rest on a stone bench. The wall, ancient and crumbling, looks like every other wall I have seen in Italy, as though they all were rendered from a single source. Tiny plants sprout from the chinks between the stones, a dozen kinds of moss and lichen grow in scaly patches of green, brown and silver. I see that the little plants have flowers and I think about how tenacious life is, and how fragile, and it fills me with rage, this constant return in my thinking to death and failure. I used to wait for it to go away, but now I know that it will not.

Thinking about this now, my mouth goes dry, and I slip my arm through Sal's. He's staring at the wall too, and I can read his mind. His thoughts are the same as mine, but they do not draw us closer together. They are a wedge driven between us, and this is the particular refinement of our torture, that we are encapsulated separately so that even my arm through his is meaningless. And everything beautiful, even the mosses and the tiny pink-and-mauve flowers, the sunlight on the pine trees, shrivels and blackens with the virus of our misery.

When we got back from our honeymoon and settled into our apartment, I took a job in my cousin's plumbing shop. I did the bookkeeping, scheduled service calls and answered the phone. It was boring, it didn't pay much, but it was only temporary, until I got pregnant. Sal and I both wanted children. I have half a dozen siblings, but Sal was an only child in an extended family where four children were considered a small family. Cousins, he said, did not make up for the lack of brothers and sisters. We wanted at least three kids.

When six months passed and I still wasn't pregnant, I spoke to my mother. She put her arm around my shoulder and laughed. "Relax," she counseled. "Later on, you'll be glad you had this time together. After the babies start coming, marriage is different."

Every month when I got my period I could see the dismay in Sal's eyes. He tried not to show it, but I knew he was worried. I went to see a doctor. "There's nothing wrong with you," he said. "Send your husband in." When I finally worked up the courage to speak to Sal, he surprised me.

"Sure," he said. "I've been thinking about it. If there's nothing wrong with you, that leaves only one person, right?" He went for the tests. Then we both sat in the doctor's office. He was an older man with a Jewish name, Greenspahn or Greenstein, and he had so many Italian patients, he had even picked up a little Italian.

"You kids," he began, shaking his head across his desk from us. "Let me tell you first off, there is nothing physiologically wrong with either one of you. You are both healthy and fertile."

"Then why—"

He cut Sal off with a wave of his hand. "Young man, I'm speaking to you like you're my own son. Hear me out." He looked first at Sal and then at me, and his eyes were kind. "You're in too much of a hurry. Parenthood is not a race. This is not medieval Europe that you have to secure the succession by providing an heir as soon as possible. Tell me, does either set of parents have any grandchildren yet?"

We shook our heads.

"See?" he said triumphantly. "You're under pressure, either by the family or by yourselves. The body knows when lovers are tense. Stop trying so hard. Relax, enjoy your life together, because after you have children, things will be different."

"That's what my mother said," I told him.

"So listen to your mother; she's a wise woman. You are both very young, with a long reproductive life ahead of you. Take advantage of your freedom now, do some traveling, stay out late. Then when you have responsibilities down the road, you won't be full of resentment."

We left the office feeling giddy, more carefree than we had in months. We went out for dinner and drank a bottle of champagne, then went home and made love on the living room floor. We promised each other we'd stop focusing on me getting pregnant and enjoy our life together. We bought a house and I quit the plumbing shop and worked with Sal on the renovation. It was a big house, with plenty of room for kids.

Sal gives my arm a squeeze. "Do you want to move on?"

I stand. "Let's see what's at the top of this hill," I say.

We start climbing again, and the wall becomes lower. We can see over it into a pretty tree-dotted meadow where a dozen or so sheep are grazing. We stop to admire them. There are two lambs among them, impossibly white, and when they see us watching, they begin to run, their long ears flopping, their slender legs stiffening with each leap so that they bounce like spring toys. They hide behind a big ewe and peep at us shyly from behind her flanks. Sal laughs, and I look up at him, surprised and grateful that something can give him pleasure. For an instant, like a flash of sun between racing clouds, I think perhaps there can be an end to this.

"I'm going to take their picture," Sal says. He slides the camera bag off his shoulder and stoops down to unzip it. I look hard at the top of his head, as though staring will reveal his thoughts. His hair, once black, is shot with silver, more than there ought to be for a man his age. I want to reach out and run my fingers in it, push it away from his face, kneel next to him and put my arms around him.

He looks up suddenly, feeling my eyes on him, I suppose. "Are you all right?" he asks.

"Sure," I say. I want to scream.

I watch Sal set up his shot. He runs up a few steps, and the lambs oblige by strolling away from the ewe and eyeing us coquettishly over their shoulders. The shutter clicks once, twice, three times. I study the pink-and-mauve flowers in the wall. Their stems end in roots no more substantial than strands of hair. The roots seem to disappear into the wall. What is the source of their nourishment?

It took us two years to finish the house. I taught myself to sew and buried myself in mountains of fabric. I made curtains and drapes, slipcovers, pillow shams, dust ruffles, napkins and placemats. Then I started on Sal. I took tailoring classes and made his shirts and pants. I got to be really good at it. "Why don't you make something for yourself?" Sal asked. I shrugged. I couldn't answer. Going through the pattern books in the fabric stores, I would inevitably come to the back where the children's and babies' things were. I stared at photos of christening robes and ran my hands through French lace and white Irish linen and cotton batiste fine as chiffon. I priced seed pearls and calculated yardage and cost.

Then Rose got pregnant. My parents were delirious. *Good*, I thought, sitting in the upstairs bathroom and holding a cold washcloth to my eyes so Sal wouldn't know I'd been crying. Now maybe everybody would stop looking at me with that perpetual question in their eyes. I bought the pattern for the christening robe and the lace and linen and batiste, the seed pearls. I told myself this would be my practice run, I'd make all my mistakes on this first one, and for my own babies, the sewing would be perfect.

We were asked to be godparents, and the pictures of us standing with Father Cappelletti on the steps of St. Catherine of Siena, the baby dressed in his stunning christening robe—an heirloom, all the relatives said—show two radiantly attractive and happy people. Holding our godchild for the camera, we were pretending, both of us, although we never spoke of it. Later, looking at the pictures, I felt ashamed.

We went to see a Manhattan specialist, very expensive, and this time the news was definitive. It was possible that I could get pregnant at some time, but not likely with my condition, maybe a chance in a thousand. We should think about starting adoption proceedings at once. We were referred to an agency, given a card with an address and phone number. Outside in the gathering twilight of Park Avenue, a woman in a lynx coat pushed a pram past us. Inside was a mound of pink blankets. Sal crumpled the piece of paper and dropped it into the gutter.

All the way home, we neither spoke nor touched. I sat immobile as a statue next to Sal, the chill of irredeemable guilt seeping into my muscles like some poison I had drunk. I felt as though I were turning to stone. When we got home, I sat down in the living room in the dark without removing my coat. On the periphery of my consciousness I was aware of Sal moving around the kitchen. Later, a few minutes, maybe an hour, he came into the living room. "Come on," he said. "I've made coffee. Take your coat off and come in and sit down with me." He bent and took my hands.

"What are we going to do?" I asked miserably.

Sal stood motionless, still holding my hands, then slowly he knelt in front of me. The light from the kitchen struck his face. "I don't know," he answered. "I guess we'll live with it. A lot of people aren't able to have kids. We'll be the world's best aunt and uncle. All the kids will come to us for advice. We'll help them grow up." Then he dropped his face into my lap and wept.

At the top of the street of steps, we find ourselves on the edge of open fields. A dog—a collie mix—barks loudly and charges at us, stopping only at the low wall that separates us. He could easily jump the wall, but he has made his point. He turns, head high, and races back toward a distant farmhouse. Sal and I laugh. There is a breeze up here, the sky is blue, punctuated by big white cumulus clouds, and I see that the sun has dropped several degrees from when we left our hotel. We are completely lost.

"Let's go this way," Sal says as we reach a fork in the path. In that direction lie tiled rooftops and trees, the way back into the town.

We adopted a dog. Not a puppy, that would have been too much. We went to the Humane Society and found a mixed-breed that looked like a cross between a German shepherd and a golden retriever. No one was going to take her because she was older and had a bad hip. When we walked past her kennel, she didn't even raise her head to check us out the way the other dogs did. She just followed us with her eyes, which were full of despair.

"What's the story on that one?" Sal asked the attendant, a kid with a name tag that said JOAQUIN. He'd told us he worked there part time while he was taking classes at City College.

"Somebody dumped her on the Rockaway Freeway. She hadn't been very well treated."

"I can see that."

"She's real sweet, though. Just depressed." He opened the cage. "It's OK, Sweetie," he said to the dog, then to me, "Sweetie, that's what we call her. We're not supposed to name 'em or get attached, but sometimes you can't help it. I'd take her home myself but my landlady won't allow dogs, just cats. I've already got three of those. I bring home another one, she's gonna throw us all out on the street."

I stepped up to the kennel. "Hi, Sweetie," I said. Cautiously, I let her smell my hands, then I stroked her head. She looked into my eyes, thumped her tail one time. She stretched out her neck and licked my fingers, thumped her tail again, then slowly got to her feet. She let me scratch her ears and I could feel her resisting, then giving into pleasure. I looked at Sal, then back at Sweetie. "How would you like to come home with us?" I asked.

Sweetie's hip got better with good nutrition and veterinary care, and on weekends when the weather was decent, we took her to Cunningham Park. When we'd had her for about four months, we went upstate for a wedding and decided to make a weekend of it. My brother Johnny came to feed and walk her twice a day. He called us on Sunday morning. "She won't eat," he said, "and she just lays in her doggie bed. I don't know if she's sick or what. You better come home."

When we walked in the door three hours later, Sweetie had that same look that we'd seen at the Humane Society. But when she saw us, she went wild with excitement. We hugged her and petted her and she ate and then we took her for a walk. She wouldn't let us out of her sight for the rest of the day, and when we had to go to work on Monday morning, she required lots of reassurance.

Sweetie was eventually joined by two cats. They were rescues too. So we became a little family, Sal and I and Sweetie and Rio and Loki. We spoiled our nieces and nephews. I opened a sewing shop and gave specialty classes in window treatments, lingerie, baby clothes, men's tailoring. Sal's business expanded and he hired more men.

Then one month my period was late. I refused to even hope that I could be pregnant because it had been such an incredibly stressful year: Sal learned that his oldest friend and most trusted foreman had been stealing from the company for two years, his father suffered a crippling heart attack, and my mother was diagnosed with ovarian cancer. Then my cousin Theresa, now a professor of astronomy at New Mexico State University with a particular expertise in hydrogen accretion in spiral galaxies, broke her spine in a skiing accident that left her a paraplegic. Steve Rabinowitz, who had been her lover since undergraduate school, left her, and Theresa descended into such a profound depression that she had to take a leave of absence from her job.

I started waking up each morning sick with dread, but when I didn't get my period for a second month, I became alarmed. All I could think about was cancer. I made an appointment with my doctor, and when she told me I was three months pregnant, I couldn't believe what I'd heard. I kept saying, "What? I don't understand. What's wrong with me?" Finally, she burst out laughing and grabbed both my hands. She said slowly, "You. Are. Pregnant. P-R-E-G-N-A-N-T. As in you're going to have a baby in about six months." I stared at her for a few seconds and then we both began to cry. Finally, she said, "I don't want you driving home alone. Call your husband and tell him to pick you up right away. I want to see you in another month, but I'm going to call you tomorrow because we have to discuss your prenatal care."

The next four months were the happiest time in my life and in our marriage. The joy that our news brought to our families after such a prolonged period of illness, fear and heartache was incalculable, and I blossomed like a bed of spring tulips. Sal and I made a nursery of the bedroom next to ours. My favorite feature was a border around the middle of the walls with elephants, giraffes, lions and zebras smiling and cavorting over a pastel savannah. There was a baby shower, and I began to design and sew the christening robe that I'd not dared think about for so many years. Each evening, Sal would lay his head against my belly and listen for the baby's heartbeat.

In my seventh month, when I went in for my regular examination, I saw a faint frown on the doctor's brow. "It's probably nothing," she said, trying to sound unconcerned, "but I'd like you to check into the hospital for some tests."

"What?" I demanded. "What kind of tests?"

That was last spring. Now it's autumn and we are in Italy. I'm walking through a strange city with a husband I no longer know, looking for a vast formal garden recommended by the guide books, carrying a wilting rose given to me by a nun who spends her days teaching and caring for orphans. We come to a turn in the street and suddenly there it is: a high wrought-iron gate and a sign: GIARDINI DI VILLA MELZI . I suck in my breath. Beyond the gate are gorgeous vistas. I see trees in autumn finery, carefully tended beds of glowing flowers in every imaginable color, classical statuary, paths disappearing among splashing fountains and vine-hung gazebos, a lichen-covered stone bench, and through the trees and shrubs, a glimpse of Lake Como, deep indigo in the late afternoon light. Sal and I look at each other in disbelief. Quickly we approach the gate and push it open. We are just standing there, looking around, figuring out which of several paths to begin walking, when a uniformed man appears. He is middle aged, with a narrow mustache and receding hairline. *"Signora, Signore,"* he says, sounding genuinely regretful, "I am so sorry, but the gardens are closed for the day. Please come back tomorrow."

There is nothing to be done but turn around and go back out into the street. The uniformed man closes the gate behind us. I look at Sal, and I see that he is worn out in a way that I never saw until now. "Why?" he says softly, his eyes exhausted. "Why is everything always closed to us?"

I take Sal's hand and we start walking back toward our *pensione.* We climb the stairs to our room at the top of the serpentine street, and as soon as I close the door behind us, I drop the wilted rose in a wastepaper can. Sal sits on the bed, his face blank and distant. I kneel on the floor in front of him and remove his shoes. I push him gently down onto the mattress and pull a blanket around us and hold him in my arms. Dusk begins to gather. On the street, shops and restaurants open for the evening's business. I hear people coming home from work, doing their marketing, filling up sidewalk tables and conversing over glasses of wine.

I close my eyes and remember the nun in the tattered sweater, the way her smile transformed her homely face as she handed me the rose through the fence. I sit up in bed. *I will not accept this,* I tell myself. I get up, retrieve the wilted rose from the trash, fill a glass with water and place it on the bedside table. Then I trim the stem of the rose and chew it until it becomes pulpy, able to absorb water. In the morning, its petals will be fresh and plump, and its fragrance will fill the world.

WHY I FAILED THE SUPERWOMAN STRESS TEST

for Barbara Merchant

AS SOON AS I GOT HOME from the supermarket and put my ice cream away, I sat down with *The Star* and took the "Are You Trying to be Superwoman?" stress test. You know the kind I mean: there are ten questions, and you're supposed to answer *Always*, *Sometimes* or *Never*. Well, my score indicated that I was on the brink of psychological meltdown from trying to be supersister, superaunt, superadmin—in short, super everything to everybody.

I had originally picked up *The Star* to read about this high-school boy in Tennessee who killed himself as a result of taking steroids. Well, I don't care what Mark McGwire and Sammy Sosa told that congressional committee a few years back, I think all those athletes are using the stuff and that it does terrible things to their bodies, not the least of which is to make them crazy, impotent and homicidal.

I threw the paper down in front of my nephew, the baseball star. He wants to go to one of those sports doctors who administers performance-enhancing drugs in so-called safe doses. "See that?" I jabbed a finger at the front-page picture of the dead boy. Ronnie was drinking his third glass of milk along with a second turkey sandwich. Ronnie always stops by my house after school, and I'm grateful for it. I never have to throw away leftovers. Ronnie drained the glass, wiped his mouth with the back of his hand, made a wild-animal sound in the back of his throat that these days passes for "Yes," and went to the refrigerator. He pulled out half a pan of rice pudding and rummaged in the drawer next to the sink for a spoon. Ronnie is sixteen.

"See that?" I repeated as Ronnie straddled a kitchen chair. "You start taking that stuff and look what happens—first, your testicles shrink away to nothing and the next thing, you're dead."

Ronnie turned bright red. "Jeez, Aunt Jewel, cut it out."

"It's time you woke up." I'm relentless. I can say things to Ronnie his mother never could. His mother is my sister Shirley, and Ronnie's father fell onto the elevated train tracks in Chicago five years ago and got himself electrocuted. I'd never tell it to Shirley, but good riddance to bad rubbish is what I say. He was drunk when he fell, and more than likely on his way home to give Shirley another black eye. If he hadn't got himself electrocuted, I'd have probably busted his legs with a baseball bat, which is what I told him the last time he hit Shirley. I'd have done it too, and I'd be in jail right now for it because that's the way I am. I was so worried over my family and my job and every other thing in my life that I was worn to a frazzle, which is why I failed the Superwoman Stress Test.

"Look here," I said to Ronnie. He was scraping at the

sides of the pan where the custard and cinnamon had crusted, the best part of rice pudding, in my opinion. "I want you to stay away from those steroids. You kids think you're immortal, that you can do anything you want because your bodies have never failed you yet." Ronnie has the physique of a young god. He can run for miles and never even breathe hard. He's never sick, there's not so much as a zit on that smooth white face of his, and worst of all, he can eat like a herd of African elephants and never gain a single ounce—another reason I've decided that God is a man.

"I don't have a choice," Ronnie said with sudden passion. "If I want to go to the major leagues, I have to. Everybody's doing it."

"That's no reason for you to."

"Yes, it is. You don't understand. Doping gives you an edge, makes you better than your best. And to get into the major leagues I have to be *best* of the best."

"Is it worth your life?" I demanded.

Ronnie stood up from the table suddenly, knocking over his chair. "Yes, dammit, it is! It's worth everything. It's the only chance I got. I'm no good at anything else. I ain't smart like Bill and I ain't gonna marry some rich doctor like Kathy did." He righted the chair, snatched up his letter jacket and lunged for the door.

"Wait!" I called. I went after him and caught his shoulder. When he turned to face me, I was ashamed to see tears in his eyes. Ashamed of myself, not Ronnie. I'd forgotten how it was to want something so badly you were willing to die for it. "I'm sorry," I said. "I guess there is a lot I don't understand. I just don't want anything awful happening to you, hear? You're like my own."

"I know, Aunt Jewel." He gave me a rough hug and

bounded off down the back steps. I stood in front of the screen door for a long time, watching the wind tug the red and yellow leaves off my trees—trees Kyle and I planted together in 2002. Well, Kyle is gone now. His kidneys went out on him seven years ago come December, and that was that. I still miss him every day of my life, but Lord, I'm barely forty and I'll live into my nineties the same way my crazy old aunts and grandma have done.

    I stood there in front of the door watching the leaves and crying. I thought, there has got to be more to life than worrying about Ronnie and Kathy and Bill and Shirley, and going to my job at the aluminum can factory every damn day of my life except Saturday and Sunday and always feeling that there's never enough of me to go around. I was going to have to make a change—something more substantial than an Autumn Moonlight rinse over at The Powder Puff Beauty Salon or a January cruise to the Virgin Islands, both of which I'd tried.

    I thought of my friend, Carlene. She had her kids young and underwent a hysterectomy at thirty-seven. Then she had some kind of nervous breakdown. She went to the psychiatric hospital over in Carbondale for six weeks. I can't say whether it helped or not and neither can she.

    Anyway, she finally took up crafts, and it made her a different person. She started classes at the community center, then scoured the stores for yarn and fabric remnants and got all her friends saving up margarine tubs and baby-food jars. Pretty soon she was turning out the cutest things you ever saw: Christmas stuff like Santa Claus faces with curly white beards and laughing eyes to hang on your front door, and braided wreaths all done up with holly and silver bells and tiny packages tied with gold thread. She made quilted albums and picture frames trimmed with lace and satin ribbon, decoupage jewelry boxes, little bitty crocheted baby clothes with flowers and birds appliquéd down the front. Her double-wedding-ring quilt won first prize up at the state fair in Springfield last year. And she's making money at it too, selling this stuff at church bazaars and on consignment at Sally's Bridal Shoppe and The Powder Puff and places like that. I saw her at Kroger's just yesterday and she told me she's got enough saved from her crafts to take her and Willard for a Las Vegas weekend.

But crafts aren't for me. About the only thing I can do with my hands is work my flower beds. By God, I can make things grow. I've got azaleas in the front yard that make you dizzy to look at in the spring. My tulips are the biggest and prettiest in Williamson County. Growing flowers is my greatest pleasure in life. I was studying that idea, still standing there at the door, when it hit me like a lightning strike. "Well, I'll swan," I said to myself out loud, standing right there at my back door looking at the light fade in the yard. I wiped my eyes on my apron, closed the door and went directly to the telephone to call my cousin Arthur.

Arthur sat across the kitchen table from me, his big, permanently dirt-encrusted hands holding one of my English bone-china teacups with a delicacy that would surprise you. For all his size, Arthur is a graceful man. When you see him at the VFW dances waltzing or doing the Watusi, you forget that he weighs two-fifty and digs graves for a living.

"You what?" he said to me now. On his head was his green-and-white John Deere cap which I swear he hasn't taken off since he came home from the Persian Gulf. He was smoking a menthol cigarette and he looked at me as though some alien life form had just crawled out of my hair.

"I said," I said slowly and precisely, "I want you to get

me a job at the cemetery."

Arthur's cup began to rattle against the saucer. "The can factory's closin'!" he burst out finally. "Great God A'mighty, Jewel, that's the end of this town—"

"The can factory is *not* closing," I interrupted. "Now calm yourself, Arthur. I just want to make a change, that's all."

"You got a good job," Arthur said in a tone that let me know he was personally offended. "You know how many women would want your job?"

"They can have it."

"You work for the president of the company, you got a benefit package and a pension and you get to travel."

"Weekends in Muncie, Indiana, inspecting the latest in aluminum-can-stamping technology and fending off the inflated libidos of equipment salesmen with their wedding rings in their pockets are hardly my idea of high romance. My boss has hemorrhoids, a schizophrenic daughter, both a wife *and* a girlfriend who sound *exactly* alike on the telephone and a nasty habit of picking at his ears. If you want to talk about job stress, Arthur, I invite you to follow me around for a week."

Arthur stared down at this teacup. I could see his bald spot through the mesh in the crown of his cap. If I'd told Arthur once, I'd told him a hundred times that wearing your hat in the house will make your hair fall out. Everybody knows that. "There ain't no women at the graveyard," he said, sullen as storm clouds.

"This is the twenty-first century and women's rights are here to stay. There's got to be a first time for everything. *You* wouldn't be prejudiced against working with a woman, would you?" I had him there. Arthur is the world's worst sexist pig. He's not a bad person—it's the way we were raised. But he likes to think he's progressive, so he'd never admit in a million years that working with a woman would threaten his precious male ego.

"Hell no," he growled through a screen of cigarette smoke. "But you have to know how to operate a backhoe." He thought he had me.

"But you can teach me that. You always say how you've got the run of the place and get to do anything you want." Arthur and I have been going at each other like this since we were children.

"Dammit, Jewel, are you gettin' the menopause or somethin'?"

I gave him a look that would wither a Brazilian rain forest. "Why is it, Arthur, that every time a middle-aged woman decides to do something a little out of the ordinary, people think she's going through the change? My mother never went through it 'til she was fifty-three and Aunt Liddy was fifty-six, and I'm nowhere near that age. I'm still a young woman, in case you haven't noticed, and I'm strong as an ox, and I'm about to drive myself plum crazy worrying over everything and everybody in my life. I can't think straight anymore because there's too much damn noise and confusion going on around me. You hear what I'm saying?"

"You'd lose your benefits," Arthur said, but I could tell he was weakening.

"I don't have any financial worries, thank God," I said. "And believe me, my pension wouldn't pay the rent on a bird house."

"What if you don't like it?" he said.

I gave him my sweetest smile. "Then maybe I'll try brain surgery."

Within three months, I had my job in the cemetery. I like

to nagged Arthur to death, but he finally got me an interview, and in the end, they couldn't legally prevent me from being hired, because I could do everything the job required, including operating the backhoe. Everybody at the can factory thought I'd lost my mind. It was the best gossip this town has had since the Holiness preacher ran off with the delivery boy from Buford's Pharmacy.

The cemetery crew was hostile at first and played some nasty jokes on me—I won't say what, 'cause if I did, folks would never bury their dead. They'd just put the casket in the living room, throw an afghan over it and set out a bowl of wax fruit. I ignored the pranks until they did a particularly vulgar thing with the coffin of a child who had died of leukemia and couldn't be buried right away. We had the worst cold spell of the century and the hydraulic system was out on the backhoe. I knew which one had thought it up, and he was four inches shorter and thirty pounds lighter than me. I went into the shed where they were all eating their lunches around an old space heater. I walked over to him and snatched him to his feet by his collar. He was eating a bologna sandwich and drinking coffee out of a Thermos bottle with a big red cup. He dropped the coffee and the sandwich and stepped in both.

I spoke very softly. "I've seen rattlesnakes that walk taller than you," I said. "If you ever do anything like that again, first thing, I'm gonna get on the telephone and call your wife. And the second thing, I'm going to pound you into the ground like a tent stake. Do you understand me?"

"Yes," he said.

I let go of him and turned on the rest of them. I felt colder and meaner than the farthest outpost of hell. "And that goes for the rest of you, too. It's time you stopped doing things you wouldn't want done to your own wives and mothers."

"Now Jewel," Joe Sisskin began. Joe and I went to grade school together, and I buy his daughter Ruthie's Girl Scout cookies every single year. "You know we didn't mean no harm."

That's one I've thought about over and over since I went to work in the cemetery. You have so much time to think in this job. No dressing for success, no more Mary Kay parties or manicuring your nails, worrying about runs in your pantyhose and how much those pointy-toe high heels hurt your feet. Nothing but birds and animals, sky, trees and flowers. I've thought and thought. One of the conclusions I've come to is that the worst hurt people do each other is usually excused by that innocent phrase, "I didn't mean any harm."

"Maybe you didn't *mean* harm," I said. "But you *did* harm just the same. Intentions don't mean jack."

I walked out then, and sure enough, after that they left me alone. Now they merely ignore me, and that's fine, because the day will come when I'll be just one of the boys, and they'll start including me in their lunches and asking me to backyard barbecues and fishing trips over to the Lake of Egypt with them and their wives and their divorced brothers. When that day comes, it will be time for me to move on. But I think I'll have it figured out by then. What I'm going to do next in my life, I mean.

I know I can't fix other folks' problems for them, like Ronnie for instance. All I can do is love him and give advice when he acts without thinking. Other than that, he's got to work it out for himself, doping and all.

Like I said, I have lots of time to think. Nothing comes between me and God in the graveyard. Everything's real simple: just death, and what we do with the little time we have before it claims us.

TREE ANGEL

THE FIRST TIME Bernadette encountered the angel was at sunset on an September Sunday. She had cooked the leftover carcass of a big chicken until the bones that collected on the bottom of the soup pot were as clean as if they'd been scoured with sand. She poured the broth through a strainer and dumped everything left in the pot into the garbage can. "Good riddance," she murmured as she twisted the bag shut. He'd been an ornery, mean-tempered old rooster and she hadn't been sorry to wring his neck.

    Bernadette thought about asking Lyle Junior to take out the garbage, but she didn't have the energy to make him do it. She grabbed an old sweater from a hook by the porch door and started across the yard to where the garbage can sat by the fence. The chickens had all gone to roost and the wind was down. It was warm for late October; most of the leaves were still on the trees. The sun was sinking into a lake of crimson and violet cloud. Bernadette dropped the garbage into the can, but instead of turning back to the house, she leaned against the fence to admire the sky, groping her sweater pockets for her cigarettes and lighter. Miraculously, she found both. She lit up a Salem and watched the sky change colors. She was thirty-four years old and she wondered what in the world had happened to her life.

Sometimes Bernadette daydreamed about Lyle's death: a train accident, a sudden heart attack. Her fantasies were so real they brought tears to her eyes. She saw herself picking up the telephone and hearing the voice of an EMT from county emergency services, or dressed in black receiving the condolences of Reverend Millburn, or standing amid a forest of umbrellas at a graveside service under a frigid November downpour.

Bernadette took another drag on her cigarette. At her back, she heard a distinct rustling sound in the old apple tree. Since there was no wind, it could mean only one thing: the Lauderbach kid from across the road. *Damn,* she said silently. She wished she had a shotgun full of rock salt for him to take home in his sorry white-trash butt. Slowly she pivoted toward the tree. She said, "Get the hell down from there right this damn minute!"

Later, back in the kitchen, Bernadette sat in the dark. In her hands was a Minnie Mouse jelly glass with an inch of Jack Daniels in the bottom. She had almost stopped shaking. In the living room, Lyle snored in front of the tube. Overhead, Lyle Junior played heavy-metal rock at a volume fit to crack the foundation of the house. Bernadette decided that she was flat-out crazy and might as well get in the truck right now and drive to the county asylum and check herself in. She wondered how long it would take her husband and her son to notice she was gone. *Probably until they ran out of socks or peanut butter and jelly,*

Bernadette thought.

Bernadette told no one about the angel. In fact, by the following morning she had come to believe she'd had a vivid hallucination. *Maybe I've got a brain tumor,* she thought. *Lord, I miss Mama.* She pictured herself in a white hospital gown sliding into one of those machines to have her brain scanned like she saw on *ER*. It would serve her right, she thought, for having bad thoughts about Lyle. That evening Bernadette set the garbage bag on the porch inside the door and didn't even look out the window. As she loaded the dishwasher, she remembered confessing her fantasies to her sister Merline a few weeks before.

"Good God, Bernadette!" Merline had said. "There isn't a woman on this planet married more than a year that hasn't fantasized her husband's death. Why don't you redo the downstairs bathroom?"

Back in August, her girlfriend Tammy suggested she have an affair.

"There's not one man in this whole county I'd care to have one with," Bernadette declared. But her nights were filled with longing, for what she didn't know. She didn't think it was sex, but how could she be sure? That night, when Lyle rolled off her and fell immediately into snoring sleep, Bernadette lay awake beside him flat on her back, the blankets pulled up to her chin, her hands folded across her waist. *Laid out for burial,* she thought, staring at a water stain on the ceiling. A rectangle of moonlight stood propped against the far wall. *I am as dead as I can be without actually being in the ground.* She got up and went to the window. A nearly full moon hung like a ripe peach, fat and satisfied. Bernadette watched its slow rise, the way the shadows changed in the yard as the colors of the landscape muted and silvered. She heard a whippoorwill, then an owl. All the vast night lay before her.

Somethingsomethingsomething, sang the pulse in her temples. *What?* she asked. *Please tell me what.* The moon stared back. Bernadette returned to bed, full of hunger or desire or yearning. Whatever it was, it refused to name itself. *Maybe I'm having a nervous breakdown,* Bernadette thought just before she went to sleep. *I wish Mama was still alive.*

The next thing Bernadette knew, it was October and there was an angel camped out in the apple tree. Most of the leaves were still on the branches, but Bernadette worried about what would happen when eventually they were bare. She was careful not to intrude on the angel's privacy, although why an angel would require privacy and why she seemed to sense this, she did not know.

She took to carrying out the garbage each evening, to the delight of Lyle Junior, who was fifteen and wanted to spend about twenty-five hours a day in his room, which was a swamp of dirty clothes, empty pizza boxes, sports paraphernalia, magazines, heavy-metal CDs and miles of electrical cable connecting computer components that he ordered through catalogs from places in California and South Dakota. Bernadette had no idea what he did with it all, and Lyle Junior volunteered nothing. Perhaps he was raiding banks in Tokyo or breaking into Pentagon files on crashed UFOs. Whatever it was, he had moved beyond his parents into a world they could not share. Bernadette assumed that if they kept feeding him, seeing that he went to school every day and avoided arrest, he would emerge in a few years as a reasonable semblance of a human adult and begin speaking to them again in whole sentences. In the meantime, she kept out of his way.

On her evening sojourns to the garbage can, Bernadette tried to avoid looking directly into the tree. She developed a sly technique of taking her cigarettes with her and pausing at the fence to smoke before returning to the house. While she smoked, she studied the apple tree out of her peripheral vision. Once she saw a foot hanging down, glowing with a faint cunning, unearthly radiance. It was a slender, elegant foot clad in a Jesus sandal, and the arch of the foot looked so tender and vulnerable that she wanted more than anything in the world to lay her cheek against it.

On another occasion she sensed as soon as she passed beneath it that the tree was empty. Her heart plummeted like a lead sinker as she lifted the Hefty bag and dropped it into the garbage container at the fence. Her arms felt as though they'd been shot full of Novocain, and tears overflowed her eyelids, making hot tracks down her cheeks. She would have gone immediately back to the house except for the tears. With quaking fingers, Bernadette lit a cigarette and put her elbows on the top of the fence to stare unseeing at the pasture on the other side. At that instant she heard a noisy disturbance at her back, a crackling of branches and rattling of leaves. She whirled around in a single movement just in time to see a great luminous snowy wingtip retract into the shadows of the upper branches. Her heart cartwheeled, joy flooded her body from the roots of her hair to her toes. She went to the trunk of the apple tree and pressed her palms against it. "You came back," she whispered. "You came back to me."

Bernadette always collected her eggs at the crack of dawn. She pushed irritable squawking hens off the nests and reached into the warm straw recesses to extract the eggs carefully and lay them in her basket. The Lauderbachs had moved in across the road just that summer, and already three of her best layers had died in clouds of feathers at the paws of the Lauderbach dog. Replacing them had been fairly easy and inexpensive, but still she never knew when the dog would dig under its fenced yard and strike again.

She washed the eggs carefully and sold them at two dollars a dozen to neighbors and Lyle's coworkers. Lyle was always telling her how the chickens were more trouble than they were worth. Nevertheless, Bernadette stubbornly persisted. The taste of fresh eggs and chickens raised the old-fashioned way were worth it, she always told him. But it was the dawn ritual of collecting the eggs that Bernadette couldn't let go of. It was something that had to be done every day, winter or summer, no matter how miserable or happy she was, sick or well. It anchored her to the world.

As the days grew shorter and colder and the leaves thinned out of the apple tree, Bernadette grew more apprehensive about the angel. Surely he couldn't stay concealed much longer. What would happen then? Would he fly south for the winter to lollygag in banana trees among brown-skinned folks who would marvel over him in Spanish? And more to the point, Bernadette thought, what was he doing there—in her apple tree—in the first place?

She determined to ask him that very evening, but at the last minute, she lost heart. Leaning on the frosty fence, dragging at her Salem menthol, she imagined him telling her, "Oh, nothing special. Just passing through." And she knew she would be crushed, broken beyond recovery. She wanted him to be there for her, Bernadette, with some special message that would lift and sustain her, that would take up residence in her soul and continue to reflect its invisible light from the edges of the universe for all her long life yet to be lived.

But that opened another, less comfortable possibility. What if the special message involved some task she was ordained to perform? She thought back through her Sunday-school lessons, trying to remember what happened to the people in the Bible when angels appeared to them. Sara, hearing that she would bear a child in her old age, had laughed and been struck dumb. Saul of Tarsus had been struck blind. Mary's life after her visit from Archangel Gabriel hadn't been any picnic either, for that matter: pregnant out of wedlock, giving birth in a wretched livestock barn in a strange city, then living the rest of her life without even the comfort of sex, only to see her son nailed to the damn cross in the end. Bernadette dropped the remains of her smoke and ground it under her shoe. She threw a single apprehensive sidelong glance at the tree as she gave it a wide berth on her way back to the house. A faint demanding radiance clung there, pulsating coyly like starlight beamed across galaxies a million light years away.

One morning near Thanksgiving when Bernadette went out to collect eggs, she found bloody feathers scattered in the chicken yard. Sure enough, when she counted, another of her hens was missing, Veronica, the most dependable layer of them all. "Damn!" she exploded. She went through the nests quickly, ignoring the nervous flapping and squawking of the remaining chickens. They were spooked all right, but she hardly noticed as one particularly vitriolic rooster made an enraged swipe at her ankle with his talons. Fuming, Bernadette marched back to the house, plunked the basket down on the stoop and headed down the driveway and across the road.

Dawn was coming on, sullen and reluctant, through heavy cloud cover pregnant with rain. There were no lights on yet in the Lauderbach kitchen, she noted with vicious satisfaction, as she hammered a gloved fist on the flimsy screen door. *Good!* she thought. *Get the lazy bastard out of bed while it's still morning for once in his worthless, no-account life.*

The porch light came on; Bernadette heard wordless snarling and grumbling as locks were released on the inner door. "What the hell . . ." Bruno Lauderbach peered out, blinking, his hair pushed up on the side of his head in a way that might have been comical if Bernadette were not so furious. She stepped back reflexively as the screen door flung open and the sour smell of human dissolution flowed out like toxic effluent.

Bernadette caught her breath. *Christ, how can people live like this?*

"Yeah, whaddya want?" Bruno had pulled his pants on but his enormous gut overhung the waistband. Bernadette stifled the urge to ask him how he managed to get his hands around it to pee.

"Your dog," she said without preamble, "has got into my chickens again, damn it! He got my best laying hen and I want you to know that the next time I see him on my property, I'm gonna blow him into the next county."

"What the hell are you talkin' about? Wasn't my goddamn dog in your chickens."

"Exactly what I'd expect you to say," Bernadette snapped. "Maybe if you'd feed him once in a while he wouldn't have to raid my chicken yard. I've got a mind to call the sheriff." She turned to stomp off the porch.

"You go right ahead," Bruno growled. "And while you're at it, ask him if he's seen my kid yet."

Bernadette turned back. Bruno still stood in the doorway, and Bernadette could see his chest heaving.

"He run off with that dog a week ago and I ain't seen hide or hair of either one of 'em since." Bruno's voice cracked, and Bernadette saw with horror that his eyes were brimming wet. "So you just go find somebody else to blame for your troubles, lady!" The door slammed in her face hard enough to split the frame. Bernadette hesitated a moment, opening and closing her mouth. Finally she fled back across the road, shame stabbing at her heels like the sharp talons of the rooster.

"Owl," Lyle said around a mouthful of cheese grits. "Dog'd leave parts behind."

Bernadette filled both their coffee cups and sat down across the table from him. Between them, Lyle Junior sat, wolfing his grits and scrambled eggs behind a copy of *Muscle* magazine. Bernadette reached over and pulled it away.

"Mom!" Lyle Junior protested.

"No reading at the table," Bernadette said.

Lyle Junior gave her a look of disgust and downed the last of his orange juice. He stood up. "Gotta go," he mumbled. He snatched up his backpack and lurched out the door.

Bernadette sighed and sipped her coffee. "An owl," she said heavily. "Owls hunt at night. When the chickens are all inside."

"I reckon this one got an early start," Lyle said, stirring Carnation evaporated milk into his coffee.

Suddenly Bernadette remembered the hoot of an owl on the night she had watched the moonrise from the bedroom window. "I heard it," she said.

"What? When?" Lyle asked.

"The owl," Bernadette replied irritably. "I heard it after we went to bed. You were asleep." She shivered, sipped at her coffee again.

"Well, there you go then. An owl got the hen."

"What can we do?" Bernadette asked.

Lyle shrugged, probing his molars with a toothpick.

"Hell, I don't know. Shoot it, I reckon. If you see it, that is. They gener'ly lay up in the daytime, hunt at night, like you said. I'd say this 'un come out 'long about dusk, before them hens was all in the roost. Got lucky. Or maybe real early in the mornin'."

"It's dark now before either one of us gets home from work."

"Then don't let 'em out no more 'til the days get long again."

"I guess that's what I'll have to do," Bernadette said. "I hate to, especially on sunny days. It makes 'em meantempered."

"Hell, they're mean to start with," Lyle snorted. "I don't know why you want to keep 'em in the first place. They're mean and dirty and smelly."

Bernadette set her coffee mug down with a thump. Coffee sloshed onto the table top. "I don't notice you refusing to eat them—or their eggs."

Lyle stood up and pushed his chair back. "We can buy eggs at Winn-Dixie and fried chicken from the Colonel," he said.

Fury rose in Bernadette's throat like sour vomit. She did not dare to move or open her mouth. Lyle clapped a hand on her shoulder as he squeezed past her chair. "I'll get out the shotgun and do some owl hunting this weekend," he said.

Bernadette did not believe that Lyle would get the owl. Owls were too cunning; this one would hunt elsewhere for a while until Lyle tired of waiting for it and then strike again as soon as they let their guard down. On Friday night, he got the shotgun from the closet shelf and sat at the kitchen table to clean it as Bernadette stacked the dishwasher.

Before dawn the following morning, Lyle was up with the chickens. Bernadette went downstairs with him to make coffee. Lyle dressed quickly and slipped quietly out the back door. He'd told her the night before that he'd decided to lay up just inside the entrance to the henhouse where could see the chicken pen without being seen. Bernadette wondered anxiously about the angel. She had never seen him in the morning. Presumably he was up and about his divine business—whatever that was—well in advance of dawn. Bernadette watched briefly as Lyle was swallowed in the predawn gloom. Then she went back to bed.

Later, at her deposition, Bernadette would testify that she woke up to the shotgun blast, but the truth of the matter was that she had awakened a second before. One moment she was asleep, and in the next she was sitting straight up in bed, wide awake, as though a switch had been thrown, and the hair on her arms was bristling. And then came the boom of the gun. Bernadette leaped out of bed as Lyle shouted from the yard. "I got the sonofabitch, Bernie! Holy shit! I got him!"

Bernadette ran down the stairs and out into the yard without pausing for robe or slippers. The eastern sky had grown rosy with the approaching dawn and Lyle stood outlined against it. At his feet was what at first looked like a crumpled bed sheet.

"Holy shit, Bernie," Lyle repeated. "Look at this sonofabitch, will you? I never seen no owl like this before around here. . . . What the hell, woman? Why ain't you dressed? Jesus Christ!" Lyle laid down the shotgun, peeled off his jacket and hung it around Bernadette's shoulders. She was too mesmerized by the thing on the ground to notice.

Lyle dropped to his knees. The sky was lighter now, and Bernadette could see blood vivid on the snowy feathers of the biggest owl she had ever seen in her life. Lyle spread its wings out on the ground. "Jesus, look at this." He looked up. "Hey, Son, look what your old man just shot." Bernadette turned to see Lyle Junior stumbling across the yard in Levis and a jacket that barely covered his naked chest. He was barefoot.

"What's goin' on? What happened? Ma, are you all right?"

Bernadette looked up at him and realized for the first time that Lyle Junior was now taller than she was, but his face was still that of a dazed child roused from sleep.

"I got the owl been killin' your mother's chickens." He looked from one face to the other. "Well?" he said. "How about it, you two? Am I a dead shot or what? . . . Well *now* what's wrong? Goddammit, Bernie, what are you cryin' for? How about some enthusiasm here?"

Bernadette felt Lyle Junior's arm go around her and she leaned gratefully against his shoulder.

"Gee, Dad," Lyle Junior said. "That's not an ordinary owl."

"*I* know that!" Lyle replied in an aggrieved tone. "This here is some bird that's got away from its natural range. These birds belong up in Chicago or Canada or some other place where it snows all year round. What the hell was it doin' this far south anyway?"

Yes, Bernadette thought. *What the hell?*

"Mom?" Lyle Junior said. "Let's go inside, Ma. . . . Ma, are you all right?"

Bernadette sat at the kitchen table and refused to go outside, even when the photographer from the local weekly newspaper arrived. By that time Lyle had nailed the dead owl to the garage door with its enormous wings stretched to their fullest extent which, according to Lyle, was six feet, one-and-a-half inches. Bernadette thought that he must have had to break the angel's wings to spread them that far. Lyle posed next to the garage door, his shotgun broken on one arm.

Bernadette drank coffee and wept inconsolably. She stopped only after realizing how upset Lyle Junior had become. "I'm all right," she reassured him after hanging her head in the kitchen sink and turning a spray of cold water on the back of her neck. "I'm okay, Son." Lyle Junior retrieved a towel from the downstairs bathroom—the one she had been advised to redo—and patted her hair nervously with it. "I'm going upstairs and take a shower now," she said, forcing a calm into her voice that was pure artifice.

She stood under the hot water until it started to run cool, then dried herself roughly and put on jeans and a double layer of sweaters. Then she went downstairs again, made a large, cholesterol-laden breakfast for Lyle Senior and started ripping the paper off the bathroom walls.

Lyle clearly thought she had lost her mind. That night, as she stirred chicken gravy at the stove, Lyle had implored with just the slightest edge of hysteria, "What the *hay-ull* is the matter with you anyway, Bernie?"

Bernadette turned toward him slowly, the big wooden spoon in her hand dripping a half-circle of gravy across the floor. "Nothing is wrong with me, Lyle," she said, enunciating clearly. She seized the skillet by its handle, and with a strong, sure forearm, arced it solidly through the big double-glazed kitchen window. The sound of exploding glass reverberated through her body like an orgasm. She looked at Lyle's chalk-white face for the briefest moment, then turned and mounted the stairs slowly and locked herself in the bedroom.

The newspaper came out on Tuesday, and Lyle's picture was on the front page. Bernadette saw it by accident in the TV room where Lyle had piled ten copies on the coffee table. The bird's eyes were wide open, startled by their glimpse of infinity, like the eyes of children who are still capable of wonder. Bernadette felt as though her own eyes had been slashed with a shard of glass.

On Wednesday morning, Bernadette answered a crank phone call from somebody with a snotty up-country accent saying she was from a news wire service, whatever that was. Bernadette told her to stick it squarely up her rear end and slammed down the phone. Then she drove to town and bought groceries. Pearl the checkout clerk made a comment about Lyle's picture in the newspaper, which Bernadette pretended not to hear. When she got back home, a strange white van stood in the driveway. Instinctively, Bernadette recognized major trouble. She pulled up next to it, prepared to throw the pickup into reverse and beat a hasty exit. There, in rainbow letters on the van's side panel, was the name of a major news network.

Then she saw two people by the garage door, apparently taking pictures. One of them—Bernadette couldn't tell whether it was a man or a woman—held a shoulder-mounted video camera, the other appeared to be taking still pictures. Bernadette sat with her hands on the steering wheel trying to absorb what was going on.

Finally the one with the video camera turned in her direction. Bernadette was pretty sure it was a woman, but who knew these days? What with men wearing ponytails and women sporting crew cuts, it was hard to tell one sex from the other. As the ponytail ambled toward her, Bernadette saw that it was a man after all. He was slight of build and he wore a small gold hoop in his left earlobe. Bernadette supposed that meant he was gay, but that was irrelevant. She swung the truck door open and hopped out. Just as she came out from behind the door, the one with the still camera, whom Bernadette now saw had breasts, raised the camera and clicked off several shots.

Bernadette stepped forward, infuriated. "What are y'all doing on my property?" she demanded.

Over the woman's shoulder she saw the man with the video cam approaching. He walked briskly, making some sort of manual adjustment, then pressed a button. Bernadette could hear an electronic whir. "Stop that," she said.

"Afternoon, Ma'am," Ponytail said. "We're from KZAM. We'd like you to tell us about the snowy owl."

"You're trespassing," Bernadette said flatly, "and you didn't ask my permission to take my picture either." The next thing Bernadette knew, the dykey-looking woman had shoved a microphone in her face, and Ponytail was taping her. "Do you routinely kill endangered species on your property?" Dykey demanded.

"Stop that," Bernadette ordered, reaching to block the camera lens. Ponytail danced skillfully backward as Dykey pushed the mike closer to Bernadette's face.

"I said *stop that right now!*" she ordered. "Princess Di was too much of a lady to give you what you deserve, but we don't worry about those niceties too much in these parts."

Ponytail was approaching again, his head nearly obscured by the video cam. He looked like some techno-human hybrid. Bernadette felt a surge, as though she'd touched a live wire, and the next thing she knew, Ponytail was on the ground and Bernadette was smashing in the passenger-side window of the network news van with the video cam. Ponytail was screaming hysterically and trying to get it away from her. "That's a nine-thousand-dollar camera!" he shrieked. Bernadette drop-kicked the camera across the drive, seized the strap of Dykey's still camera, which hung around her neck, and began dragging her toward the road. Just then Ponytail tackled Bernadette from behind. Bernadette dropped Dykey, pivoted and chopped Ponytail hard on the left shoulder just above his collar bone. He went down like a hog in the slaughterhouse. Bernadette stood over both of them, gasping for breath. Ponytail was crying and Dykey was making gagging sounds.

"Now get off my property," Bernadette said briskly, "before I get *really* pissed."

Bernadette sat in the kitchen waiting for Lyle to return her phone call. How could she have been deluded all those weeks into thinking an angel was living in her apple tree? But on some level she must have known the truth. After all, she'd been careful to not really look at him after that first heart-stopping encounter—the one in which she'd seen what she wanted to see—telling herself she didn't want to violate his privacy. But it had been only a poor dumb bird and now it was dead, and poor dumb Lyle had called the local newspaper and insisted that somebody take his picture with it. And that had resulted in the network news people trespassing on their property and her sending Dykey and Ponytail down the road whining like whipped dogs. Bernadette supposed that she'd now be arrested for assault and destruction of property and God knew what all else. And Lyle would probably be arrested too, for killing an animal that was on the endangered list. Wasn't that a federal crime? A felony? Bernadette shuddered. Here she'd been fantasizing about Lyle getting killed, and now he was probably going to jail, which was even worse.

Her cell phone rang, and Bernadette jumped reflexively.

"Hello?"

"It's me, Bernie. What's goin' on?"

"The network news people were just here, looking at your dead owl and wanting to know if we routinely kill endangered animals on our property."

"Wha—?"

"And they stuck microphones and cameras in my face and I ran them off—"

"You what?"

"I said I ran them off. And Lyle, that's not all—"

Just then Bernadette heard the crunch of tires on the driveway. She looked out the window and saw the county sheriff's patrol car. "Lyle," she said, "I think you'd better come home right away."

By the following spring, the entire matter had been settled. After wrangling with the county sheriff, the Fish and Wildlife Service, the FBI, and the TV network's lawyers, after thousands of dollars in legal fees, it was decided that none of the parties owed each other anything. The cost of the camera and damages to the van were offset by the naked fact that the reporters had been trespassing. Bernadette had the right to defend herself and her property when they continued to harass her after she'd asked them to leave, a fact confirmed by the contents of the camera's voice recorder, which the reporters had thoughtfully left lying next to the driveway. The snowy owl enjoys protection under the Migratory Bird Species Act, but is not on the Endangered Species List, so the nightmare of a jail term for Lyle became moot. The Fish and Wildlife Service, which had taken possession of the owl carcass, determined that it was the largest example of its species ever recorded.

Over the winter, Bernadette grew pensive. She quit

smoking, stopped fantasizing about Lyle's death. She applied for a job in housekeeping at the county hospital and left the candy factory where she'd worked since Lyle Junior started first grade. Across the road, the Lauderbach kid came back home along with his dog. Bernadette learned that the boy's mother had died just before he and his father moved in the previous summer. One spring morning, she crossed the road with a freshly roasted chicken and a dozen eggs. Lauderbach himself answered the door. Bernadette was shocked at his appearance. He was freshly shaved and wearing a clean shirt and overalls. The draft from the door didn't smell as bad as Bernadette remembered. "Yeah?" Lauderbach said coldly.

Bernadette swallowed hard. "I—uh—I want to apologize for how I behaved last fall when I thought your dog killed my chickens. I should have done this sooner, but this past winter has been, ah, pretty hectic at our house."

To Bernadette's immense surprise, Lauderbach grinned. "Yeah, I heard about that owl your old man shot, and that business with the Fish and Wildlife outfit and those reporters. Did you really smash their camera and drag them off your place?"

"Yessir, I really did." Bernadette tried to look serious, but then she started to giggle. "I can't tell you how satisfying that was." She thrust the foil-wrapped chicken and the carton of eggs at him. "I'd like you and your son to have these. I cooked the chicken last night and gathered the eggs this morning. I hope I can be a better neighbor now."

Lauderbach took the chicken and the carton as a blush gathered on his cheeks. "That's real nice of you Ma'am," he said.

"Please call me Bernadette. I'm glad your son's home. I hear you've been through a bad time. I hope things are getting better."

Lauderbach nodded. "Slowly," he said. "It's slow. It's hard to raise a boy without a mother."

"I can't even imagine," Bernadette said. There was a small silence and then she stepped back down the stoop. "Well, I guess we'll be seeing you then. You and your boy take care now."

That evening after supper, she and Lyle sat on the back-porch swing. Lyle Junior was doing his homework. For some mysterious reason, he'd taken an interest in jazz; the days of heavy metal seemed to be over. Miles Davis drifted down from upstairs. Bernadette sipped at a glass of wine. The lilacs had begun to bloom, and their seductive perfume filled the cool night air.

"How's your job goin'?" Lyle asked. He was drinking a Bud Light.

"I like it," Bernadette replied. "I really like the nurses and the CNAs. I work on the hospice unit in the afternoons, and I like that the best."

"With all those folks dyin'? I'd think you'd like that the least. It's gotta be depressing."

Bernadette shook her head. "I thought it would be too, but it's not. I can't explain it very well—you actually have to be there—but there's something special about taking care of folks who are on their way to the next world."

There was a long silence. Just when Bernadette thought their conversation was ended, Lyle said, "Bernie, I've done a lotta thinkin' over this winter . . ."

Bernadette felt a thrill of alarm. "Yes?"

"I know I'm not much. I mean, I ain't handsome or rich or even very smart. We got married right outa high school, and

I guess if you'd waited a little longer, you coulda got some guy who was all those things I ain't and never will be. But I do love you, Bernie, and I hope you'll stay with me."

Bernadette put her hand in Lyle's. "I don't have any intention of going anywhere," she said. "I was never interested in looks or money. I married you because you're a good person. I'll never forget how kind and patient you were with Mama when she was so sick and angry about having to leave her home and come to live with us. You've been a great dad to Lyle Junior. And besides, you never once got nasty with me over what I did to those reporters, even though we've had to refinance the house to pay off the damn lawyers."

"I was proud of you. *Am* proud of you."

Bernadette squeezed Lyle's hand. For a few minutes they listened to crickets singing in the grass. "Lyle, there's one thing . . ."

"What?"

"When I was a little girl, I always dreamed of being a nurse when I grew up."

"Yeah?"

"I guess that was part of why I applied for the housekeeping job at the hospital when I couldn't stand the candy factory anymore. I wanted to be around nurses. But it's occurred to me over the last few months that maybe I could still be one."

Lyle shifted his position on the swing and looked directly at her. "Go on," he said.

"Well, I've been doing some asking around. There are scholarships and financial aid programs, and I think I can do it. I—I *know* I can do it. And once I actually got my RN, I'd be earning more money and we could get the mortgage paid off a lot faster and help Lyle Junior with college."

The Search for the Villa Melzi Gardens...and Other Tales

"You're really serious," Lyle said.

"Yes." Bernadette took a deep breath. "But I can't do it without your help. Yours and Lyle Junior's."

There was a short silence before Lyle answered, "Sure, Bernie. I reckon we can do whatever we have to."

By the time autumn color began painting the landscape, Bernadette was enrolled for the fall term in the associate-degree-in-nursing program at the community college. She still worked twenty-five hours a week at the hospital, and sometimes she was so tired at the end of the day she could barely speak. But Lyle kept his word. He and Lyle Junior learned to use the washing machine and vacuum cleaner, even how to make some simple meals, and to Bernadette's astonishment, Lyle took on maintenance of the henhouse. Bernadette still began her mornings collecting eggs.

One crisp evening as the days grew short, she decided to pick a bag of apples to share with her workmates next morning at the hospital. The branches of the tree were heavy with fruit. Squirrels and birds and raccoons had gorged themselves and fruit lay rotting on the ground, but there were still so many apples. She'd have to take a few hours this coming weekend to deliver a big box to the soup kitchen in town and to make some pies for the freezer. She would take one to Merline's family and another to the Lauderbachs. She got a grocery bag and put on a hoodie. Outside, across the pasture, the sun had set in a froth of orange and pink. She paused at the fence where only a year earlier she'd been smoking cigarettes after emptying the garbage. What a year it had been.

She turned back to the tree and began plucking fruit from the low branches. Suddenly, overhead, a silvery luminosity shimmered as though a sailing cloud had uncovered a full moon. Bernadette froze, her hand on a particularly fat red apple. She remembered the snowy wingtip, the sandaled foot. She lifted her face to the light.

COLUMBA LIVIA

I DREAMED LAST NIGHT of Uncle Stash. I was walking across a big green field, but it wasn't like the ball field at Comiskey Park or any other place in Chicago. This was like way out in the country. I couldn't see any houses or buildings or even trees. The grass was an unnatural bright green, like in the old Technicolor movies of the fifties, and although everything was lit up like daytime, the sky was midnight black. There was a white bird winging around, and it made me think of my uncle and the pigeons he kept when I was a boy and we lived in Hegewisch on the top floor of a three-flat on Saginaw Avenue.

Uncle Stash had a job at the South Works Steel Mill, and he had this routine. He'd come home from work, set his hard hat and lunch box on the kitchen table, then climb a ladder on the back porch up through the trap door that led to the roof. That's where he'd built his pigeon loft, and he'd spend hours feeding and petting his birds. His favorite was Livia, who was, with the exception of some dark tail feathers and her rainbow neck, almost pure white. She would sit on his finger and rub her head against his cheek while he fed her millet seeds and bits of apple and dried apricot. He told me he had named her for her species, *Columba livia*. He had long conversations with Livia, and she had complete freedom to come and go. One time, she didn't return at dusk, and Uncle Stash sat up next to the loft all night long, wrapped in an old quilt. He'd told Ma he wouldn't be down for supper, so she made his favorite dish and sent me up with a plate of pierogi and boiled potatoes and cabbage. I asked him if I could wait with him, and when he nodded silently, I went back down the ladder to get my own quilt. I remember how the sky over the south shore of Lake Michigan glowed red from the fires of the open-hearth furnaces of East Chicago, Gary and Burns Harbor. When Livia finally flew home at dawn, Uncle Stash wept like a child.

Uncle Stash never talked much. Ma said he used to talk a lot before Vietnam, but he came home from the war silent. So he communed with his pigeons and went to work and slept in a little room off the kitchen. Although he wasn't a conversationalist, he was never unkind to me, and I wanted him to love me. This was at a time when Pop worked two jobs to pay off Ma's medical bills, so I never saw much of my old man. I used to daydream that Uncle Stash would take me to the park and play softball with me, but I was too young to know how to ask.

Nevertheless, Uncle Stash gave me a cartridge from the M60 machine gun he fought with in Vietnam, and one time he let me hold a shell that the VC had fired into his hooch. It was a dud. He and his buddies had been playing seven-card stud when somebody screamed "Incoming!" The next thing they knew, this shell came through the roof and punched a hole in the floor. Uncle Stash said he'd seen Death that day, not the death of enemies or of fellow soldiers, but his own personal death, and that he'd known from then on he wouldn't die in Vietnam.

So he started doing crazy shit like running into the line of fire to hurl grenades into enemy positions, and carrying wounded guys to the Medevac helicopters with bullets flying from all directions. Once, he pulled some villagers out of a flaming hut and his hands got burned so bad he had to have skin grafts. As a result of all this, he was awarded a Purple Heart, a Bronze Star and a Silver Star. But I never saw them and Uncle Stash never spoke of them. Pop told me about them the day we buried him in Holy Cross Cemetery next to my grandparents. Right after he came home from Nam, Pop said, he'd pitched his medals into the Calumet River.

Uncle Stash never married. He had a woman he saw every Saturday night. She was older than Uncle Stash, a Vietnam widow. Her name was Theresa and she'd cook supper and they'd go for walks in nice weather or to the movies. Then he'd come home after breakfast on Sunday morning. This went on until his death.

I was twenty-two when my uncle died. I'd left home to work on the oil platforms along the Louisiana gulf coast, and Ma called one night to say that Uncle Stash had had a heart attack up on the roof. When she'd found him, she told me, the pigeons were making sounds that she'd never heard before, like they were crying.

So in the dream of the green field and the dark sky and the white bird, I knew Uncle Stash had to be close by. I sat in the cool grass to wait. Sure enough, a smudge of dull-orange light appeared, like the glow of the sky over the South Shore the night we waited for Livia. The smudge grew and Uncle Stash floated down to me. Livia, with a flash of opals, flew to perch on his shoulder. I stood up to meet them, and suddenly I was a little kid again. I caught the acrid odor of the steel mill, and when Uncle Stash reached out to me at last, I could see the scars on his hands.

THE TRESPASSER

LILY GETS THE PHONE call at the office. In fact, she has only just arrived. She doesn't even have a cup of coffee yet, and she's immediately alarmed, hearing the voice on the phone identify itself as Joan Radley's sister, Ellen. Lily stands in front of her desk, still wearing her coat, listens to Ellen apologizing for calling her at work, explaining that she tried to reach Lily several times at home without success. Lily feels an upwelling in her chest, a dangerous tide. Slowly she sits down in one of the upholstered guest chairs. Her secretary walks in, mouths good morning and drops off a Xeroxed memo. Lily sees that it has to do with the summer vacation schedule. She also sees that her Swedish ivy needs water. Ellen says, "Joan has cancer and she's not expected to . . ."

"Oh, God," Lily breathes. She turns toward the window and sees the January sunlight glitzing off the surface of Lake Michigan. It's enough to make her eyes smart.

"Lily, you were so close at one time," Ellen sighs. "I

thought you'd like to know."

Lily's husband and son smile at her from a Plexiglas frame next to the Swedish ivy. Her son wears braces on his teeth, so he is smiling with his mouth shut and he looks as though he has just sucked a lemon. Lily is particularly fond of this photograph. She hasn't seen the Radleys in years. She doesn't even think about them much anymore. Nevertheless, she feels as though she's just been whacked across the chest with a two-by-four.

It occurs to Lily that she is the same age as Joan when she and Joan's son began living together. Lily sits on the 147 bus watching Michigan Avenue slide by. It's a damp, gray March day. She sees break dancers twirling on their heads in front of Tribune Tower and wonders why their necks don't snap like dry sticks. She's on her way to Northwestern Memorial Hospital to see Joan Radley, and she's permitting herself to think about Joan, something she hasn't done in a long time. Joan had been beautiful back then. Her most striking feature was her hair, which was shiny blue-black and fell away from her face in great luxuriant waves. Lily had always longed for black hair, so it was the first thing she noticed about Joan. That and the fact that Joan didn't look like the other women doctors. Joan wore makeup and perfume and fashionable clothes. But despite these eccentricities, she was devoid of pretension. She treated everyone the same, from the chief administrator to the Mexican and Polish cleaning women. Everyone one loved her. Joan's specialty was childhood leukemia. Lily often wondered why Joan didn't go crazy or become hardened from seeing so many dying kids. But Joan had some sort of secret; magic perhaps, or indestructible faith. Lily never saw it flag, not until later, when everything came unwired.

Lily had gone to work in Joan's department as a clerk-typist and immediately fell under Joan's spell. This was less than a year after the punch-press accident that had crushed the forefinger of her left hand. "Don't go back to the factory," her father had said, driving her home from the emergency room. He had come straight from the mill, still wearing his hardhat. "Get a job with some class, someplace where you'll meet a guy who makes money with his brains instead of his back." Lily had sat studying her hand. The injured finger throbbed like a little heart under its balloon of snowy gauze.

For some reason that was unfathomable to Lily, Joan took an interest in her. "You're too bright for this job," she said. "Why don't you go back to school and get a degree?" No one had ever told Lily that she was bright.

That winter, Joan worked late a lot, and she gave Lily theater and ballet and symphony tickets that Joan was unable to use. Until then, Lily had never seen any kind of live performance. She attended entranced, comprehending nothing, loving the sounds and movements, feeling like a trespasser in the carpeted aisles of the Auditorium, the Civic Opera House, Orchestra Hall. Eventually, Joan had seen the little sketches Lily made whenever she talked on the phone. "Why, these are delightful," Joan had said, turning her perfect smile on Lily. A few mornings later, she found a catalog from the Art Institute of Chicago on her desk. With Joan's help, she signed up for a drawing class. She did well. She started with still life, then moved on to figurative, where she did even better. Lily did not associate with the other students. She kept her mouth shut. That way, no one would guess that she didn't belong.

One day, Joan said, "I'd love for you to meet my son. Can you come to dinner this Saturday?" The Radleys owned a three-story Victorian house in Evanston. They had four cats and two dogs. Joan's husband, Ben, was a professor of chemistry at Northwestern University and looked exactly like a professor of chemistry ought to look. He was tall and thin. He wore horn-rimmed glasses, a neatly trimmed beard and a tweed jacket with suede elbow patches. He smoked a pipe. When he questioned Lily about her classes at the Art Institute, he focused his complete attention on her.

The Radleys had three children, the youngest of whom was still in high school. His name was Alex and he didn't talk much. The oldest, Erica was in Boston at medical school. The middle child was Ferrell. He played the cello. He had just moved back to Evanston from two years of study abroad. He was developing a solo career. Lily could hardly speak to him. He looked exactly like Joan. He even had Joan's hair, which he wore long, fastened in a neat ponytail on the nape of his neck. When he and Joan sat at the piano playing duets before dinner (Mozart, Lily thought; she had been listening to a lot of music that year), they had laughed like children. Lily watched their heads bobbing up and down as their eyes moved from the sheet music to the keyboard. The light from the lamp next to the piano made blue-and-white sparks in their hair. Lily pressed her hands together and looked away.

Dinner consisted of stuffed Cornish hens and other things Lily had never before tasted and couldn't name. It was cooked and served by a tall skinny black woman named Carrie who lived in. Lily had never known any colored people. At school, the colored and white kids didn't mix. Carrie was a paid servant, which Lily could understand, yet in the kitchen, Alex and Ferrell put their arms around Carrie and kissed her or teased her about riding in the back of the bus. When Carrie told them they weren't too big to whip, she wasn't kidding. Lily sucked in her breath as Carrie came from the kitchen with a large platter and served Lily first. She looked around quickly, saw that everyone was absorbed in a conversation about the upcoming Democratic National Convention and the antiwar protesters who were planning to camp out in Grant Park. She swallowed, took the fork from the platter and scooped a Cornish hen onto her plate. She hoped that no one had seen her hand trembling.

After dinner, Ferrell took out his cello and played the Bach Unaccompanied Cello Suites. Lily listened in anguish. She stared at her hands. She wished she understood the music. When Ferrell was finished, he sat for a moment with his face lowered, the bow still poised above the strings. Then he slowly raised his head. Lily thought he looked like a swimmer emerging from the water. His eyes rested on Lily. Six weeks later, they were lovers.

Lily suddenly sees the Water Tower pass by. "Damn," she says softly. Now she'll have to walk back. She reaches for the signal cord. It's windy on Michigan Avenue and Lily winces, buttoning the collar of her coat. She looks up at the Water Tower. She read once in a magazine that the Water Tower was an architectural horror and this makes her feel guilty. She has always loved the Water Tower, and surely no one with genuine taste can love an architectural horror. For a few months after reading the article, Lily tried to dislike it, but she finally gave up. She knows what this indicates, but what can the world expect from someone who grew up in the shadow of the Bethlehem Steel Works in a two-flat reeking of boiled cabbage?

When she arrives at Northwestern Memorial, she is directed to the tenth floor. She gets off the elevator and avoids the nurses' station. She looks at the room numbers and arrows posted on the wall and begins walking, passing a solarium where an old man wearing a Cubs hat sits in a wheelchair reading *People Magazine*. When she reaches Joan's room, she hesitates in the doorway. It's a semi-private room, which surprises her, and one of the beds is empty. In the other is an elderly woman, her face turned toward the window, eyes closed. Lily hesitates. She wonders if Joan is in the bathroom or off getting therapy or something. She's trying to decide what to do when the old woman opens her eyes and turns her head.

"I'm sorry," Lily says. "I didn't mean to disturb you. I was looking—"

The old woman's hands move spasmodically on the blanket. She says, "My God." Lily stares. "My God," the woman repeats. "Lily."

Lily walks to the bed. The old woman's face opens in a smile, and the smile is the same: wide mouth, perfect teeth, a deep dimple in the left cheek. "Hello, Joan." She bends and kisses Joan's cheek. It's as dry and yellow as old newspapers, and the smell of cancer is unmistakable.

"Sit down," Joan says, still smiling out of her ruined face. She gestures toward a chair and Lily pulls it up to the bed. Joan holds out her hand, and Lily takes it in both of hers. "So," Joan says, "How did you know I was here?"

"Ellen called me. I didn't know you'd been ill."

"I'm dying," Joan says matter-of-factly, in a tone of voice one might use to discuss the weather or the merits of a particular make of automobile. Lily doesn't know what to say. "I had an astrocytoma." Joan taps a spot on her head with her free hand. "Malignant, unfortunately. They took it out, but now it's metastasizing. I had some chemo and I felt pretty good for a while. I was even able to go back to the lab. I'm grateful for that. It gave me time to get my work in shape for my assistant. She's good. Really good . . . It makes it easier, you know? . . .

Lily, don't cry. It's all right."

Lily blushes. She frees her hands from Joan's and gropes in her coat pocket for a Kleenex. "I'm sorry," she says, blowing her nose.

"It's all right," Joan repeats.

Lily mops her eyes and cheeks, blows her nose a second time. She bets her mascara is a mess. Finally she dredges up the courage to look at Joan. Joan is still smiling. Her skin is sallow and her neck is creased and flabby. Lily wonders what happened to Joan's hair. There isn't much of it and what remains is white and wispy. The chemo probably. She wants to burst into tears again and she bites the inside of her cheek until she tastes blood. She swallows blood and saliva and forces herself to smile back at Joan.

"I'm rather lucky, actually," Joan says.

"Lucky?"

Joan nods. "That sounds strange, I suppose, but I've had a lot of time to think. I believe it's better this way."

Lily shakes her head. "I don't understand."

"It gives one time," Joan replies. "To prepare, I mean. To prepare one's family . . ." Joan looks out the window, then back at Lily. "There are things that I've been able to say to my children, to Ben, that otherwise might not have been said."

Joan looks down at her lap. "Does Ferrell know?"

"It's hard to say. Ben went to see him, but no one knows whether he hears or not."

"He's never . . ." Lily can't finish the question.

"No," Joan says.

Lily had just come from the Read Zone Center. She stood in the kitchen of the apartment on Wells Street. It was a suffocating August night. All the windows were open and the air was clamorous with crickets, but there was no breeze. The Peace Now mobile hung immobile from the light fixture. The kitchen was neat, spotless. It was one of the things that always gave her away. Her hair grew to her waist, she wore faded jeans with psychedelic symbols and she did not wear a bra. But she was a fraud. She saw Ferrell's shirt folded over the back of a chair. She picked it up and smelled his familiar smell. They had told her the prognosis was hopeful, but Lily knew. She pressed the shirt against her face and wept.

Lily looks at Joan. Joan is examining the scenery outside the window. A silence stretches between them and Lily gropes for words. If the silence is not broken, she doesn't know what will happen. "Are you," she begins tentatively, but her voice comes out small and defeated. She clears her throat. Joan looks away from the window and back at Lily. Her eyes are yellow and tired and Lily sees a hunted look. "Are you," she says again, her voice strong now, "in pain?"

Joan plucks at the bed covers. "No," she says, "at least not enough to matter." The corners of her mouth turn down sardonically. "That's one of the advantages of being a mover and shaker in the world of medicine. I get all the drugs I want."

Lily smiles.

"I'm afraid of pain," Joan says. "I always have been. I don't know how I managed to have three babies. Do you think I'm a coward?"

Lily swallows. Ferrell had once asked her that.

It was two days before his Orchestra Hall debut. Lily was going to the Art Institute full time now. She was working in oils. All her teachers were impressed. She no longer felt like a trespasser. She knew what codas and adagios were. Ferrell's family adored her. Ferrell adored her. His career was burgeoning and his agent talked about a European tour. Lily would go along; they'd make a honeymoon of it. The future was unfurling like the petals of spring flowers. On this particular night she had come home from a class and found Ferrell sitting alone in the twilight at the kitchen table. She had thought the apartment empty, so when she turned on the light and saw him there, she was startled. "Good God!" she said. "Why are you sitting in the dark?"

Ferrell inspected the calluses on the fingers of his left hand. "I smelled something burning," he said. "I thought it might be the wiring. Did you know that this building is ninety-seven years old? Electrical fires can't be faked, you know." He interrupted the examination of his calluses and looked at Lily, and she wondered much later why she hadn't run out of the apartment shrieking. Instead, she set her portfolio carefully against the table. She reached out and touched Ferrell's hair. It hung loosely around his shoulders and it wasn't very clean. She said, "Maybe we should call the janitor."

Ferrell said, "Do you think I'm a coward?"

"No," she tells Joan. "There's nothing to be learned from that kind of pain, and it isn't ennobling. If I were you, I'd take whatever is necessary to make me comfortable."

"I've paid my dues, haven't I." Joan says, and it isn't a question.

"Yes," Lily answers.

Joan draws a shuddery, uneven breath. "So," she says. "How is your son? Tell me about your boy."

Lily runs her tongue along the back of her teeth. Her mouth tastes coppery. "He's fine. He's a good boy." She grins. "Of course, adolescence is only a couple of years away."

Joan chuckles. "Most parents survive it," she says. "Is he a good student?"

"Yes, he loves school. He's very disciplined. I don't know where he gets it. Not from his mother certainly."

"From his father?"

Lily nods. "Probably." She thinks of her husband, the meticulously arranged tools in the basement, the lists printed neatly on index cards: p/up dry clning. mail visa. sears—oil filter. "My son likes math and science. And he loves to read. I read to him from the time he was an infant."

It was Joan's turn to nod. "Children watch too much television. A child who loves reading has a great advantage."

"He's a good boy," Lily repeats.

"I'm glad," says Joan. "Are you still working for the same company?"

"Yes."

"How many years now?"

"Sometimes I think too many," Lily replies, making a mirthless sound. "But I can't complain. It's a good company. They pay me well and they promote women. I started out as a typist and now I'm buying food ingredients, corn syrup and related products, to be specific. I'm lucky. I've never been aware of any sex discrimination, or maybe I just haven't recognized it." She and Joan both laugh.

"That's good," says Joan. "And your husband?"

"He's fine too. He has an administrative job now. He works at a desk."

"That must be a great relief. I've never understood how policemen's wives keep their sanity."

Lily only nods. She does not tell Joan that after Ferrell nothing has ever truly shaken her again.

Ferrell screamed, kept screaming. It was a white sound, and it tore the inside of Lily's skull like talons. Six men—two paramedics and four cops—were getting Ferrell into a strait jacket and Ferrell kept screaming that Lily mustn't let them do this to him. Ferrell's cello lay in splinters around the fireplace. Lily was unable to answer. She was too busy coughing blood. It would be three days before she could speak, a month before the fingerprints on her throat went away.

Joan coughs. There's a ghastly resonance to the cough, as though it's coming from somewhere deeper than her lungs. She leans forward, gags. She makes a strangled sound and Lily springs from her chair. She grabs tissues from a box on the bedside table and presses them into Joan's hand. Joan expels whatever it is she's coughed up. She breathes heavily and her face is slick with oily sweat. Lily strokes her back. "I'm sorry," Joan gasps.

"Nonsense," Lily says. "Would you like a drink of water?"

Joan nods. She flops bonelessly back against the pillows. There is a green plastic flask on the table. Lily picks it up, but it's empty. "I'll get this filled," she says. When she comes back with the fresh water, Joan's color is back to gray-yellow. Lily pours water into a glass and hands it to Joan. Joan takes a few tentative sips and hands the glass back.

Lily sits down again. Joan's eyes are closed and Lily sees how deeply they lie in their sockets, the lids smudgy violet as though someone has tried to apply eye shadow in a bad light. She wonders if Joan is going to sleep. She wonders if she should leave.

Joan says, "I'm glad you came. I've been thinking about you. As a matter of fact, I've been thinking about you quite a lot."

Lily says nothing. She takes Joan's hand again, and the hand is cool and light, insubstantial as a pile of dry twigs.

"We weren't very kind to you, I'm afraid."

Lily explores a rather large cavity in an upper molar with the tip of her tongue. The filling fell out two days ago. She has an appointment with the dentist tomorrow. She is grateful that the nerve is dead. The tooth hasn't hurt a bit. Joan's eyes are still closed. "We were—there was a need to place blame. Anywhere but on ourselves."

Ben Radley and Lily stood facing each other in the middle of the corridor of the psychiatric unit. It was the third psychiatric unit she had become familiar with in the past sixteen months. The vinyl tile floor shone with fresh wax and the air reeked of Lysol and urine. Ben's eyes raked her. "Why were you always pushing him?" he said. "Why couldn't you leave him alone?"

Lily stood speechless, hugging her middle. Alex came up to them, placed a hand on his father's arm. "Dad," he said, and Ben shoved the hand away, keeping his eyes on Lily.

"Answer me!" he shouted. "Who did you think you were to pressure my son the way you did?"

"Dad," Alex said again. Ben whirled toward Alex. Two orderlies and an intern at the nurses' station interrupted their gossip to stare. "She's nothing but an ignorant Polack!" Ben shouted. "Who did she think she was?"

Joan's eyes are still closed. Lily continues to say nothing. Joan says, "You were—heroic." She pronounces the word in three distinct syllables. "People don't use terms like that much anymore, do they? Words like *heroic* and *loyalty* and *honor* are rather old-fashioned. One must always say them with a deprecating smile if one says them at all." Joan opens her eyes.

"I was not heroic," Lily says. "I loved him. It never occurred to me that I had a choice."

Joan closes her eyes again. "That's why you were heroic."

There's a squeaking noise from the doorway. Lily turns to look. A young black woman in a pink-and-white uniform approaches the bed with a tray. There's a little plastic bar pin on her blouse that says *Patricia*. She smiles a cheery professional smile. It's her shoes that make the squeaking noise. "Dinnertime," she says, and she busies herself cranking up the bed, settling the tray in front of Joan.

"I'm not hungry," Joan says.

Patricia pretends not to hear. "In honor of St. Patrick's Day," she says, removing the stainless-steel cover from the tray, "corned beef and cabbage."

Stem rises from the plate. Patricia walks out of the room, shoes squeaking energetically. The fragrance of cabbage fills Lily's nostrils. She thinks she may throw up.

It's almost dark when Lily reaches Michigan Avenue, and the 151 bus is crowded. Luckily she gets a seat after only a few minutes. She will get home at about her usual time. Her son will have taken the beef stew out of the freezer and put it in the microwave. The only thing she'll have to do is a make a salad and set the table. Her husband has a Fraternal Order of Police meeting tonight and won't be home until late.

The bus turns into Lincoln Park and Lily gazes out at the naked trees and benches, the white fence of the Farm in the Zoo, the looming glass domes of the conservatory. The azalea show is still on. She ought to take her son this weekend before it closes. The boy likes flowers. This worries his father. It doesn't worry Lily. The boy's father knows his worry is ridiculous. "It's the way I was raised," he says, shaking his head. He's a good husband and father. Lily knows how lucky she is. There were a few years when he was drinking that were really touch-and-go, but then he had seen what was happening. He transferred out of homicide and now he hardly drinks at all, just a beer once in a while, usually during Monday Night Football. Lily hasn't painted in years. Her husband found some of her watercolors when they moved into the house. "These are real pretty, Lil," he had said, looking at her with something like awe. "How come you stopped?" They have a nice house. Their son is healthy, and Lily knows how lucky she is. And they're saving to buy a farm, somewhere downstate where the winters are shorter. Nearly all of Lily's salary goes into the farm account. That and the boy's college fund. Lily is good at her job and she's well paid. She knows how to get along with people. She's able to extract information from vendors and competitors that no one else can get, and she does it without creating enemies. It's generally conceded that what she doesn't know about corn sweeteners nobody knows, and the prices she recently negotiated on a multi-million dollar purchase are the lowest in the history of the company. This year she's eligible for four weeks of vacation. This year she'll make vice president. Lily knows how lucky she is, and sometimes she wakens in the night and her pillow is wet with tears from dreams she cannot remember.

SNAKES

I ONCE HAD AN AFFAIR with a man who disliked snakes. He told me this very early in our relationship, so there's no excuse for me not knowing what he was really about. I was purely blinded by lust. There was something about the taste of his skin that made me feral and shameless.

He told me he'd found a huge king snake in his garage— or rather his daughter had found it— and that he'd blown it apart with a shotgun.

"A shotgun?" I echoed pointlessly.

"I wanted to make sure I hit him."

At the time I was licking his collarbone. I tried to imagine the concussion a shotgun would create in a suburban garage— even with the door open.

"King snakes are harmless," I said, biting softly. "They eat rodents. Why didn't you just carry it off into the field behind your house?"

"I. don't. like. snakes." He placed an audible period after each word.

I had my own snake story, although I didn't tell my lover. I may be reckless but I am not altogether stupid. This man had a repertoire of variations on the ancient theme that kept me in a languor of half-arousal for days on end. I wanted as much as I could get for as long as I could get it.

One summer when I was home from college, I found a snake in Aunt Liddy and Uncle Will's barn. Or rather Aunt Liddy found it. Uncle Will wasn't around, and it was getting on for sundown, which meant that the cows would be wandering down from the pasture for evening milking. I was in the garden picking lettuce and tomatoes for supper when Aunt Liddy made me come to view the snake. It was the biggest one I'd ever seen outside a zoo, a timber rattler as thick as my forearm. It lolled in a series of graceful S-curves in a pool of lambent sunshine just inside the barn door.

Now this snake, you could tell from its size alone, was older than God; by inference a smart snake, or it wouldn't have gotten so old. I studied it from a respectful distance. It ran out its long, delicate tongue and snicked the air. This struck me as a gesture of great refinement.

"I wish you'd just go on," I said. "That field yonder is full of fat mice, any one of which would be a snap for a wily old varmint like you." The snake stared back at me, unblinking. It was plain as death that it would be right there when the cows came in.

"Shit," I said. I walked back to the house and fetched Uncle Will's twenty-two, which lay alongside the twelve-gauge on top of the dining room breakfront. Uncle Will hunted rabbits and squirrels with it mostly, but kept it loaded for the occasional barnyard pest—like the rattlesnake I was going for now.

I made short work of it. I had to, because sometimes if you think about a thing too long, you end up not doing it at all. I came up close, took careful aim at the head and squeezed off the shot. A twenty-two doesn't make a whole lot of noise, just a pop, like a toy gun. But that old rattlesnake arced into the air, falling down in a cascade of opalescent light, a shower of pink and golden spangles where the setting sun shimmered off its skin.

I waited a long time to drag the body by the tail out to the edge of the garden. I dug a deep hole so the dogs and cats couldn't get at him. I cried while I spaded up the earth.

Later, after I'd stopped sleeping with the man whose taste drove me wild with desire, I thought about the snakes. Why would a man kill a thing, anyway, when he really didn't have to? Even snakes have beautiful skin.

HOSPITALITY

MAGGIE PUTS DOWN the pastry bag and carefully licks her fingers clean of pink butter-cream icing. Then she rinses them under the faucet and dries them on her apron. It is precisely 11:35 AM. The phone continues to ring as she walks unhurriedly to the hallway telephone stand. She hopes that by moving slowly the phone will stop ringing before she reaches it, but it doesn't. It will keep ringing until she picks it up, just like it does every morning at 11:35. The only exception to the pattern since it began nearly three weeks ago is weekends, when she's not alone in the house.

Like it knows, she thought. *Like it's watching me.*

Now she stands before her ringing phone, hands smoothing her apron. She reaches out.

"Hello," she says dully. She holds the receiver slightly away from her head, as though pressing it against her ear in the normal way will invite an intimacy she doesn't want.

The usual static, punctuated by quick, metallic beeps comes through, then finally The Voice, as she has come to think of it. "Wake up, Maggie!" it says.

"I *am* awake," Maggie answers, "and I don't know why you think you have to tell me this every day of the week." The only reply is more clicks and beeps.

Maggie hangs up. She returns to the kitchen and picks up the pastry bag again, meticulously squeezing out the petals on the rose she is building. She needs fifteen butter-cream roses for the spray of blossoms she envisions for the top of the cake. Then come the pale green leaves and the gold latticework on the sides of the cake. Finished, it will look like a basket of roses. The cake is for Grace—or Graciela, as she has recently announced she wants to be called—who will celebrate her *quinceañera* tomorrow.

Maggie does not know where fifteen years have gone. She used to roll her eyes when she heard her mother express similar thoughts. Now Maggie is the same age as her mother was then—thirty-six—and she still feels like she's about eighteen. She has recently begun to register a mild shock at the sight of her own image in the mirror. She's put on weight—not much, but she certainly can't wear size-six jeans anymore, and her breasts have gone slack from three babies. Miguel doesn't seem to mind, though. At least he doesn't complain. He's put on a few pounds himself over the years. The other day she caught him in front of the big mirror on the bedroom-closet door, sucking in his gut and turning sideways to flex his biceps. He'd blushed darkly when she'd walked in on him. Quickly he grabbed his shirt off the chair, pivoting away so she wouldn't see the blush spreading over his chest. Maggie wonders if he's flirting with some girl down at the dealership. They're all so young, with the kind of blank, uncritical faces that married men of a certain age seem to fancy.

Maggie hasn't told anyone about the phone calls, not even Miguel, nor about the event that preceded their start. Who would believe her? Half the time she doesn't believe it herself. Sometimes, after the kids are off to school and Miguel has left for work, she pulls out her journal, which she keeps in a locked drawer, and rereads the entry for that day, just to remind herself that it really happened, that she's not crazy after all. Her handwriting is jagged, as though she'd been writing in a moving vehicle (which she hadn't) or been really upset (which she had). Maggie finds this oddly comforting. If her imagination had manufactured the whole thing, she believes, there'd have been no reason to be that upset.

It had been a Wednesday evening, about seven o'clock, just as the sun was setting, and she was driving home from the big Safeway over in Durango. It had been a fine, warm spring day, and she'd worked in the garden a long time, carefully removing her tomato sets and bedding plants from the cold frame and placing them in the ground. That was the reason she'd been so late going to the grocery store, leaving the kids at home with instructions to Grace—Graciela—for starting dinner.

She was driving along Route 141 with the windows down a few inches, listening to Waylon Jennings sing "The Highwayman" on KKOW ("your cowboy-country radio heaven, playin' country-western twenty-four/seven"). A green pickup truck whizzed past, going in the other direction, but there wasn't much traffic. Suddenly a flicker of light out the driver-side window caught her eye. She glanced quickly to the left, expecting to see another vehicle or the rising moon. Whatever it was, it was brightly lit, and when she glanced again, she saw a glistening ball, maybe fifteen feet in diameter, overtaking her about a dozen feet above the ground.

Maggie doesn't remember feeling anything after that except for a tight, scalding sensation on the top of her head, as though boiling water had been poured over her scalp. The ball of light shot past her and then dropped directly over the road, blocking her way. Maggie braked to a stop, spilling shopping bags onto the floor. Her hands stayed on the steering wheel. She didn't move at all, just watched as a door appeared in the sphere and three men stepped out. Only they didn't really step—there were no steps—they glided to the ground slowly, like underinflated balloons, and began walking toward her.

They were ordinary-looking youngish men, dressed in navy-blue coveralls with some sort of insignia embroidered in white thread over the breast pocket. At first Maggie thought they must be military, but that couldn't be right because they all had shoulder-length blond hair. In fact, they looked enough alike to be brothers.

Open the window, said one of the men, grinning broadly, though he didn't say the words aloud; Maggie heard them inside her head. She watched her left hand release its grip on the steering wheel and move to the automatic window button on the armrest. The window slid down.

The grinning man leaned over as he reached the car. *Nice weather,* he said pleasantly. *Where are you from?*

"Socorro," Maggie heard herself answering, "but I live outside Durango now."

The second man grinned too. *Do you have any cookies?* Asked the third one.

"Uh—sure," Maggie said. She rummaged in the spilled groceries until she found some Archway windmill cookies, Miguel's favorite. She handed them through the window and watched in amazement as the second man attempted to bite into the closed package. He pulled it away from his mouth and looked with bewilderment first at the package, then at Maggie.

"Here," Maggie said, holding out her hand. She broke

open the plastic at one end and pulled out three cookies. She had a sudden memory of Miguelito at age two, shrieking in frustration over an unopened bag of Oreos that she'd just brought home from the supermarket. She recalled his smile of undiluted joy, tears still streaming down his red little cheeks, as she'd removed a cookie from the bag and placed it in his upraised hand. The three men had that same look of innocent delight right now as she distributed the windmills.

Thank you, they murmured, munching happily.

Maggie thrust the package toward the first man. "Here," she said, "why don't you take the whole thing?"

He accepted the gift with a broadening grin. *You are very generous,* he said. *Can you tell me what time it is?*

Maggie looked at the dashboard clock. "A quarter past seven," she replied.

Have a nice day, he grinned. *We'll come to your house sometime.*

Abruptly, the men turned, walked back to the glowing sphere, and rose into the doorway, which swallowed them seamlessly. For a moment, the sphere hung against the rosy sunset. Maggie thought later that her ears popped at about that time, just before the sphere shot straight up into the twilight and disappeared.

Maggie sat there, unable to move for several minutes, until a pair of headlights rounded the curve ahead of her and swept across her windshield. It was nearly dark, and there she was, stopped dead in the middle of a country highway, alone, and a cold wind was blowing through the open windows. At some point, the engine had died. She turned on the ignition, rolled up the windows, and drove home.

Maggie finishes the fifteen roses and leaves them drying on a sheet of waxed paper on the countertop. Ever since that night, she has been unable to think of anything else.

We'll come to your house sometime. Maggie doesn't want them to come to her house. She doesn't understand why they stopped her on Route 141 to begin with. Or who they were. The more she tries to make sense of the event, the more absurd it becomes. She's not ignorant, of course. She's seen Geraldo and Jerry Springer and listened late at night to George Noory and the stories of people abducted from their beds. But her experience was nothing like theirs. No bald little grays in skin-tight suits, no preying-mantis-type monsters conducting physical examinations or taking her for flying-saucer rides to Andromeda. She'd always thought those people were wacko anyway, but at least their stories had a kind of logic to them.

Maggie doesn't know what to do. Maybe she should go into therapy, but how would she explain it to Miguel? Briefly she considers making an appointment with Father Julio, the pastor at Our Lady of Holy Mysteries. Maybe it's a spiritual issue after all. She tries to imagine herself sitting in Father Julio's office, talking to him across his immaculate antique oak desk. What would he make of those blatantly Anglo brothers and their glowing vehicle?

Father Julio tries to act as though he's at home with his Anglo parishioners; he tends to mention too often that he graduated from Notre Dame. Miguel finds this amusing, but Maggie feels a subtle current of distrust emanating from Father Julio whenever she goes to confession, as though he thinks she's hiding a secret life of *gringa* sins he can only imagine. She wishes old Father Willis were still alive, but by the time he'd died two years ago, the parish was more than half Hispanic, and so Father Julio had been inevitable. "Make a novena," he'd tell her, or "Say ten Hail Marys and ten Our Fathers and see me in a week." As usual, Maggie circles back to the conclusion that she has to just forget about the whole thing. Only she can't.

Maggie completes her morning chores and returns to the cake. It comes out beautifully, the best cake she's done so far. She drives into Durango to buy wrapping paper for Grace's birthday present and a fat *piñata* for the party on Saturday. All the relatives will be there: both sets of grandparents, the fair-haired, fair-skinned aunts and uncles; the dark-haired, dark-skinned *tías* and *tíos,* all the cousins. It had taken a few years, but finally Maggie's family and Miguel's family are able to relax in one another's company. Maggie's sister, Vivian, has actually become friends with Miguel's sister Marisol; their children are the same ages and attend the same grade school.

Maggie is just emerging from the Hallmark store, a large shopping bag in hand, when she sees the three brothers from the glowing sphere coming up the street. She can hardly believe her senses. They are walking toward her, dressed in what look like brand-new Levis and plaid shirts and western boots and hats, like eastern tourists gone native. They pass other pedestrians, nodding pleasantly, the same manic grins on their faces. When they reach Maggie, the grins widen in recognition as they make eye contact. One of them even winks, but they don't slow down to chat. Maggie turns and watches them disappear around a corner. She feels as though she has stepped off a cliff and is falling into a vast chasm too deep for daylight to penetrate. Somehow she reaches her car and throws the shopping bag into the back seat. She locks the doors and starts the engine, at the same time punching out on her cell phone the speed-dial number for Our Lady of Holy Mysteries.

Father Julio sits across the desk, his hands tented thoughtfully, elbows resting on the clean blotter. He wears

Levis and a threadbare green Harley-Davidson sweatshirt. He nods at the bottle of tequila at his left. The pale worm lies curled shyly at the bottom of the bottle. "Would you like another?" he inquires politely.

Maggie shakes her head. "No thank you," she declines. She places the empty shot glass carefully on the desk. Normally Maggie doesn't drink much, but she'd been trembling so badly when she arrived that Father Julio had pulled the bottle from a desk drawer and insisted she take a drink. It had had the desired effect. She'd stopped shaking and stammering and told Father Julio the whole story. He listened attentively, not interrupting, while she finished her account.

Now Maggie waits for his response. She thinks he is about to refer her for psychiatric evaluation; in fact, she hopes he does. A prescription for Prozac will probably fix her right up. She looks at him expectantly.

At last Father Julio reaches for the bottle of tequila and produces another shot glass. "Do you mind?" he asks.

"No, of course not," she says.

He pours a shot and drinks it in a single swallow, then pours another. He sighs, stares out the window, drums his fingertips on the blotter and finally looks back at her. "First of all," Father Julio says, "I don't think you're crazy. Without breaking confidence, I can at least tell you that you're not the first person in this parish to have . . . strange experiences." He takes a sip of tequila. "But aside from that, I don't know what to tell you. We live in a strange world, and things happen for which I have no theological explanation."

Maggie looks down at her hands.

"I'm sorry," Father Julio says. "I know you came here for help, for answers, and I don't have any."

Maggie looks up again and is surprised to see tears in

Father Julio's eyes. He glances away in embarrassment; he clears his throat. "There's only one thing I can think of," he says slowly. "Did you ever read the story in Genesis about the three men who visited Abraham?"

Maggie shakes her head. Father Julio takes a Bible from a small collection of books between brass bookends in the image of Kokopeli. "These three guys show up unannounced," Father Julio explains, "and Abraham invites them to rest in the shade while he prepares an elaborate meal. They tell him that they're going to return the following year, and that when they do, Sarah will have borne a son."

"Now I remember," Maggie says. "Abraham and Sarah were already old—Sarah didn't even have her periods anymore."

"Right," Father Julio nods, flipping pages. "But those men were correct: Sarah miraculously conceived a son, Isaac."

Maggie squirms in alarm. "Holy Mother," she breathes.

"What?" Father Julio asks.

"Nothing," Maggie answers.

"Anyway," Father Julio continues, "listen to this, from St. Paul's letter to the Hebrews." Father Julio has put on reading glasses and he holds the Bible at an angle to catch the light from the window, through which Maggie can see into the courtyard where masses of pink tulips bloom around the feet of the Virgin. "'Do not neglect hospitality,'" he reads, "'for through it, some have entertained angels unaware.' See, those three guys who showed up at Abraham's tent looked like ordinary men. Abraham didn't know they were angels; he simply did what he apparently always did when travelers passed through his neighborhood. He offered food and water and rest."

"So St. Paul was referring to Abraham's visitors," Maggie says. A small silence stretches out as both she and Father Julio think about the implications of St. Paul's admonition.

"I think," Maggie says, drawing an uneven breath, "that means that as Christians, we should show hospitality—kindness—to everyone, without judging them, because they might turn out to be angels."

Father Julio nods. "I think so."

"But doesn't it go further?" she asks.

Father Julio raises his eyebrows. "In what way?"

"Shouldn't we be hospitable because it's the loving thing to do and not just because we're afraid of offending angels?"

Father Julio gives her a long look. "Of course, Mrs. Ramirez," he replies after a moment. "That is exactly what we should do."

Maggie remembers the windmill cookies. "Tell me," she says, "without violating confidence, have any of the other people who've had these, uh, 'strange experiences' been harmed in any way?"

"You mean other than being scared out of a year's sleep?"

"Right."

"Not to my knowledge," Father Julio concedes. "Not that I know of."

Maggie finishes folding the I ♥ SANTA FE T-shirt and makes her way to the bedroom, wet stains spreading across her shirt as the cries escalate to a furious wail. She bends over the crib and scoops up the baby, feeling the diaper, which, thank God, is still dry. There is a rocking chair by the window, the one in which she'd nursed and rocked the older children. In honor of the new baby, Miguel had refinished it and reupholstered the seat in corduroy in a shade of blue that presciently matches the baby's eyes perfectly.

Maggie sits down, unbuttoning her shirt, and the baby seizes the swollen nipple greedily.

At first Miguel had been shocked. "How the hell did it happen?" he wondered. "Did you miss a pill or something?"

Maggie shook her head and burst into tears. "I don't know," she sobbed.

Miguel had immediately put his arms around her. "It's all right, *Querida*," he murmured. "Not even the pill is foolproof. It was meant to be, that's all."

He rested his chin on top of her head until she stopped crying, then eased her onto the bed. He spread his palm on her belly, although it was much too early to feel anything. "It must have been the night of Gracie's *quinceañera*," he chuckled.

Maggie recalled how they'd danced together like high-school kids. When a slow song came along, they'd held each other close, and Miguel had whispered things into her hair. She could feel his excitement as he pressed against her, and to her surprise, desire swept through her in a quick, hot flood. It seemed as though weeks passed before the last of the guests left and the children were in bed.

After the initial surprise, Miguel was as enthusiastic about the new pregnancy as he'd been about the first one. He bloomed out in full *machismo*, bragging to everyone who would listen, glowing with pride as Maggie's belly ballooned. They decided to build an addition onto the house, one that would nearly double their current square footage. Miguel's brother Ramon built custom-designed houses, and they began work the very next month.

They also decided not to learn the new baby's sex until the birth. "I hope it's a girl," Miguel said, "but I'll be happy either way as long as it's healthy."

Late one night they lay awake thinking up baby names

according to the formula they'd used for the older kids: Maggie's choice if it was a girl and Miguel's choice if it was a boy. "Lucinda Elizabeth," Maggie said, "for my grandmother on Mom's side."

"That's pretty," Miguel agreed.

"And if it's a boy?" Maggie prodded.

"Isaac Pacifico," Miguel answered decisively.

"Pacifico for your dad's dad," Maggie said cautiously, "but where does Isaac come from?"

"It's a nice, old-fashioned name," Miguel replied. "There's a story in the Bible about Abraham and Sarah. They had a baby in their old age—just like us."

Maggie punched his shoulder softly. "We're hardly old," she protested.

"I know," Miguel said, "but this baby is a surprise, just like Isaac was to Sarah and Abraham."

Maggie studied her husband's face in the moonlight pouring through the window. It contained no hint of secrets or guile.

It had been an easy pregnancy and an easy birth, the easiest by far of her four babies. Maggie had dreaded the drudgery of diapers and night feedings, but she found herself, after the passage of so many years since the last child (Roberto was ten) a much more confident and relaxed mother. And to her delight, Graciela was a tremendous help. She came straight home from school or basketball practice every day instead of hanging out with her friends. She did loads of laundry, helped Maggie with the cooking, and doted on little Isaac. Miguelito and Roberto were proud and protective.

Lying now in Maggie's arms, Isaac gradually stops suckling as his eyelids grow heavy and finally close. He has lived up to his middle name, for he is a contented baby who sleeps through the night and smiles readily. Maggie admires his long eyelashes and pale skin, the mop of white-blond curls that has begun to fill out on his tiny, perfectly round head. The older children have her features and their father's coloring. Isaac has his dad's high forehead and prominent cheekbones, but Maggie's fair skin, hair and cornflower eyes. As Maggie rocks, Isaac's mouth releases its hold on her nipple.

The 11:35 AM phone calls stopped as abruptly as they'd begun, right after Maggie learned she was pregnant. She doesn't know if it was coincidence or something more.

Any day now there will be a knock on the door. Maggie has read and reread the eighteenth chapter of Genesis, but there is no mention of the angels' promised return. That doesn't mean it didn't happen, though, and Father Julio agrees: angels always keep their word.

Maggie has already baked the cake for the christening party. Its chocolaty layers lie in the lightless depths of the freezer, awaiting only the butter-cream frosting and decorations. Father Julio will officiate, of course. Maggie and Father Julio have actually become friends. Where before she saw coldness and anti-Anglo judgment, Maggie now recognizes fear of rejection and doubt about his efficacy as a pastor.

There will be three angels on the cake, Maggie decides. The rich irony will be appreciated only by her and Father Julio. The angels will have shoulder-length blond hair and plaid robes. Maybe cowboy hats too, if she can pull it off.

It's spring again, almost a year since her twilight encounter on Route 141. And there *will* be a knock at the door. Maggie believes this as surely as she believes in the love of her family and in ultimate justice. And when it comes, she will be ready. This time she will be awake.

ALL OF IT

IT WAS WHEN MY stepsister Regina waved to me from across Central Avenue that bright May morning that I first began to suspect I was dead.

Regina died a year ago—breast cancer. She weighed seventy-two pounds and her skin had turned a ghastly yellow the day she drew her last breath. Or at least that's what they told me. I didn't make it to the hospice. Regina was a great gal, but she never showed any common sense about money. Whenever she managed to accumulate some, she'd blow it on feeding the homeless or taking care of some old codger on Social Security—like there aren't social-service agencies for that sort of thing—or rescuing dogs and cats from the local animal shelter. As a result, her wardrobe came from local thrift stores, and she died penniless.

So naturally I was surprised to see her walking down Central Avenue looking better than she ever had in life. Her auburn hair was lustrous and professionally cut. She wore a crisp pale-pink linen suit, white high heels and a white wide-brim hat with a big pink rose on the band, and she carried a smart white handbag. Very soignée, very un-Regina. Her step was energetic, and one of her favorite dogs, a crippled, worm-infested old black lab named Loki she'd gotten at the Humane Society the day he was to be gassed, tugged at a leash she held in her left hand. Come to think of it, Loki was dead too. He'd drunk antifreeze on a dreary December afternoon not long after Regina departed. Anyway, Regina gave me a jaunty wave and flashed me a big wink and continued up Central as if she saw me every morning of the week. I noticed that Loki no longer limped.

It drew me up short, I can tell you. I began to wonder exactly where I was and what I'd been doing lately. I ducked into Great Harvest Bread Company for a complimentary slice of nine-grain bread and butter and then walked three doors down to Starbucks and bought a double espresso. I carried it to a table on the sidewalk next to a big planter filled with purple hyacinths and yellow daffodils and sat down to think things out.

I was fifty-nine years old, twice married, and I had two children who lived with their mother in a North Shore neighborhood overlooking Lake Michigan, with lots of mature elm trees and black nannies pushing expensive English prams through carefully manicured parks. I thought about my children's mother. A charming and intelligent woman, a good homemaker, but plain-looking, I recalled. After the children were in grade school, I'd realized that she was not the wife I needed to move ahead professionally, so we'd parted. I had another wife now, rather younger than myself and quite decorative. For some reason, I couldn't picture her face nor could I recall much about my children. A boy and a girl—surely they were in college by now. Or were they grown up with families of their own?

I sat with my espresso and watched people pass by: harried young parents, preschool-age children in tow, struggling parcels into a Beemer parked at the curb; an elderly couple moving slowly, arm-in-arm, engaged in some acrimonious debate that had doubtless been going on forty years or more; two adolescent boys dressed in the repulsive current fashion of jail pants, oversize T-shirts and baseball caps turned backward, faces ablaze with acne and boredom; a young magenta-haired woman who was at least fifty pounds overweight, wearing skin-tight jeans and a sleeveless yellow stretch top. Her arms crawled with tattooed cobras and she leered at me suggestively.

God, people were depressing! I sipped some more espresso and felt the caffeine begin to rev up my energy. I had to figure out what I was doing here on Central Avenue on a spring morning. What had I been doing before I saw Regina waving from across the street?

I remembered playing racquetball at the East Bank Club—when? Last night? My partner was actually my law partner, Don, and we'd talked about an upcoming trial. What the hell was it about? Ah, yes. We were defending some LaSalle Street *ganef* who'd been indicted for securities fraud. He was guilty as Cain, but he had deep pockets and we'd mounted an ingenious defense.

But after the East Bank Club, my memory was blank. I was thinking about going back inside Starbucks for a latte, when my old high-school algebra teacher, Mr. Kovachek, walked by, holding hands with a really hot piece of ass, all long blond hair and long tan legs and big tits. I recalled that his wife had died of multiple sclerosis. She'd been a looker too—and a blonde—before disease ravaged her beauty. *Well, good for old Kovachek,* I thought. *He's moved on with his life. He even looks younger.* He'd flunked me for an entire semester after he caught me using a crib sheet on the final. I'd had to go to summer school. A couple of my buddies and I had set off a cherry bomb on his front porch. Unfortunately it killed the family cat, who'd been nursing a litter of kittens there. But how could we have known about the cat? Kovachek looked straight at me and nodded curtly. I was unpleasantly surprised that he recognized me.

Just then a shadow dropped across my empty espresso cup and I felt a hand on my shoulder. I looked up. "Robert!" I exclaimed. "My God, what are you doing here?" I jumped out of my chair and threw my arms around him.

"What are *you* doing here?" Robert laughed, slapping my back.

My older brother looked just as he had when he'd left the last time for Vietnam, his lieutenant's uniform immaculate, just one month to the day before his plane was shot down near the Cambodian border. Or perhaps *over* the Cambodian border. I'd wondered about that a lot over the years.

"Listen," I said. "I'm a little confused. I thought you were dead. I thought Regina was dead, but I saw her too, not half an hour ago. And I can't recollect where I slept last night or my children's names."

Robert smiled patiently. Around us, the crowd had begun to thin and I saw that the sun was setting.

"Am I dead?" I asked.

Robert smiled.

"I'm dead, aren't I?"

Robert continued to smile. Behind us, Starbucks lay dark and shuttered.

"I never imagined that it would be this way," I continued. "I mean, I never really thought about it at all, I guess. But isn't there supposed to be a tunnel and a white light and then Jesus or somebody? . . . And Rob, I hope you didn't believe what they told you about me hitting on Sarah while you were in Nam. No way would I do that, Bro."

Robert smiled.

I drew a deep breath and Robert tucked his arm through mine. Those ghastly sodium-vapor street lights had come on and a breeze blew trash and dead leaves ahead of us down the empty street.

"It takes some getting used to," Robert said.

"I can see that," I answered, shivering against the wind. For the first time I saw that I was wearing only shorts and a singlet. "Is it always like this?"

"Like what?" Robert asked.

"Like what we left behind—ugly women and unhappy marriages and boat payments and war?"

"The whole package," Robert replied somberly.

I considered this as we walked into the gathering gloom. Gray and brown leaves showered from the trees overhead. I realized that it was late autumn. Robert tightened his grip on my arm and I laughed bitterly.

"What?" Robert asked.

"People always say, 'You can't take it with you,' and I believed that. I actually believed that!"

Robert stopped and looked down at me. "Oh, little brother," he told me, his eyes full of terrible compassion, "we take all of it with us. All of it."

NOVA

THIS IS HOW I MOURNED Raf's death: After Alex told me the news, after I phoned the florist to wire the usual ghastly hothouse chrysanthemums accompanied by the requisite condolence note, after I spoke to Father Barsini about a special mass, I gathered up all our old Rolling Stones tapes and drove up into the mountains, all the way to Clingman's Dome. The sun was setting as I arrived; there weren't many people around. The famous blue haze is mostly industrial smog these days and acid rain is killing the pines. Their denuded tops thrust upward along the horizon like rows of rotting teeth, unspeakably melancholy, as though the valleys are open mouths about to announce the end of the world, which perhaps they are.

I swung into a slot in the parking lot and plugged a tape into the cassette player. *Paint It Black* jumped out of the speakers. After a few bars of that amplified bass line, my whole body contracted and I bent over the steering wheel. I saw Raf, sitting in Dan and Dolores' yard with the moonlight on his face. The image was so immediate, so pure, that I wanted to scream to erase the keenness of unbearable longing.

The body never forgets.

I met Raf in the summer of seventy-nine. Alex and I had been married for nearly seven years and Maria was just starting to crawl. We'd gone out to Long Island for Alex's nephew's grammar school graduation. There was a big family get-together at his brother's house. My sisterinlaw Dolores had been cooking for a week and her face was beginning to take on the look of all the older women of that family: lined with determined gloom and permanently flushed from standing over endless pots of sauce. As I helped her slice pepperoni, dish up coleslaw, carve immense loaves of bread and balls of provolone, she chattered nonstop about *The Young and the Restless*, our motherlinlaw's prolapsed bladder and whether or not to have her hair streaked for her cousin's wedding.

Alex's Aunt Gisela came into the kitchen. "Angie, did you bring those coupons?" she asked, kissing me.

"They're in my purse."

"Good. Pathmark's giving double rebates to seniors next Thursday."

While Aunt Gisela hovered, I rummaged in my bag. I pulled out the book I had been reading on the drive up, a translation of Reillard's poems from his years in Avignon. The clumsiness of the translation irritated me: I had read those poems in the original fourteenth century French, and I knew I could do a better job. "What's this?" Aunt Gisela asked, opening the book.

"Poetry," I said. "A book I'm considering for my class next term."

Aunt Gisela clucked and shook her head. "Books," she said. "You're always with your head in a book. I like TV myself. It takes you away, you know? But you'll find out, now you've got Maria. That TV is the best babysitter in the world."

I found the wad of coupons for mouthwash, artificial sweetener, room deodorizers and detergents. I handed them over with a smile. Aunt Gisela meant well, I knew, which was more than I could say about Alex's mother who regarded all my interests—especially my postdoctoral studies—as a waste of time.

"Raf's coming later with his son," Dolores announced out of the blue. "I can't believe you're finally gonna meet my brother."

"Really," I replied mildly. "How's he doing?" It was a rhetorical question. I had managed to avoid meeting Dolores' brother only through default. When Alex and I got married, Raf was in Florida working; during holiday visits he was occupied with side jobs or his wife's relatives.

"Who knows?" Dolores said glumly. "Brian is getting better now, he's not so hyperactive, but Sherry has the flu. She just started a new job out at the race track and now she has the flu, can you believe it? When I talked to her this morning she had a hundred-and-two fever but she wanted Raf to come anyway and bring Brian so she could at least sleep for a while."

"What's Raf doing?" I asked, losing interest fast.

"Working in Manhattan, a high-rise job."

There was another gloom-pregnant sigh, as though high-rise construction were in some way morally suspect. Raf had been assigned a role in the family that no amount of maturity on his part would ever erase. I knew his story well enough. It had already developed the patina of family legend, with all the more spectacularly tragic elements of Italian opera.

Dolores had been eleven years old and Raf thirteen when their mother contracted cancer. She had taken four years to die, and in the end, her long crucifixion was marked by intractable pain. Raf, seventeen by then, made connections in New York City, traveled there regularly and brought back heroin for his mother. By the time she died, he was shooting up too. The father turned his back on both children after his wife's death, remarried within a year and sent Dolores to live with her grandmother. Raf was in and out of jail, in and out of treatment. Finally, when Dolores and Dan were newlyweds, they had taken Raf into their home. He had been able to get himself straight, but he had continued an odyssey of feckless wandering, dead-end jobs, inability to manage money and judge the trustworthiness of his friends. He got married at last, not long after Alex and I, to an older woman whom he met while working in Florida. She had given birth to Brian a short time later. She was reported to be shrewd, hardworking and homely.

I carried an ice bucket out to the umbrella table in the yard. The kids were already playing in the pool. Older relatives sat in the shade drinking highballs and lemonade. Neighbors began to drift in and out. Dan and Alex were readying the barbecue.

I scooped up Maria from a blanket where Aunt Gisela was minding her and carried her to an upstairs bedroom to change her diaper. She was a happy baby, the delight of my life—my flower, the seed that had grown inside my body and emerged a tiny closed bud. The dark petals of her curls fanned out against my hand as I nibbled her neck and sucked the fingers she poked joyously into my mouth. Since her birth, my senses were as finely tuned as those of a feral cat: Nothing I had read or heard in all my conscientious preparations for motherhood had even hinted at the tidal wave of love that engulfed me the first time she was placed in my arms. I returned her to the yard with reluctance.

When the party was in full swing, Raf arrived with his son. I heard an exclamation out in the yard, Dolores' voice above the others: "I didn't think you'd come. How's Sherry?" The deeper answering voice was not loud but had a resonance that made it carry. "She's beat. I didn't want to leave her alone but she said she'd be able to sleep if the house was quiet."

I was back in the kitchen again, filling a tureen with sausage and peppers. Something about the voice arrested my attention. It was definitely a New York working-class voice, but there was something else. It drew me like a magnet to the back porch and down the steps.

Over the years I had developed a vague image of Raf as a sort of male version of Dolores, with a short, stocky Mediterranean body, a face coarse-featured and prematurely aged from outdoor work. And there was something deeper, an impression so subtle that I was never even conscious of it until that startling moment in the yard. I had also pictured insecurity, hesitation and unease. The man who stood talking to Dolores was as different from this picture as sun from shadow.

He was at least a head taller than any other man there, maybe six-three, slender and long-limbed like a dancer. He wore faded jeans and an azure tank top, but even casual clothes couldn't conceal a certain elegance, all the more remarkable because I saw instantly that it was natural and unself-conscious, a gift of God like the color of one's eyes or hair.

I swear that in that instant I heard a crackle inside my head as Raf turned abruptly from Dolores and looked straight at me. Dolores followed his eyes. "Oh, Angela," she said, "you've never met my brother Raf."

"Hello," I said, moving forward. I was carrying the tureen. Without speaking, Raf took it from my hands. "This go on the table?" he asked, jerking his head in the direction of the buffet.

I nodded mutely. I followed him past Dolores and pushed around baskets and trays to make room. As he set the bowl down, I noticed his hands. They were as elegant as the rest of him, the kind of hands one always thinks should belong to pianists or surgeons. He wore a plain gold wedding band. "Thank you," I said. I met his eyes again and even they were extraordinary, deep-set and long-lashed, a vivid pale green which made me think ludicrously of forsythia buds in March. They made an arresting contrast against the background of summer-tanned skin and black hair.

"You're Alex's wife," Raf said.

His son was tugging at his pockets. "Please Dad, can I go in the pool?"

Raf looked down at him and I saw a momentary flash of bewilderment as though he had forgotten who Brian was. "Sure," he said, ruffling the boy's hair. "Say hello to Angela."

Brian looked boldly up at me and held out his hand. "Hi," he said. He looked very much like his father.

I shook his hand formally. "How do you do?"

"Stay at the shallow end," Raf admonished. "I catch you anyplace but the shallow end, it's outa the pool and no going back in, period. Got it?"

"Right, Dad!" Brian broke into a run.

Raf's eyes lingered on him with an amalgam of love and angst that moved me to say, "Steve's got pool duty. He's switching off with Jennifer, the diving champion."

Steve and Jennifer were older cousins, already sober and responsible at sixteen. Raf looked back at me. "Kids and water make me nervous."

"I know," I replied. I thought of Maria's fingers in my mouth. "Why don't you get a plate and have something to eat? I'll get you a drink. There's beer and wine."

"Any Dr. Pepper?"

"I think so. I'll look."

Just then a group of relatives surrounded him and I went to hunt down a Dr. Pepper, relieved to be out of range of those eyes. I had felt naked somehow, not undressed in the sense of superficial sexual assessment, but revealed, as though he recognized my most ridiculous flaw, my most sterling virtue, and accepted it all without judgment.

The party stepped up a note, more people arrived. I occupied myself with keeping the buffet table in order, gathering abandoned plates and cups, filling the dishwasher. I kept a water tumbler of cheap white wine with plenty of ice within reach. I had finished breast feeding, and the wine kept me in a state of mellow, detached relaxation that let me go through the motions of the party without feeling too forlorn. When I could, I watched Raf.

Eventually Alex found me in the kitchen. Dolores had not bought enough plastic cups, so I'd retrieved a couple of dozen from the trash and was washing them out at the sink. "You all right?" Alex asked.

It was his standard question at family events and I gave the standard reply. "Sure," I said.

"Where's Maria?"

"Upstairs asleep."

"You meet Dolores' brother?"

"Yes. He's nothing like I expected."

"He looks good," Alex said. "I haven't seen him since before we got married." He opened the refrigerator and pulled out a couple of six-packs. "He got a notice of audit from the IRS," Alex added. I looked at him, questioning. Alex is a tax lawyer, and he is inevitably dragooned into service whenever anyone in the extended family has a tax problem. He shrugged and gave me a rueful smile. "What could I do? I told him to bring his records and his returns around tomorrow and I'll take a look." He kissed the back of my neck and went out the back door with the six-packs.

After I had taken the clean plastic cups back to the umbrella table, I settled into a chair in the shade. Raf came and sat next to me. "So you and Alex been married what, six-seven years?"

"Almost seven," I answered. "I believe it was the summer before you got married."

"Yeah, that's right," Raf said. He popped the cap off another Dr. Pepper. "I was invited to the wedding but I couldn't make it. I was down in Sarasota, slappin' up beach houses. That's where I met my wife." He took a long drink. "He's a good man, Alex. He helped me out, him and Danny, after I got outa the slam a few years back." Raf's eyes patrolled the swimming pool. Brian jumped off the edge and into the water at the shallow end. There was a lot of splashing and screaming. "So I hear you're a teacher," he said.

"Yes," I answered. "French literature." He was sitting very close to me, so close that I could smell him, a mingling of soap, sweat, aftershave and tobacco that seemed to go right to the back of my throat.

"I used to read a lot of poetry," Raf said. I had not anticipated this until he said it, but of course it made flawless sense. I looked at his hands. "Not so much since Sherry had Brian. Not much time anymore. But I liked Victor Hugo."

"Victor Hugo?" I repeated. I suppose I had expected Rod McKuen or Khalil Gibran.

"Yeah, you know, *Les Miserables*. He wrote poetry too."

I turned quickly away and coughed, I am sorry to say. Raf missed nothing. "It's all right," he said. And then he laughed, a wonderful, disingenuous laugh like that of a child, without resentment. "It's all right. I guess you know who Victor Hugo is." He grinned. "I heard Hugo's much better in the original French. Is that true? I never learned French."

"Yes," I said. "But it's also true of most literature we read in translation. And even if we can read the original language, it's very difficult to understand the underlying cultural nuance, the deeper layers of meaning based on the common experience of a particular period of time." I had a blinding instant of standing outside myself listening in, and I heard the unmistakable cadences of my lecture-hall voice. "Oh God," I said. "I'm sorry. I can't seem to leave the classroom behind." I could feel the heat in my face.

"It's all right," Raf repeated. "I know what it's like to be with people who don't know nothin' about you. It makes you so uptight that every time you open your mouth, the words come out wrong." He smiled at me in that direct, uncomplicated way that I had rarely seen in an adult. I smiled back, and relaxed suddenly into a place of such ease and comfort that I realized—and then only for the briefest moment—the level of self-protective tension with which I armored myself in every waking moment. What would it be like, I wondered, to lay down the dead weight of it once and for all?

"And anyway," he continued, "you're right about that cultural nuance stuff. How could anybody who wasn't young in America in the sixties really understand 'Hello darkness, my old friend, I've come to talk with you again'?" Someone, Alex perhaps, had put Simon and Garfunkel on the stereo and the music wafted around us like an aroma evoking the taste of our separate yet mutual pasts.

"Exactly," I said. The blood was humming in my ears, something exquisite and terrible began to stir at the center of my body.

"Sometimes I think about Brian and his friends. The music they'll be digging in ten years won't be what we listened to. We probably won't be able to stand it, just like our folks couldn't stand Elvis and the Beatles. I wonder what they'll make of Woodstock?" The anniversary of Woodstock had been getting a lot of media coverage that summer. As if programmed specially for our conversation, a Rolling Stones album followed Simon and Garfunkel. The first song was *Paint It Black*. We looked at each other and began to chuckle. Raf grabbed an imaginary guitar and grimaced an excellent mime of Mick Jagger. I laughed harder.

"Woodstock," I gasped. "I was at Woodstock."

Raf's eyebrows arched. "You were?"

"Yes, in the mud and the rain." I did not add that I was also at Berkeley in the sixties, and the worst sort of left-wing radical snob. Sometimes, emerging from dreams I cannot later recall, I taste tear gas at the back of my throat. "We didn't draw a straight breath or sleep for five days. How will I ever explain to my daughter what Woodstock was, the vision of the new world we were sure we were creating?"

"I was at Woodstock too," Raf said. We stared at each other. "Yeah, you and me and a million other stone freaks." Raf lit a cigarette and shook his head, laughing. "Christ," he said.

I felt light and happy. I sat up straight in my chair. "You must have had long hair," I said, looking at his hair. It was trimmed fashionably short.

"Down to my ass," he grinned. "And you?"

"Nearly. I wore it in a single braid. I used to envy the black girls with their hair out to here." I held my hands apart at the sides of my head. "The afro was so pretty, so sexy and free."

"Yeah," Raf said. "And now black kids are into doing all that shit to their hair again. I don't know why, it looks like hell, like nothin' you'd want to touch. I was going with a black chick then, and I loved her hair. It was so soft."

"What happened to her?"

Raf shrugged and chuckled, taking a deep drag on his cigarette. "Hell, I don't know. She took off the second day we were there, some white dude from Southern California with long blond hair. A surfer. She thought he looked like Jesus Christ. She was doing a lot of acid." We were giggling almost uncontrollably.

I took another drink from my tumbler. "I wonder how close we came to meeting?" I said. "Maybe we were waiting in those same awful lines for the Portajohns."

"Naw," Raf said, "we never came near." He was suddenly serious, his eyes looking into me again in that way that made me feel naked and accepted at the same time. "I'd have remembered you, I don't care how tripped out I was or how different your hair was. I'da never forgot you."

I couldn't hold his gaze. I looked down, then across the yard where Jennifer was reprimanding one of the kids for getting too close to deep water.

"You there with a boyfriend?" Raf asked.

"Yes," I answered. "A musician. He was into rock, but he would have gone back to classical, I think."

"What happened?"

"A brain aneurysm, just three months later. A cerebral accident, they called it. I remember when the doctor came to talk to me and his parents, I couldn't quite grasp it. I got this picture of things crashing together in his head." It was distant enough now in time that I could manage a lopsided smile.

"I'm sorry," Raf said.

"I was too. I was pretty screwed up for a while, I was so young. And then I met Alex."

We sat in a companionable silence of acknowledged mutual loss, of the passage of time, of the inevitable cumulative weight of chance and choice. Then Brian ran up, begging his father to join the volleyball game starting in the front yard. Raf rose from his chair reluctantly and looked down at me. "You come too," he said.

I heard the wavery treble of my daughter's voice drifting down from the upstairs bedroom. "Thanks," I replied. "Maria just woke up." I watched them walk away, admiring his work-hardened body, wishing I'd stayed at home to teach summer school.

It was later in the day and most of the yard was in shade. The crowd had thinned a little, and people were lying or sitting around in the drowsy aftermath of good food and alcohol, enjoying the fine afternoon and looking forward to coffee and the many kinds of desert that would come later. I loaded up a big restaurant-size tray with half-empty bowls, cups, flatware and plates. All around me voices droned in a pleasant buzz. Even the children had quieted down, and there was a golden haze around everything. The sky was piled high with great billowing cumulus clouds which might or might not bring rain later in the night. I lifted the tray and started past the swimming pool for the back door when for no particular reason I glanced down.

There, deep in the water, hair undulating like seaweed, blank eyes staring up, was Brian. His mouth was open. Not a single bubble broke the surface.

Alex told me later that the tray hitting the concrete sounded like a high-speed auto crash. I never heard it. I dived into the water. In the few seconds available before the sting of pool chemicals blinded me, I found Brian and dragged him to the surface. Hands grabbed him; I heaved myself out. I could hear the women shrieking, the curses of the men. I pushed my streaming hair out of my eyes and saw my motherinlaw clutching Brian against her chest. She was sobbing.

"Lay him down," I said. She clasped Brian tighter, howling. "Lay him down!" I beat at her arms with my fists. Shocked, she dropped him. Brian flopped onto the grass. I tried to stretch him out but all around us was a forest of legs and plucking hands. "Please!" I implored.

Someone grabbed my arm and tried to pull me away. "Don't touch him, wait for the paramedics." Another hand forced my shoulder back. "She's hysterical, get her away."

Raf was suddenly beside me. "Get back," he said. "Give her room." There was such authority in his voice that everyone instantly obeyed. Our eyes locked briefly and I saw in Raf's face a plea and something I had not expected—trust.

We laid Brian out on his stomach. It seemed as though I pressed half the contents of the swimming pool out of him, but when he didn't start breathing, we rolled him onto his back. I felt for the carotid artery. His neck was as frail and tender as the stem of a flower and I thought immediately of Maria. I pressed my fingers into his flesh; there was no pulse. I started CPR and time stopped; I was very lucid as I told Raf how to pinch Brian's nostrils and breathe for him in tandem with my chest compressions. I remember how cold Brian's chest was, the spasm of nausea that seized me as I felt ribs separating from sternum. Someone was praying the rosary. *Where were the paramedics?* I did not want this appalling responsibility. Water, tears and sweat dripped from my face onto Brian's torso, I felt panic rising in my throat. And then Brian coughed. He began to vomit onto the grass. The paramedics arrived.

After that, there was only the exhaustion of anticlimax. Dan and Dolores drove Raf to the hospital behind the ambulance. My motherinlaw wouldn't look at me. Aunt Gisela found me a pair of Dolores' jeans and a pullover, Alex brought me coffee. He got Maria up from her nap and sat with her on his knees, one arm around me. Neither of us could speak.

"How did you know what to do?" They all wanted to know. "Pure luck," I said. "At school, they're requiring at least one instructor per shift to have CPR training. In the humanities department, we drew straws. I finished the course just before the end of this term."

At last, long after dark, Raf, Dan and Dolores came back from the hospital. "He's okay," Raf said. "He's got a couple of busted ribs, but he's okay. Sherry's with him now."

Dolores and Dan began recapping what had happened at the hospital for Alex, my motherinlaw and the aunts. Raf poured two cups of coffee and motioned me silently out the door. We sat at a table in the yard. There were a few clouds and plenty of stars, a nearly full moon. Raf had put on a chambray shirt over the tank top, unbuttoned, and he fished a pack of cigarettes from the pocket and lit two. He handed one to me. I hadn't smoked in years, but I took the cigarette gratefully and inhaled. It was wonderful. We sat without talking, drinking our coffee and smoking.

Presently, Raf reached for my arm. He turned my hand over and rubbed it thoughtfully with his thumb. He did it in an open, unhurried way, as though time streamed in front of us, abundant and slow-moving as a great wide river. Then he lifted my hand and placed the palm against his cheek and held it there, his eyes closed. We drifted in a state of perfect suspension. Every particle of sense and consciousness eddied away from my brain and flowed out into the place where my hand lay against his cheek. After a moment, he pressed his mouth against the inside of my wrist. A cloud passed, the moonlight poured over his face and he looked at me. "Thank you," he said. Our eyes held for a long time.

The screen door clicked and the others came out with more coffee and a plate of cake. Gently, with great reluctance, Raf lowered my hand to the table top. I think Alex may have seen us, but I'm not sure. He has never said.

We talked while the moon dropped lower and lower, and

then we realized that we were all half asleep. "I've got to get back so Sherry can rest," Raf said. We walked him to his car. As we said good night, he turned to me and Alex. "You know," he said softly, not looking at Alex at all, "we almost met one time before."

"When was that?" Dolores came to stand at her brother's side.

"It was that Fourth of July bash just before Alex and Angela got married, right before I split for Florida."

I ticked back in my memory and found the referenced picnic. It hardly seemed like my own life. I remembered the boredom of that party, my feeling of alienness. It was then that I first discovered that, beyond superficialities, there was nothing I could have a conversation about with anyone in Alex's family.

"Yeah," Raf said, "I was planning to come. I'd been off smack for a year and I felt like I could live forever. Some jerk ran a red light and totaled my car. It was the day of the party. Just totaled it. I was lucky he didn't total me too." Raf smiled and shifted his shoulders in a gesture so minimal it might have been missed by everyone else. His eyes held mine again. "It was just timing I missed that picnic. I was on my way to the store to pick up a case of Dr. Pepper to take along, and this guy nails me at the light there on Jericho where the chair factory used to be. If I'd left a minute sooner or a minute later, either one, I'da met you years ago." He turned to Alex.

Alex stuck out his hand. "You take care, Raf," he said. "Drop your files off at my mom's and I'll give you a call. We'll work something out."

"Thanks." Raf glanced out into the darkness beyond the street light, then back at Alex. "You got one helluva woman, Alex," he said. "Take good care of her."

Alex's arm tightened around my waist. "I do," he said evenly.

Raf placed his hands lightly on my shoulders and brushed my cheek with his lips. "I'll see you again sometime."

"Yes," I said.

But I never saw Raf again. I was bathing Maria when he stopped the next day with his tax records. I stayed in the bathroom, holding her wrapped in a towel against my breasts, until I heard the front door close, the sound of his car fade down the street. It was an hour before I could stop shaking.

Raf died from the same kind of cancer that killed his mother.

By the time the Stones tape was finished, it was dark and the parking lot at Clingman's Dome was empty. Fog had begun fingering its way up from the valleys. I got out of the car and tilted my head back. I stood for a long time watching the slow cartwheel of the heavens, the shape-shifting moon, the sky smudged with clouds and the secrets of spangled galaxies.

Time is so cunning. It grins its trickster grin as you play with your dolls, choose a major, a job, a husband, a neighborhood. Children shock you by growing up, parents stun you by growing old. Before you know it a lifetime has accumulated, and a lot of it feels like stones and broken glass.

I continue to teach. I specialize in French poetry of the late medieval period, and last year I published a volume of translations that was received with gratifying critical acclaim. I have a family, a career; I am a woman with responsibilities. And I have learned that commonplace that each of us has to learn alone: There are no permanent satisfactions, only moments. And I have learned not to dwell on the past, on the times when the cosmic gears do not mesh faultlessly, but instead clash and shriek and fling the fragments of one's spirit into darkened corners where their glow gradually fades and winks out like novaed stars.

THE HUNTING SEASON

for Rick

HE PULLED AN OLD jacket out of the back of the closet, one he hadn't worn in God knew how long. It was too narrow through the shoulders now and the cuffs were raveling, so it didn't matter if he got it dirty. He slipped it on over the red plaid shirt Eva had given him on his last birthday before her death. That had been more than three years ago, and he'd worn the shirt so much that it was nearly threadbare. He wondered if he ought to launder it one more time and just fold it away in the drawer where he kept other mementos of their life together: the wedding pictures, anniversary and birthday cards, the letters they'd written during the war, the ticket stubs for that Rolling Stones concert, the packet of condoms they'd forgotten to take on a canoe trip in the Upper Peninsula that had resulted nine months later in the birth of their only child, Jared.

He went to the shed for a shovel, brushing away cobwebs and dead leaves from where he'd hung his tools in neat rows on the wall. How long had it been since he'd done any yard work? He lifted a spade from its mount and carried it into the daylight.

He'd chosen a spot in the garden—or rather what used to be the garden. Eva had grown vegetables there, but he hadn't kept it up after her death. The grave didn't take long to dig. He went back to the porch for the blanket-wrapped body. Judy, that was her name. Judy, aged seventeen, had produced some magnificent pups, kept him company on countless hunting trips and had been his closest companion since Eva's passing. Judy had died in her sleep, thank God. He'd dreaded having to take her on one last trip to the vet. They'd both been spared that.

He lifted her body and lowered her awkwardly into the hole, tucked a red rubber ball and a package of her favorite biscuits under the blanket. *You sentimental fool,* he thought. He hefted a shovelful of earth and swung it over the grave, then stopped just as he was about to dump it in. Tears blurred his vision and without warning, he heard himself sobbing. He dropped to his knees and covered his face with his hands. For a brief moment he tried to stop, but the tears came in an irresistible torrent, a flash flood of grief for Judy, for Eva, for his parents and his brother Todd, who'd died of polio at eight, for his buddies face down in the rice paddies of Vietnam, for the son who had failed, despite every advantage, to achieve responsible adulthood. He wiped his face first on one jacket sleeve and then the other. At last he stood up and dug in the pockets for a handkerchief. There was none, of course. But he did find a key, to what lock he couldn't imagine, and a book of matches. *My God,* he thought. Had it been that long since he'd worn the jacket? He hadn't smoked since Jared's seventeenth birthday. He opened the matchbook. Only one match was missing.

But there was something else, a phone number written

inside the cover. That was all. No name. He read the ten digits over and over, as though staring long enough would force them to reveal the identity of their owner. He folded the matchbook shut and stuck it back in the pocket. Then he filled the grave, tamped it down and cut some spruce boughs to lay over the raw earth.

The sun had begun to set. The days were so short now, heading for winter solstice, the deep, dark ditch of the year. He hung the spade back in the shed and returned to the house, threw a couple of logs into the wood stove and poured himself a shot of Johnny Walker. He was about to peel off the jacket when he remembered the matchbook. He opened it and stared again at the number. How long had it been in his pocket? Twenty years? He tossed it onto the kitchen counter and turned on the news, poured himself another shot.

He was awake the next morning at four, just like every morning. No matter how late he stayed up, Jack couldn't sleep past four. The sky was still ink black; not even the birds were awake yet. He got up, registered the jolt of not finding Judy asleep at the foot of the bed, then wept in the shower. He dressed, fed the stove, put on a pot of coffee. He picked up the matchbook and tossed it into the trash, walked to the end of the driveway to collect *The Milwaukee Sentinel.*

After breakfast, he was about to drop the filter full of coffee grounds into the trash when he saw the matchbook again. He dropped the grounds on top of it and turned to the unwashed dishes. "Aw, hell," he said, stacking the last plate in the drainer. He reached into the trash, dug through the coffee grounds and retrieved the matchbook.

He had no idea what he was going to say. On the fifth ring, a small hope blazed that no one would answer. After all, with the passage of two decades, it was hardly likely that the number existed anymore, and even if it did, surely it now belonged to someone other than the original caller.

"Hello."

Jack caught his breath.

"Hello?"

"Uh, hello," he stammered. "I, ah, I found this number in the pocket of my jacket. A really old jacket, as a matter of fact, but I don't know who the number belonged to . . ."

"Who is this?"

"Jack Poplowski. I live near Stevens Point, and I, ah . . ." Jack fizzled into embarrassed silence. His face flushed hot and he was about to hang up the phone when the man at the other end said, "Jack Poplowski? Is this really Jack?"

"Yes, yes, of course. Who's this?"

"Dave Torvaldson. Manitowoc High School, class of sixty-two."

"Oh my God," said Jack. Who the hell was Dave Torvaldson anyway? Jack wracked his memory but could not summon a face.

"Remember Mrs. Binstock's freshman English class? You sat next to me and we took turns drooling over Donna Tallaksen."

Memory flooded back. "Yes," Jack declared, "of course I remember. But how did I get your phone number? I found it written in a matchbook in this jacket I haven't worn in about a hundred years."

"It must've been nineteen years ago when I was helping to organize our thirtieth class reunion. I called a bunch of old classmates, and I guess you musta been one of 'em."

"And I never called you back," Jack said flatly. Of course he hadn't. That had been during the awful ordeal of Jared's first arrest.

"No, I guess not," Dave said. An awkward silence intruded.

"Well," Jack said. "How the hell are you anyway? What's it been, forty-seven years? A few things must've changed."

"I'm doing okay, I guess. You know, I played minor league baseball for a few years after high school."

"I remember now. You pitched for the Manitowoc Wolverines. You were pretty good."

"Unfortunately, not good enough for the majors. But I coached Little League for a few years. I married Arlene Stern, one of our classmates."

"I remember Arlene," Jack lied. "Any kids?" They talked desultorily for twenty minutes or so.

"So I hear there'll be a fiftieth reunion in 2012," Dave said. "You gonna go?"

"I don't know. A lot can happen in a couple of years."

"You got a computer?"

They exchanged email addresses and said goodbye.

Jack thought all day about the phone call. He hadn't been in touch with his classmates since graduation. He'd gotten as far away from his parents' home as fast as he could get. He'd gone into the merchant marine and worked the ore boats until the winters on Lake Superior became unbearable. Then he'd ended up in the army, the infantry, Vietnam. Now there were fewer years ahead of him than there were behind and it seemed the older he got, the more the past dogged him.

Toward mid-afternoon, the Jespersen kid from up the road came by with a broken beaver trap. The boy's family lived in a shack. The mother drove forty-five miles one way to her job in a chicken-processing plant. The father mainly drank. The boy trapped beaver and hunted whatever he could shoot. There were several younger children.

Jack repaired the trap and oiled it. He gave the boy a box of .22 cartridges. When the kid started to refuse, Jack said, "They're no damn good to me. I sold my .22 last spring." That was a lie, of course, but ammo had gotten so expensive and the kid had to put food on the table.

"Thanks, Mr. Poplowski."

"You're welcome. Your old man hunt deer?"

"No Sir."

"Well, I drew a tag this year. Doe. I'll be going north next weekend to hunt. I'll be up around four on Saturday if you want to come."

Jack saw the brief flash of excitement in the kid's eyes.

"Yessir," he said. "Thank you. I'll see you then."

"You ever shoot a thirty-aught-six?"

"Yessir. My uncle taught me. I don't own one, though."

That night when Jack looked at his email, he saw Dave Torvaldson's message with the subject line CLASS ROSTER. Pam Osterhaus, one of their classmates, had apparently been tracking people down. There'd been only seventy-eight kids in their graduating class, but obviously Pam had been doing a thorough job. Nick Abbatti was the first name listed. Jack remembered Nick from grades one through twelve. A short, dark little dago. He'd gone to state championships as a wrestler. "Married 43 years to Nancy Kosternak (class of '65). Retired from Wisconsin Tool & Die. 4 children, 7 grandchildren." There was a Janesville address, a phone number and email address.

Jack scanned the list leisurely. Most of his classmates had stayed in Wisconsin, a few had drifted down to Chicago and its suburbs, up to the Twin Cities, and a handful to the western states and the south. More than a few were divorced or widowed. Then he saw Rose Johnson's name and a single word:

Deceased. His heart gave an arrhythmic thump. Rose Johnson had been his first love, in the first grade. They'd ridden the school bus together, and Jack had given her sticks of Juicy Fruit gum, and one time, a brand-new fat pink eraser. There was no other information, no date of death, no mention of husband or family. He couldn't imagine Rose Johnson of the platinum-blond pigtails and blue-blue eyes dead. Tears rose in his eyes. He saved the roster document and turned off the computer. Angrily he wiped his eyes and blew his nose. What the hell was happening to him anyway? He was going to have to call Dave Torvaldson and try to find out what had happened to Rose.

In the freezing dark of 3:45 on Saturday morning, the Jesperson kid knocked on the back door.

"You had any breakfast?" Jack asked.

"No Sir," the kid said.

Jack put a plate of eggs and fried potatoes and sausage on the table, told the kid to eat, poured him a cup of coffee. "Gonna be a long, cold day. You can't start out on an empty stomach."

Twenty minutes later, they were on the road.

"You ever shoot a deer?" Jack asked.

"No Sir."

"Well, today might be your lucky day. I'll make you a deal. If you get a deer, we'll put my tag on it and we'll split the meat. If I shoot something, we'll still split the meat."

"That doesn't sound fair to you," the kid said.

"I'm too damn old to drag a deer outa the woods alone," Jack lied. "It's fair."

"Okay," the kid said.

Jack had been scouting the woods all autumn, following the herds, counting heads. They parked on an unpaved road and headed into the area where he thought the most deer would be. It was a moonless night, and there were several inches of snow on the ground. In addition to his rifle, Jack carried a backpack with extra cartridges, hand warmers, a Thermos of coffee, a bag of cookies, his .45 semi-auto, field-dressing tools and a first-aid kit. There was a big hill about a mile in diameter, carved out by the retreat of the last great glaciation. Jack kept the kid close to him. He had no idea what kind of hunter the kid was, whether he knew the safety rules or how to control his impulses.

The snow made it possible to see where they were going without a flashlight. They walked slowly, stopping every few yards to stand and observe. As daylight began to come on, they paused at the edge of a meadow. A blob of black detached itself from the greater blackness of the trees on the opposite side of the meadow and moved leisurely into the open space. They waited in silence for dawn and watched as the light grew and the blob resolved itself into a full-grown deer. But it was still too dark to tell whether there were antlers. The minutes trickled one into another until the deer stood in sharp relief against the rising sun. There was no breeze, nothing to alert it to their presence. At last, Jack whispered against the kid's ear, "Doe."

The kid squirmed with excitement. Jack handed him the rifle and motioned to him to take the shot. Jack was pleased to see that his movements were sure and deliberate. Jack held his breath and watched the doe. Twice she lowered her head to feed; twice she raised it and turned to look over her shoulder at the tree line. Jack saw the kid's finger tighten on the trigger.

"No!" Jack hissed, and reached out to push the rifle barrel toward the ground. Jack saw the flash of anger and confusion in the kid's eyes. Jack shook his head emphatically. Then as they turned their gaze back to the meadow, they saw what had claimed the doe's attention. From the tree line emerged two fawns, their flanks still sprinkled with baby spots. The kid's eyes widened and his mouth opened in silent amazement.

"She mated real late in the season," Jack said softly. "They may not make it through the winter. But at least with their mother they've got a chance."

The man and the boy watched for a long time as the doe and her twins browsed slowly across the meadow and melted once again into the trees.

"How did you know about the fawns before they came out in the open?" asked the kid.

"Did you notice the way she kept looking back at the tree line?"

"Yeah, but I didn't know what it meant."

"Better to take no shot at all than one that'll haunt you later," Jack said. "And it's easy to do when you're young and your blood's hot—just shoot at whatever moves. Remember that, son."

"Yessir," the kid said.

They drank coffee, ate some cookies, then moved on and circled the hill. They didn't see a single other deer for the rest of the day.

On Sunday morning, Jack called Dave Torvaldson. "Thanks for sending that class roster," he said. "It's kind of a shock to see how many of the class of sixty-two are dead."

"Yeah, it sure is," Dave said. They talked about deceased classmates for a few minutes.

Jack brought up Rose Johnson. "Any idea how or when she died?" Jack asked.

"No," Dave said, "I don't know anything about her, but she was pretty close to Jeanie Dykstra. Maybe Jeanie kept up with her."

Jack fired up his computer and opened the class-roster document. Sure enough, there was Jeanie Dykstra, right after Ralph Dudley, who'd been on the swim team with Jack. Jeanie's name was Kaufman now. The listing said that she was widowed with three children and two grandchildren. Where the e-mail address should've been was the notation "No computer." However, there was an address in Friendship and a phone number. Jack would have preferred the impersonality of email, but that wasn't an option. He would have to call. He was relieved to hear a recorded message inviting him to leave his name and number.

She called back that evening. "Jack Poplowski," she said. "Jeanie Dykstra. I just found your picture in the senior yearbook. You still as good-looking as you were when you were eighteen?"

They talked for a few minutes about their lives since high school. "Kinda hard to summarize nearly half a century in a few sentences, isn't it?" Jeanie chuckled. "My life's been the usual catastrophe—lousy marriage, but at least it lasted thirty-eight years. Felt like a hundred. He died in oh-two. Motorcycle accident. But I got a fantastic daughter out of it."

"I lost my wife in oh-six. Ovarian cancer."

"I'm sorry," Jeanie said.

"Look," Jack said. "I remember you used to be tight with Rose Johnson. I was wondering if you'd kept in touch with her, if you knew when she passed."

There was a brief silence. "Passed?" Jeanie echoed. "Rose Johnson is alive and well. At least she was on Thursday, which was the last time I talked to her. I think Pam Osterhaus had her confused with Rosalie Johnson, class of sixty-one. She died fifteen, twenty years ago. You want Rose's phone number?"

Monday morning dawned cloudless and chilly. A thick rime of frost clung to everything, flashing like jewels on trees and shrubs. After breakfast, Jack tackled the job of removing all of Judy's things: a large unopened bag of Purina Dog Chow went out to the truck to be taken to the animal shelter in Stevens Point. Judy's bed, a big, round red-plush cushion, long blackened by muddy paws, went into the pile to be hauled to the dump. Shredded toys went into the trash. Jack had to pause a couple of times to blow his nose and wipe his eyes. "Damn damn damn," he chanted.

In the afternoon, he dialed the number Jeanie Dykstra had given him. She picked it up on the third ring. "Jack Poplowski!" she exclaimed, the excitement in her voice unmistakable. "Jeanie told me you were going to call!"

Rose told him about her years as a diplomat's wife, her two children, their return to Wisconsin after her husband's retirement. "I know," she laughed. "You're thinking why would anyone want to come back to Wisconsin with its long, dark winters to spend their old age, but the kids and grandkids are here, you know? And Robert's had some health problems the last few years." Jack thought about his own son, far away in Colorado.

"Do you ever get down to Milwaukee?" Rose asked. "You've just got to come visit me! Promise me you will."

Saturday came, the last weekend of hunting season. The Jespersen kid was at the door at 3:45, just like the week before. They ate breakfast in easy silence. Unlike the week before, there was a full moon and it reflected off six inches of new snow. If they didn't find their doe early, chances were they wouldn't find her at all. The deer would have been up all night feeding in the bright moonlight, then bedding down among the trees, hidden from sight.

They spent an hour before sunrise paralleling a line of sandstone bluffs, their sheer sides rising out of impassable thickets of balsam, jack pine, alder, hemlock and birch. The temperature was barely above zero. They stuffed hand warmers into their gloves and boots. They drank coffee. Jack was about to suggest that they go back to the truck to warm up, when he saw a flicker of movement off to his left. He touched the kid's shoulder and pointed. About 150 feet away, several deer were passing through the trees in complete silence. Jack and the boy followed them, watching carefully where they stepped, their cold hands and feet forgotten. Twenty minutes later, the trees had thinned to the point where they could see distinct bodies. But it was nearly impossible to distinguish doe from buck. Antlers looked like tree branches, tree branches like antlers. As they watched, one deer lowered its head, silhouetted briefly against a clear patch of bright snow. Jack held his breath. The head was without a rack. It was a beautiful mature doe, four or five years old, in her prime. The kid saw her too, and nodded to Jack. Jack shook his head and handed him the rifle. "She's yours," he whispered.

The shot rent the silence as though the universe itself had cracked open. The doe went down, her companions exploded in terror through the trees.

"Good shot, kid!" Jack said, slapping the boy's back, the need for whispering gone. The boy could barely contain his excitement. They trudged quickly through the trees to where the doe lay. The bullet had struck her chest. She lay panting in great gasps of white vapor; blood flowed from her nose and mouth, steaming. "Put her down," Jack said softly. "Don't stand too close. She could still thrash around and hurt you. Aim your shot at her forehead."

The kid quickly did as Jack instructed. A paroxysm shuddered through the doe's body, there was a last great sigh, the light went out of her eyes and she lay still. Jack turned to the boy. "You did great, kid. That was a fine shot. Your old man's gonna be proud of you." But the kid turned away from Jack, his shoulders quaking. Jack realized that he was sobbing.

Jack drove down to Milwaukee the next week. Rose and her husband lived in one of the old neighborhoods with a good view of Lake Michigan, which, on this day looked like a sheet of cobalt under a cloudless sky. Standing on the doorstep, his fingers resting on an old-fashioned brass knocker, he felt suddenly foolish. What was he doing here, visiting a woman he hadn't seen in so many decades he couldn't even remember her face?

The door swung suddenly open. "I saw you coming up the sidewalk," said Rose. "How are you, Jack?"

Jack couldn't speak. Rose was so little changed from the last time he'd seen her on graduation day. True, the blond hair was now silver, her face bore the evidence of responsibility and struggle. What were still the same were the upturned corners of her eyes and mouth. Rose had always been quick to smile and laugh.

"Hello, Rose," he said. He thrust a paper cone of flowers into her hands, rust and gold chrysanthemums with sprigs of eucalyptus and evergreen that fitted the Thanksgiving holiday that was only two weeks away. She thanked him and led him through the house to the kitchen where she arranged the flowers in a blue-and-white Chinese vase. Then they stepped onto an enclosed sun porch and Rose gestured at a loveseat.

She sat opposite him on an identical loveseat.

"When we spoke on the phone," Rose began, "we really didn't talk much about my husband."

"You said he'd had some health problems the past couple of years," Jack recalled.

"Robert has ALS," Rose said, "Lou Gehrig's Disease."

"Jesus, Rose."

"So far, we've been able to keep him here at home, but he doesn't see visitors anymore. I hope you understand. It's just family and hospice people at this point."

"Of course I understand." Jack remembered Eva's final weeks. "What's his—uh—"

"A few weeks, perhaps."

"Does Robert know I'm here?"

"Oh, yes. He encouraged me to invite you."

"Why did you invite me, Rose?"

She gazed frankly at him for a few seconds, then dropped her eyes. "I don't know if I can explain it," she replied, "but when Pam Osterhaus emailed the class roster, it just floored me. My school years weren't very happy. My parents—well, they never got along. There was always so much tension in the air, and it seemed that no matter how hard I tried, I could never please them. You know how little kids are. If Mom and Dad aren't happy, they think it's their fault. Oh, I know how utterly banal all this is. It's not like my childhood was traumatic or that I was abused or anything like that, but when we were in the first grade and we rode the school bus together, you were so sweet to me. You told me once how pretty I was, and nobody had ever said that to me." Rose stopped and chuckled. "And I remember you sometimes gave me chewing gum—"

"Juicy Fruit," Jack grinned.

"Yes! And once you gave me a new eraser. It was pink. I

put it away and never used it. I think it's still in one of the boxes Robert and I hauled all over the world when he was in the foreign service."

"You're kidding me."

"No, no, I'm not," Rose laughed. "And I wanted you to know how much you helped me back then and how often I've thought of that over the years. I think it was my first lesson in the importance of kindness."

"I was in love with you," Jack smiled. "You were my first love."

After a while, Rose brought out coffee and a tray of sandwiches. They ate at a little table overlooking a thickly wooded back yard and talked about Rose's children. "You said on the phone that you have a son out west. Tell me about him. What does he do?"

Jack swallowed his bite of sandwich, drank some coffee. He took a breath, let it out slowly.

Rose looked at him, her face full of concern. "What?" she asked softly.

"He's in a maximum security prison in Florence, Colorado. He's serving life without parole for killing two police officers and a hostage during a bank robbery back in oh-four."

By the time Jack left to drive back to Stevens Point, dusk was closing in. The roads were dry and clear, no snow in the forecast, thank God. Jack had noticed the last couple of years that driving in snow made him nervous. He turned on the radio, found a Milwaukee jazz station. The highway ribboned out in front of him, the way ahead visible only as far as the reach of the headlights. But it was enough; it would get him home.

They had talked a long time. Rose's face had not closed up as had the faces of so many others, including neighbors, fellow church members, even family, when they learned the truth about Jack and Eva's son. She had held his eyes steadily for a few seconds, then reached across the table and touched his arm. "Oh, Jack, I am so very, very sorry. I can't even imagine how terrible that must be for you."

"It killed Eva," Jack said. He found himself, as he had so often in recent weeks, fighting tears. He had to reach inside his jacket for a handkerchief.

Rose waited patiently as he composed himself. "Do you want to talk about it?" she asked at last.

Jack shook his head. "No," he said, then, "Maybe. Maybe I would like to at some point in the future, but not right now. You have enough sorrow of your own to deal with."

She'd nodded, they'd changed the subject to old classmates, to recollections of teachers, a Halloween when they'd been nine years old. A neighborhood spinster had dressed up as a ghost, complete with white-face makeup, and answered their shouts of "Trick or treat!" with homemade caramel apples from the tree in her yard.

When the sky over Lake Michigan began to take on the pale aqua and pink of late afternoon, they said their goodbyes. Rose kissed Jack's cheek and squeezed his hands. "You were very brave to come and see me," she'd said. "Let's stay in touch."

Darkness fell swiftly and Jack's thoughts drifted to the Jesperson kid. The kid had been unable to make eye contact with Jack after his outburst of sobbing. They'd field dressed the doe, then dragged her back to the truck, heaved her into the bed and driven to Jack's place. Jack threw a strong rope over a rafter in the garage and they'd hoisted the carcass well off the floor where it was left to cure for a week. Butchering would take place tomorrow.

The kid had left with his head sunk in shame. Jack hadn't known what to say, what to do. He'd failed the kid somehow. Later that evening, as he turned it over and over in his mind, all the agony and helplessness that had characterized his relationship with Jared came rushing back. He scrubbed at his his eyes and stayed up late watching Jay Leno in the dark, his hand fisted around a clump of paper towels, the bottle of Johnny Walker on the table beside his chair.

Jack had told the kid to come around 7:00 AM. He half expected him to pull a no-show, but at seven on the dot there was a knock on the door. Jack invited the kid in.

"You eat breakfast?" Jack asked.

The kid ducked his head, not looking directly at Jack. "Yessir, I ate already."

They went to the garage, where Jack had set up a table of planks and sawhorses and laid out his tools: knives, a meat saw, a cleaver. They carefully lowered the carcass onto layers of butcher paper on the table. Jack gave instructions, the boy did what he was told, but the camaraderie of the hunt was gone. Finally, Jack lay down his tools.

"What's going on, kid?" He tried to keep his voice neutral.

The kid wiped his hands on a scrap of toweling, his eyes on the floor. "I acted like a wuss," he said simply.

Jack wiped his own hands, placed them on the edge of the table and paused. He looked at the kid's lowered head, at the carcass of the dead deer. Slowly, the planks and sawhorses took on the gravity of an altar. The doe lay between them, her white bones and red flesh numinous as a sacramental offering.

"No you didn't, kid," Jack said. "Killing should never be

easy. Don't ever let yourself get hardened to it. That goes for the rest of life, too."

With great care, Jack picked up the meat saw and separated a rear leg from the pelvic girdle. When he looked up, the boy's eyes were at last on his. "Sometimes," Jack said, "tears are the only thing you've got to remind you that you're still a man."

SECRETS

MARTHA JEAN WAS my cousin. She and Aunt Muriel and Uncle Bill lived just a few houses down from ours, so she always babysat me whenever Mama and Daddy went square dancing in the grade-school gym on the first Saturday night of each month. Like everybody else, I loved Martha Jean. Unlike my older brother, Donny, who always went to Uncle Paul's house on square-dance night to play pool with our male cousins, she never made me feel like I was in the way. She was in high school and she was very pretty and popular with her beautiful red-gold hair and sweet disposition. Martha Jean had that rare gift that I was able to articulate only much later in life: joy was her natural state. To Martha Jean, all weather was beautiful, no baby was homely, no one could possibly be deliberately cruel or unkind. Her expansive heart embraced everyone, no matter how dull or venal. When she entered a room, her radiance turned people toward her like iron filings drawn to a magnet.

When square-dance nights rolled around, I would be excited from the moment I woke in the morning, wondering what Martha Jean and I would end up doing that evening. Once she brought over a basketful of sewing scraps. Martha Jean made her own clothes—even the formal dress for her piano recital—and we spent the hours cutting out little outfits for my favorite doll, Annabelle. She taught me simple garment-construction stitches, as she taught me in later years how to knit and crochet. By the time my parents came home that evening, Annabelle had a new wardrobe.

On other evenings, we made peanut butter fudge or ate popcorn and apples while we listened to the radio—*Jack Benny, The Cisco Kid,* or my favorite, *Mr. Keen, Tracer of Lost Persons.*

On this particular Saturday night—I remember it was in early November, not long after Halloween—we were going to play checkers and have ice cream. Mama and Daddy already had their coats on; Martha Jean was a bit late. Finally there was a knock on the door. When Daddy opened it, Martha Jean came wordlessly inside. I saw Mama and Daddy exchange glances. "We'll be back around midnight," Daddy said. Martha Jean nodded, her eyes averted, as Daddy pulled the door shut behind them. I could tell she'd been crying.

"What's wrong, Martha Jean?"

"Nothing," she said but we both knew that wasn't true.

"Did you have a fight with Aunt Muriel?" Aunt Muriel was, of course, Martha Jean's mother, my father's older sister. I'd overheard my parents talking one night a few months earlier when they thought I was asleep. Daddy said Aunt Muriel was way too hard on Martha Jean and not nearly hard enough on Jeffrey, Martha Jean's younger brother.

"She's going to break that girl's spirit," Daddy said

grimly. I wasn't sure what that meant, but by the tone of Daddy's voice, I knew it was something terrible. "And," Daddy continued, "that fool Bill doesn't have the backbone to stand up to her."

Now Martha Jean sat down on the sofa and lowered her face to her hands. Her shoulders began to shake and I watched helplessly as tears slid through her fingers and made dark splotches on her red skirt. "Mom said I can't date Lou anymore," she sobbed.

I didn't know how to respond. Everybody admired Lou (that was short for Luigi) Santori, the high-school track and field star, the straight-A student, who was nice even to dummies like Tommy Snow who couldn't tell *was* from *saw*, and the darling of every neighborhood mom because of his dark good looks and polite manners. Most of the Italian immigrants in our part of Illinois were uneducated folks who came to work in the coal mines, but the Santoris were different. Lou's father played a violin that he had made himself and he repaired musical instruments for a living. He also had a cousin in Italy who was a famous opera singer. Martha Jean and Lou had been dating for a couple of months. Just a week before, Lou had given Martha Jean his class ring to wear on a slim silver chain around her neck. That meant they were almost engaged. Lou was a senior, a year ahead of Martha Jean. Next fall, he'd be going upstate to Champagne-Urbana to study geology, which had something to do with rocks. He was what my mother called "a real catch."

Finally I asked, "Did Lou do something wrong?"

Martha Jean produced a handkerchief, wiped her eyes and blew her nose. "No," she said. "She says it's because the Santoris are dagos, which means they're not really white, and because they're Catholics, which Mom thinks is even worse, because they're idol worshippers."

I felt queasy way down in the bottom of my stomach. Mom's two older sisters, Aunt Marcena and Aunt Irene, had both married Catholics, and as far as I could tell, my uncles weren't bad people at all. In fact, Uncle Ray was my favorite uncle. He told funny stories about priests and rabbis and even the Pope. I didn't always understand them, but the way Uncle Ray told a joke made everybody howl with laughter. Awkwardly I patted Martha Jean's shoulder. I'd always thought that when people fell in love, it meant they had to get married. What would happen to Martha Jean if Aunt Muriel wouldn't let her be engaged to Lou?

Weeks passed. Martha Jean came to babysit twice more, but she had changed. She seemed nervous and jumpy all the time, and just wanted to watch our new TV instead of playing Monopoly with me or listening to *Mr. Keen*.

"Martha Jean," I asked finally, "are you mad at me?"

She gave me a blank look, then shook her head. "No, Sugar," she said, but there was no further explanation.

The next morning, I asked over breakfast, "What's wrong with Martha Jean?"

There was a small silence as my parents traded looks across the table. "What do you mean?" asked Mama.

"She's sad all the time," I said. "She doesn't smile, ever since Aunt Muriel told her she couldn't date Lou anymore because he's not white."

"What?" My father set his coffee mug on the table with a clumsy thunk. "Where did you hear a thing like that?"

"From Martha Jean," I said indignantly. "She said Aunt Muriel told her she couldn't date Lou anymore because he's a dago, which is not white, and a Catholic too. Mama, is Uncle Ray an idol worshiper?"

"Hush, Baby. *Dago* isn't a nice word."

"I don't understand my sister," Daddy said angrily. "We weren't raised that way."

"What way is that?" I asked.

"To despise people who have different religions or skin colors. The Santoris are fine people and Lou is a good boy. A smart one too. If Muriel had a lick of sense, she'd encourage that romance."

"Maybe you could talk to her . . ." Mama said diffidently.

"That would only reinforce her attitude. You say *black*, Muriel says *white*. She's never been wrong about anything in her life, ever since she was this high."

The next Saturday was square-dance night, but I wasn't looking forward to spending it with Martha Jean. When she arrived at seven o'clock, I was reading a book in my bedroom, *Little Women*, by Louisa May Alcott. I didn't come out. I heard Mama and Daddy shut the door behind them and pretty soon Martha Jean came to find me.

"What're you doing?" she asked.

"Reading," I answered.

"Ernie Kovacs comes on in twenty minutes. Want to watch it with me?"

"I guess not," I sighed, raising the book once again to my face.

Martha Jean sat down on the edge of my bed. "I know I haven't been good company lately," she began. "I've been awfully sad, ever since, you know . . ."

"Ever since Aunt Muriel made you give Lou's ring back," I finished.

Martha Jean nodded. She began to smooth her skirt with both hands, something she always did when she was nervous. "Nan, can you keep a secret?"

I dropped the book on my lap. "Uh-huh," I said. I loved secrets. Secrets made you important. Once, Judy Gately had told me a secret, that her mother was PG, and that I was the only one she had told, and I mustn't tell anybody else ever. Then I had to cross my heart and hope to die. I didn't know what PG meant, but I knew it was serious, so I carried Judy's secret like a treasure, as Donny always carried his lucky marble in his right pants pocket. I knew something only Judy and I knew and I prided myself in never telling anyone. Finally, I asked Mama one day what PG meant. "Where did you hear that?" she demanded.

"At school," I answered truthfully. "One of the girls was talking."

"Well," Mama said hesitantly, "it means . . . expecting."

"Expecting what?" I asked, totally confused.

"Why, a baby," Mama said. "PG is short for *pregnant,* but we don't say that word in polite company and we don't say *PG* either. We say *expecting.*"

"Oh," I said.

Five or six months later, Judy announced that she had a new baby brother. So now, sitting on my bed with Martha Jean, I leaned forward eagerly. "What?" I demanded.

"You have to promise me that you won't tell anybody no matter what."

"Cross my heart and hope to die," I swore, making a big X on my chest with my index finger.

Martha Jean hesitated, as though she wasn't sure telling me her secret was a good thing.

"What?" I asked again.

"Lou and I are going to elope."

"What's elope?"

"We're going to go away and get married and not tell

anybody until afterward."

I was speechless. Martha Jean and Lou were going to be together after all! I flushed with pleasure and delight. "When?" I asked.

"Next Friday night," she said. "I'm going to go to bed early, and then I'll climb out onto the garage roof. Lou will be there with a ladder. We'll drive down to Kentucky and find a justice of the peace. You can get married in Kentucky when you're seventeen."

"Aunt Muriel will be awful mad at you."

"I know," Martha Jean said, and for the first time I saw a flash of fear in her eyes. "But she'll just have to get over it. Lou said she'll come around when the baby arrives."

I looked blankly at Martha Jean. "What baby?"

Martha Jean blushed and looked down at her hands. "I'm going to have a baby," she said.

Now I was really confused. How could you be PG if you weren't even married yet? But I didn't pursue the issue. It was obvious that there were still a lot of things I didn't know about falling in love and getting married.

"Anyway," Martha Jean said, smiling at me, "I just wanted you to know, because come Saturday morning, there'll probably be a lot of excitement. I don't want you to be upset. Just promise me you won't tell anyone, not even your mama and daddy, okay?"

"When will you come home again?" I asked.

"We'll be back on Monday," she assured me. "Then the fireworks will really start, but it will be too late to stop us 'cause we'll already be married."

I felt so excited and proud. No one else would know, just me, and I knew that nothing could persuade me to tell Martha Jean and Lou's secret.

We went into the kitchen and made popcorn in time to watch Ernie Kovacs' TV show. There was a skit with men dressed up as gorillas playing musical instruments. They were called The Nairobi Trio, and we laughed so hard I almost wet my pants.

The next morning, I realized what a long week it was going to be before Martha Jean and Lou eloped, and I was bursting with excitement. The days dragged; each one felt like a week. I wanted so much to tell my best friend Janelle, but I had crossed my heart and given my solemn word, so I didn't. When Friday finally came around, I woke up all happy and excited. Tonight was the night. I was afraid that somehow Aunt Muriel would find out and ruin everything.

"What's the matter, Nan?" Mama asked me over breakfast that morning. "You haven't touched your food. Aren't you feeling up to par?"

"No, I'm fine," I said, plunging a spoon into my steaming oatmeal. I forced myself to empty the bowl, then grabbed my books and headed out the door. The autumn had been unusually warm, but today it was cold, and Mama made me wear my winter jacket. "Weather man says that we may get snow this weekend," she said as she kissed me out the door.

When school let out in the afternoon, the wind had picked up and I was glad to get home and into the warm kitchen. I looked at the clock. It was only three PM., and Martha Jean hadn't told me what time Lou was coming to get her. What was it she'd said? "I'll go to bed early," or something like that. What time did Martha Jean usually go to bed? My bedtime was nine o'clock, but older kids got to stay up later, especially on the weekends.

After supper—Mama had made chili—we watched

television. *Judy and Jimmy and the Cinnamon Bear,* an annual Christmas radio show, was on TV for the first time that year. We'd listened to it every December since I was a little tiny girl, so I was really excited that it was going to be on TV. But what a disappointment! The characters looked artificial and stupid, nothing like what I pictured when I listened to the radio. I didn't want to tell Mama and Daddy, so I said I didn't feel well and wanted to go to bed early. Mama insisted on taking my temperature, but it was normal, as I'd known it would be. The only thing wrong with me was that I couldn't stop thinking of what was about to happen just down the street. I lay in bed with my eyes wide open, trying to picture Martha Jean climbing down a ladder to Lou, the two of them driving slowly away down the alley with the headlights turned off until they reached the street that would take them to the highway and on to Kentucky.

I woke on Saturday morning full of a mix of dread and anticipation. If everything had gone as planned, Martha Jean and Lou would be in Kentucky looking for someone to marry them. Did Aunt Muriel and Uncle Bill know yet that Martha Jean was gone? I crept down the stairs to the kitchen, trying to act like everything was normal, but already I felt as though Martha Jean's secret was written across my forehead in red ink. Mama and Daddy were sitting in the kitchen drinking coffee and reading *The St. Louis Times Dispatch*. Donny was still asleep. Daddy wore a plaid flannel shirt and cotton wash pants, unlike during the week when he always dressed in a suit and tie for his job at the high school, where he taught American history and coached basketball. Just as I approached the kitchen door, I saw Daddy reach across the table. Without looking up from the paper, he touched Mama's hand. She twined her fingers around his and smiled, although her eyes never left the funnies.

Suddenly Daddy looked up and saw me. "Good morning, Honey Bee," he smiled. Daddy had started calling me his little honey bee when I was just a baby because, according to Mama, I was the sweetest thing he'd ever seen.

"Hi, Daddy," I said. My parents were acting like nothing had happened, so I assumed that they didn't know yet. Or worse, something had happened to destroy Martha Jean's and Lou's plans to elope.

Mama said, "Would you like some silver-dollar pancakes, Nan? Daddy and I already ate."

"Sure," I said. I loved Mama's pancakes. For everyone else, she made them normal size. But for me, she made little ones, no bigger, Daddy said, than silver dollars. She always served them with her homemade peach syrup and bacon.

"Get dressed and wash your hands and braid your hair," she instructed as she rose from the table.

I quickly obeyed. It was a chilly morning, and from my bedroom window, I could see frost on the roof of the house next door. The skies were heavy and dark. I put on a pair of slacks and an undershirt, then pulled open my dresser drawer. There was the sweater that Martha Jean had knitted for my last birthday, when the weather was still too warm to wear it. I admired the twisting pattern of cables and the softness of the yarn. It was rose pink, which was my favorite color. I slipped it over my head now, in honor of Martha Jean. Wearing it made me feel closer to her and that was important today. Just as I was pulling my pigtails out of the neck opening, I heard knocking at the front door, and our little brown-and-white spaniel, Tulip, barked a couple of times. A lump rose in my throat, and the next thing I heard was Aunt Muriel, speaking in low, frantic tones. I couldn't understand her words, but her mood was very clear. Then I heard Mama and Daddy and Uncle Bill, who was trying to calm down Aunt Muriel. I decided that it would look funny if I didn't come back downstairs, especially since Mama was fixing pancakes for me.

I stood next to Daddy at the foot of the stairs. Uncle Bill and Aunt Muriel were wearing coats and Mama was pushing the front door closed. Aunt Muriel said, "How could she do this to us?" She was colorless and tears had started up in the corners of her eyes. I almost felt sorry for her.

Daddy said evenly, "Muriel, we don't know that she's done anything. All we know is that she's left the house without letting you know. Were you arguing with her last night?"

"No!" Aunt Muriel hissed. "She just said she didn't feel well and was going to bed early. And then this morning when she didn't get up, I knocked on her door. When she didn't answer, I went in—"

"—and her bed was empty," Uncle Bill said unnecessarily. "Hadn't been slept in."

"Maybe she got up early and went out," Daddy said.

"Why would she do that?" Aunt Muriel snapped.

I saw Daddy and Mama exchange a quick glance. "Maybe she met a friend."

"Why would she do that?" Aunt Muriel repeated.

"Perhaps," Daddy said slowly, "because you told her she couldn't see him anymore." The silence was deafening as I saw the possibility dawn across Aunt Muriel's cramped face.

"Oh, my God," she breathed. "She couldn't. She wouldn't." She whirled on Uncle Bill. "If she's seeing him behind our backs, I'll make her wish she'd never been born."

"Muriel," Uncle Bill began.

"I think," Daddy said calmly, "that perhaps you ought to pay a visit to the Santoris and see if Lou is home this morning."

Aunt Muriel's face was gray, except for her lips, which were white. "Come on, Bill," she ordered. "We're going over there right this minute."

"Oh dear," Mama said, as she shut the door behind them. "I hope Martha Jean hasn't done anything foolish. Muriel will just make her life miserable."

Daddy's face was sad and angry at the same time. "I think she's already done that," he said. "But this was bound to happen. Martha Jean isn't a baby anymore, and she's sure to rebel if she isn't given any room to breathe." Just then, Daddy realized that I was standing beside him. He tugged gently at one of my braids and smiled. "Come on, Honey Bee," he smiled. "It's breakfast time."

My stomach felt like a clenched fist as I followed my parents into the kitchen. I was seized with something I hadn't expected—guilt. I knew that Martha Jean and Lou were together and that before the day was over they'd be married. But I hadn't been prepared for how upset everyone was. I ate my pancakes and bacon in silence, then went upstairs to finish my arithmetic homework so that I could go outside. By the time I put on my jacket, I could see snowflakes falling lazily out of the pewter sky. I was so excited. Snow was a rarity in our part of the state. The radio was on in the kitchen, where Mama was rolling out pie dough. The weatherman was saying that a major winter storm stretched all the way to the Ohio River Valley and was quickly making roads impassable. I wondered about Martha Jean and Lou. Were they caught in the storm?

I walked to Janelle's house to see if she could come out and play. We went to the end of her street where a narrow ribbon of water ran along the railroad embankment. In summer, there were tiny minnows and even frogs. There were willow trees too, and on one was a low branch that overhung the stream where we would sit and talk. We edged out onto the branch and were surprised that it dipped so low—our feet nearly touched the water.

"We're a lot heavier now than we were last year," Janelle observed solemnly.

It was true. I'd grown a couple of inches at least and was not the skinny little kid I'd been in first and second grades. I had the sudden urge to confide in Janelle, to tell her about Martha Jean and Lou and how they were getting married that very day. I even opened my mouth to speak, but then I clapped my hand over my lips. I had promised not to tell. I remembered the oath I'd made to Judy Gately about her mother being PG. I'd never been tempted to tell anyone, not even Janelle, so why was it so hard to keep my promise to Martha Jean? It must be because I was feeling nervous. Aunt Muriel and Uncle Bill were really mad—at least Aunt Muriel was mad. Uncle Bill just seemed worried. I knew where Martha Jean and Lou were but I couldn't tell because I'd crossed my heart and hoped to die if I did. Just last year, a fourth-grader, Buddy Spitz, whom everyone called Buckshot, had got himself killed in a combine accident on his uncle's farm. One of his cousins, Jimmy Ranfranz, had said that it was because Buckshot had broken a promise not to tell Jimmy's daddy that Jimmy had stolen dirty magazines from the Rexall drugstore. Jimmy's daddy had given him a real hiding. I wondered what it was like to get run over by a combine, and I shuddered.

"You cold?" Janelle asked.

The snow was falling hard around us. The hood of Janelle's jacket was covered in big white flakes. I supposed mine was too. "There's not enough snow to make a snowman," I said.

"Why don't we go to my house?" Janelle said. "I've got a new book of paper dolls."

Janelle's mom made us cocoa with tiny little marshmallows floating on top, and we drank it at the kitchen table, laughing at the marshmallow moustaches that collected on our upper lips. Then we played with the new paper dolls in Janelle's bedroom. There was a blond one and a brunette one, just like me and Janelle, and they had the cutest outfits. We dressed them up for a tennis game, a day at the beach and finally, an evening out. It was hard getting the tiny high-heeled shoes to stay on their feet, but I loved my doll's ball gown. It was deep blue with a bell-shaped skirt that was full of sparkles like a summer night's sky.

Finally Janelle's mother came out of the kitchen wiping her hands on a faded dish towel. "Nan, it's getting on for dark. Your mother will be wanting you home along about now."

"Yes, Ma'am," I answered reluctantly. I didn't want to go home, but I knew I had to. I helped Janelle put away the paper dolls and pulled on my jacket. I thanked Janelle's mama for the hot chocolate and Janelle saw me out the door. The streetlights were coming on, and everything was bright as day because of the snow. Several more inches had fallen while Janelle and I were playing. Maybe tomorrow we could make a snowman.

When I came in the kitchen door, I smelled split-pea soup. The big stock pot was on the stove and Mama was making cornbread in her old iron skillet that had belonged to her mama's mama. It sits in a cupboard in my own kitchen today. "Hi," I said hesitantly. Mama turned toward me, her face tight.

"Hi, Sweetie," she said without smiling. "What did you do this afternoon?"

"Janelle and I went down to the railroad tracks and sat on the willow branch. Mama, we're getting too heavy to sit on it together. We almost had our feet in the water."

"You're growing up so fast," she said. "It seems like just last year that Martha Jean was your age." Mama poured batter into the skillet and set it inside the oven. "Nan, it looks like Martha Jean and Lou ran away together. Lou didn't come home last night and his car is gone." Mama suddenly pulled me to her and hugged me. "Promise me, Nan, that you'll never run away from home."

"I promise," I said. I felt really awful to see Mama so worried. Nobody said much during dinner, not even Donny, who usually had to be shushed up so he wouldn't be sitting at the table after everyone else was finished.

On Sunday morning, the snow was so deep that everyone on the street was out clearing their sidewalks with coal shovels so they could at least walk downtown to church. Automobile traffic was impossible. Daddy gave me a tiny shovel and a bucket of ashes from the furnace to scatter on the icy spots so that no one would fall down, especially Miss Ludie Finch, who lived next door and was real old, at least fifty, according to Donny, who liked to think he knew everything.

We went to the Methodist Church for the early service. When Reverend Dedmon read the names of the folks who needed special prayers, he mentioned Aunt Muriel and Uncle Bill. After the last hymn, we met them on the front steps. Aunt Muriel looked older than Miss Ludie Finch.

"You run along, Honey Bee," Daddy said. I knew he didn't want me to hear them talk about Martha Jean. But as I walked slowly down the steps, I heard Uncle Bill say something about the police.

Janelle was waiting on the sidewalk. "Wanna make a snowman?" she asked. "My mom gave me a big carrot for the nose. We could make him in my yard and then make a girl snowman in your yard. We could get Donny and the Garber twins to help."

I had been excited about making a snowman, but now I shook my head. I felt exhausted and vaguely sick. "I don't think so," I said.

"You're upset about your cousin, aren't you?"

"Uh-huh."

"My mom and dad think Martha Jean and Lou Santori ran away together. Is that true? Boy, if they did, they are in s-o-o-o much trouble. Is it true?"

"I don't know," I lied. And then I felt even worse. It wasn't like I'd never lied before. I lied to Donny all the time, like about where I'd hidden his baseball mitt after he tore up a special picture I made at school for Daddy. But I'd never lied to Janelle, and I knew I'd done something bad.

When I got home, I went straight upstairs to my room and sat on the bed. This was not turning out at all the way I'd thought it would. It had been pretty easy keeping Judy Gately's secret. And when Judy's mom wasn't PG anymore, everybody was really happy about the new baby. But with Martha Jean's secret, everybody was worried and sad and angry. I wanted more than anything to say, "Don't worry, they got married, that's all, and they'll be back home tomorrow, and then there'll be a baby and everything will be all right." But I couldn't. I had promised. I had crossed my heart and hoped to die.

Sunday was the longest day of my life. I kept looking at the clock, willing the hands to turn faster so that this day would be over and Monday would dawn with Martha Jean and Lou coming home. I wished that Martha Jean hadn't told me her secret after all. It felt like a big weight that I had to drag around, like one of those anvils that was always falling on Wile E. Coyote in the *Roadrunner* cartoons.

Donny finally made me come outside with him. Mama and Daddy saw how upset I was and told him to get my mind off Martha Jean. Donny hauled my sled out of the basement and we slogged through the snow to a hill on the edge of town. At the bottom of the hill was a pond, but it wasn't very deep and it had frozen over. We took turns dragging the sled up the hill and then riding it down onto the ice.

"Martha Jean and Lou ran away together," he said.

"I know." Donny and I were standing at the top of the hill, watching the shadows of the trees stretch out across the snow. The sky had cleared and Mama had said that it would be very cold tonight. Our breath came in clouds.

"Did Martha Jean say anything to you about running away?"

I stopped breathing.

"Well? Did she, Nan? Because if she did, you'd better tell."

"She never told me anything!" I yelled. I picked up a handful of snow and threw it in Donny's face and ran all the way home.

For once, I was glad the weekend was over. I got up the first time Mama called me, and went downstairs for breakfast. I couldn't look anybody in the face. I ate quickly and left the house. It was four blocks to school, right through the center of town. The day was bright and sunny, and I saw Mr. Rose emptying the parking meters on Union Avenue, which was the main street. Mr. Rose was blind, and he'd had to go away to blind school for a while. He came back with a big German shepherd named Bopie, who helped him find his way around. Instead of a leash, Bopie wore a red harness that Mr. Rose held onto while they made their way down the street and collected change from the meters. Nobody was permitted to pet Bopie or even speak to him. He was what Daddy called a Working Dog, which meant that he wasn't a pet like Tulip. Bopie had serious business in the world, which was to help Mr. Rose do his job and support his family.

"Hi, Mr. Rose!" I called out as I approached. The sunshine, the normalcy of the morning's activities, had ignited a small flame of optimism in my heart.

"Good morning," said Mr. Rose. "It's little Nan, isn't it? Martha Jean's cousin? Has Martha Jean come home yet?"

"No, Sir," I replied, "but I think she'll be back later today."

"Well that's good news," Mr. Rose said. "Her folks sure are in a dither."

"Have a nice day, Sir." I broke into a run without waiting for a reply. Martha Jean would be home today. Maybe she was home even now.

But Martha Jean didn't come home and neither did Lou. I could tell as soon as I got in the door after school by how quiet Mama was. I went up to my room and started on my homework. Tulip followed me and sat under my desk on my feet. Even she knew something was wrong. I practiced memorizing the multiplication tables, something we had to master before we could begin studying long division. How long did it take to drive back from Kentucky? I had no idea. But Martha Jean had insisted they'd be home today. I looked out the window. Monday wasn't over yet. It was still daytime outside.

When Mama called me for dinner, I was working on my geography lesson and it was pitch dark. We'd been given mimeographed maps of Europe, but the names of the countries were left out. We had to fill them in and write, on a separate sheet of paper, a sentence about each one. The assignment was due on Friday. I was having trouble with Eastern Europe, all those little countries along the coast of the Baltic Sea that were somehow now part of the Soviet Union. The Soviet Union was ruled by a king named Uncle Joe Stalin who Daddy said was an evil man. I decided that those countries must be cold and gray all year round, and that the people who lived there probably weren't very happy.

I went downstairs and silently set the table. Mama had made round steak with mushroom gravy in the big aluminum electric skillet Daddy had given her for her birthday in July. There were collard greens and mashed potatoes too. It was one of the best things Mama made, but tonight I had no appetite. When Donny and Daddy sat down, Mama asked, "Any word from Bill and Muriel?"

"They're turning in a missing-person report to the state police tomorrow. The Santoris are doing the same for Lou."

"Something's wrong," Mama said.

"Well, that's obvious," Daddy said.

"I don't mean just that they ran away together," Mama replied. "It's been three days now. Surely one of them would have called their parents. Or at least called *us*. I can understand them running away, but to not come back or even get in touch? Something's just not right."

Donny hated collard greens. He was pushing them around on his plate with his fork. "Nan knows something," he said sullenly.

I froze with my fork halfway to my mouth. Mama and

Daddy stopped chewing and looked at me. "Nan?" Mama said.

I couldn't speak. I felt as though I'd been scalded.

"Nan," Daddy said sternly. "Is Donny right? Do you know where Martha Jean is? Did she tell you something?"

Suddenly I could no longer bear the weight of the secret. I dropped my fork onto my plate and burst into tears.

"Nan!" Mama said. "Stop that right now. If you know anything about where Martha Jean and Lou are, you have to tell us immediately."

"I promised," I sobbed. "She made me promise. I had to cross my heart and hope to die!"

Daddy spoke again, but this time his voice was gentler. "Who made you promise, Honey Bee? Martha Jean? What did she make you promise?"

"Not to tell her secret."

"Do you mean about where she and Lou went on Friday night?"

I nodded silently.

Daddy pulled a clean handkerchief out of his back pocket and handed it to me across the table. "Blow your nose," he said. "Wipe your eyes." I did as I was told. "Now," Daddy continued, "I want you to look at me, Nancy Eugenia, and listen carefully to what I'm going to tell you."

Slowly I raised my eyes to my father's. For the first time, I noticed the lines around his eyes.

"Martha Jean was wrong to ask you to keep such a secret. I know you love Martha Jean, but what she and Lou did was wrong too, and she had no business involving you in it on any level. I can't tell you how much pain she and Lou have caused her parents, Lou's parents—even our family. You won't understand this until you're grown up and have children of your own, but not knowing where your child is, if she's dead or alive, is the worst thing that can happen to you."

We sat in silence for a few moments. I looked at Donny, and he was counting the little clocks and birds on the kitchen wallpaper, something he always did when he was bored or scared.

"To keep your promises in life is sacred, Nan," said Mama. "But there are times when you have to break a promise if keeping it brings harm to someone. That time is now."

"She told me they'd be back home today," I said, trying hard not to cry again.

"Back home from where?"

"From Kentucky, from getting married. She said you can get married in Kentucky if you're seventeen."

"Oh, my God," Mama whispered.

"Did she say where in Kentucky?" asked Daddy.

I shook my head. "No, she just said they'd find a trustee of the niece." I watched Daddy mouth those syllables, then smile involuntarily. "But I don't know what that means. Mama, Martha Jean's PG. I didn't know you could be PG if you weren't married already."

It was Daddy's turn to say, "Oh, my God."

I hardly slept that night. Mama and Daddy had gone to Aunt Muriel's and Uncle Bill's house directly after dinner and didn't return until after I'd gone to bed. I cried and cried, guilty with my betrayal of Martha Jean and Lou. I kept wondering how I would die, picturing over and over Buckshot falling under his uncle's big green John Deere combine, which now sat in a pasture near Route 32 with a big FOR SALE sign on it. Maybe I'd be hit by a car or get a ruptured appendix or leukemia, like Darlene Hagermeyer who had been a year ahead of me in school.

I couldn't eat any breakfast the next morning. Mama and Daddy looked exhausted, and I guessed that they hadn't slept much either. Only Donny seemed unaffected. He gulped down his Cheerios and orange juice and left quickly for school. After the front door closed behind him, Daddy turned to me and said, "How are you this morning, Honey Bee?"

"Okay," I said. I could feel tears coming on and I tried to will them from spilling down my cheeks.

"You don't look okay," he said. "Talk to me."

That did it. The floodgates opened, and the next thing I knew, I was in Daddy's lap. "I don't want to die!" I wept.

"What makes you say that?"

"I promised Martha Jean I wouldn't tell about her and Lou eloping. I crossed my heart and hoped to die, and when Buckshot told Jimmy Ranfranz's daddy about the dirty magazines, that's when he got run over by the combine."

"What?"

I explained about the Rexall drugstore magazine heist and how Jimmy had made Buckshot promise not to tell, cross his heart and hope to die. And then Buckshot had told Jimmy's daddy. The rest was known by everybody in the county.

"Oh, God," Daddy whispered. "My poor Honey Bee!" He pried me off his shoulder and held my hands. "You are not going to die—at least not until you are an old, old lady with about a hundred great-grandchildren. Buckshot did not get killed because he told Jimmy's secret. He died because his uncle was dead drunk while he was operating that combine. Now go wash your face with cold water and run off to school."

I did as I was told. The dark burden of Martha Jean's secret was lifted from my soul at last, and I felt as though my feet never touched the concrete as I flew, light as a bird, down the sidewalks toward school. But I was very careful crossing the streets. I looked left, right, and then left again before I stepped off the curbs, a habit I continue to this day.

On Wednesday, Aunt Muriel and Uncle Bill learned that Martha Jean and Lou had obtained a marriage license in the Daviess County seat, Owensboro, on Saturday morning and had been married by a justice of the peace that afternoon. They had spent two nights in Owensboro at the Starlight Motel. Where they'd gone from there was anybody's guess.

The temporary euphoria at my reprieve from certain death faded as Thursday dawned and there was still no news of Martha Jean and Lou. That evening, as we were sitting down to dinner, our telephone rang in the hallway. Daddy answered, and after a brief conversation he came back to the kitchen, his face creased with pain.

"What?" Mama asked.

"That was Bill. The news is not good."

My stomach somersaulted.

"The Kentucky State Police found Martha Jean and Lou about two hours ago."

"Dear God," Mama said, pressing her fingertips against her mouth. "Where? What happened?"

"Their car went off the road in a rural area with a lot of trees, over an embankment. A local woman saw tire marks in the snow and stopped to investigate. It must have happened on Monday. It was very icy on Monday."

"And? Are they—" Mama couldn't finish.

"Martha Jean is alive but in critical condition. I'm sorry to say that Lou didn't make it. Bill and Muriel are leaving for Kentucky as soon as they can pack a bag."

Martha Jean had been trapped between the front and

back seats when Lou's car came to a halt among the snowy trees. Both her legs were broken, and the only reason she did not die of cold was because there were two warm blankets with which she managed to cover herself. To this day, I cannot imagine how terrible those three days must have been, knowing that Lou was dead and that she might never be found alive.

She spent a month in an Owensboro hospital. In the meantime, Lou's body was returned home for burial. Mama and Daddy went to the funeral at St. Anthony's, which was right across the street from the Methodist Church. When she was well enough to be brought home, Martha Jean asked that I come to see her. I went with a heavy heart. I was afraid of Aunt Muriel and I had no idea what to say to Martha Jean. Aunt Muriel, without one word to me, pointed to Martha Jean's bedroom. I found her propped up on pillows, looking as pale and thin as I had feared. Both lower legs were in casts.

She smiled at me as I stood beside the bed. "I broke my promise," I blurted.

"I know, Nan," she said. "Thank you for telling—" She bit her lip.

I waited for her to continue, but she merely patted the mattress, inviting me to sit on the bed. "You're not mad at me?" I asked.

"No, Nan. I'm not mad at you at all. I should never have burdened you with a secret like that in the first place."

"That's what Daddy said," I replied, "but I don't agree with him. If you hadn't told me, maybe you wouldn't have been found at all."

Martha Jean nodded.

"I'm sorry about Lou," I said, because I was afraid of asking what I really wanted to know.

"I couldn't even go to the funeral," Martha Jean said.

"I know." I took a deep breath. "When will you be able to walk again? Martha Jean, are you still PG?"

Martha Jean's eyes dropped and she placed a hand reflexively over her belly, which was, I just then noticed, the only part of her body that didn't look wasted. "Yes," she said. "And my casts come off in two weeks. After that, I have to go away for a while, to Dad's sister in Peoria."

"Why?"

"To have the baby."

"Can't you have it here?"

"Mom doesn't want anyone to know. I have to give it up for adoption."

I'd had a conversation with Mama about adoption only the past summer. It had left me unsettled and full of questions that I couldn't quite articulate. The tears that had been puddling in Martha Jean's eyes finally ran down her cheeks.

"But why?" I was suddenly angry. "You can't give your baby away!"

"No one knows but just us, just my family and your family, and Mom says I'm too young to be a mother and that it's best for everybody for me to give it up." Martha Jean suddenly grabbed my hand. "Please don't say anything to your folks!"

I jerked my hand away from Martha Jean's. "You mean keep another secret?" I demanded.

"No—I mean yes, please. It will just make everything harder for me."

Looking back on that conversation from the advantage of many years, I think that moment marked my entrance into moral adulthood. "No, Martha Jean," I said. I jumped off the bed. "I'm going to tell everybody!"

The Search for the Villa Melzi Gardens...and Other Tales

And I did. I went right home and found Mama fixing dinner and Daddy at the kitchen table reading aloud from *The Saturday Evening Post*. When I told them what Aunt Muriel had decided, Daddy was furious. "Did it ever occur to my sister," he said to Mama, "that Lou's parents might have something to say about what happens to their grandchild? I can't believe they don't know about this pregnancy!" He stood up from his chair and went right to the coat closet. He yanked his jacket off a hanger.

"John, where are you going?" Mama asked. "Please don't make a scene with Muriel and Bill. Wait until you've calmed down."

"I'm not going to Muriel and Bill's," Daddy said grimly. "I'm going to visit the Santoris."

And that's how Martha Jean went to live with Lou's parents. That following spring, she gave birth to a baby boy, whom she named Luigi Santori, Jr. Martha Jean got a job at the First National Bank in the accounting department, where she performed administrative tasks. Eventually, she studied accounting and became a CPA. She and her son continued to live with her inlaws until he was in grade school. Then she married one of Lou's cousins, Marco. Aunt Muriel had, to quote my father, "an utter and complete conniption" when Martha Jean joined the Catholic Church prior to her remarriage.

I took a job in Memphis after college where I still live today, but Martha Jean and I continue our close friendship. She eventually had two daughters with Marco, and I believe they are very happy. Every once in a while, Martha Jean will say to me, "Thanks to you, I have the most beautiful son in the whole world. And that is no secret." Then we hug each other and laugh.

THE VISITOR

HENRIETTA SAW THE rooster tail of red dust way off down the road well before she heard the whine of the engine. She sighed and leaned back in the rocker. Her dress stuck to her back. She wished she could go in the house and take off her corset, but that was nonsense of course. She'd worn a corset every day of her life since she was fifteen years old with the exception of her five pregnancies, hot weather or cold. She was too old to change.

"Nobody'll know the difference," Ruby Mae had told her only yesterday. Her granddaughter chewed gum all the time and wore black stuff in rings around her eyes that put Henrietta in mind of two holes burned in a blanket. The temperature had climbed to one-hundred-and-six according to the thermometer nailed to the maple tree in the front yard. The thermometer was rusty from the elements but you could still read JENSEN'S FEED AND GRAIN in black letters down the side, and it recorded the weather accurately. Or as accurately as Henrietta was inclined to care.

"Half the girls in my class don't even wear a *bra* anymore, Grandma. And nobody—but *nobody* wears a corset. You are absolutely the last woman alive in Saline County that wears a corset."

Henrietta had nodded and sighed. "That may be true, but I'd feel naked without it and I expect to be buried in it."

"Jesus," Ruby Mae said, rolling her eyes and taking a Coca Cola from the refrigerator. Ruby Mae wore the tightest blue jeans Henrietta had ever seen. She didn't know how Ruby Mae got them on nor how she sat down once she did.

"And don't take the Lord's name in vain," Henrietta snapped. "Not in my house, anyway. You know that just aggravates me to death."

"Sorry, Grandma," Ruby Mae said, dropping her eyes. "I don't know what gets into me sometimes."

"Well I'm sure I don't either," Henrietta replied archly. She immediately regretted her tone. Ruby Mae was a good girl after all, even if she did wear tight jeans and dreadful eye makeup. She was the only one of Henrietta's grandchildren who ever came to see her.

That had been yesterday, and now Henrietta was sitting on the front porch watching the dust cloud of the approaching car and wondering who it was driving out to her house in the afternoon heat. She picked up her fan and opened it. It was a silk fan. MADE IN OCCUPIED JAPAN was stamped on one of the wooden ends. It was pale yellow and painted on it was a picture of a little arched bridge over a splashing brook. Next to the brook was a tree with long trailing branches. A white bird sat in the tree and a lady in a peacock-blue bathrobe dress was starting across the bridge on the far side. She had an elaborate hair-do and carried a tiny parasol. She looked as dainty as a doll. Henrietta loved the fan and the scene with the bridge, the tree, the bird and the lady. It made her feel peaceful to think that somewhere in this world cool water flowed and a woman could put on a pretty dress and go out for a walk with only a white bird for company.

Henrietta squinted at the dust cloud. The vehicle was invisible now on the other side of the corn field, but presently it came around the bend in the road and she saw a blue Chevy coupe with a tall antenna. The antenna arched back from the drag of a huge fox tail. The Chevy slowed abruptly and turned into the yard. The fox tail drooped. The car was coated with dust, the windshield and front grill splattered with bugs. After a minute the driver-side door swung open and a man got out. Henrietta had never laid eyes on him in her life. He wasn't more than twenty, Henrietta guessed. He wore jeans and boots and what Henrietta had heard Ruby Mae call a motorcycle jacket, although why on earth anybody with a lick of sense would be wearing a jacket like that in heat like this was certainly a mystery to her. In fact, she found it alarming. A man who'd wear a motorcycle jacket when it was a hundred degrees in the shade must be flat-out crazy. Maybe he had a long-handled knife or a gun stuck in his britches. You heard stories all the time these days about drug-crazed hippies killing people in farm houses and writing things like "Death to the pigs!" in lipstick—or was it blood?—all over the walls.

And here she was alone on this farm, not a single man on the place anymore. By God, if this crazy person didn't kill her and steal her egg and butter money out of the sugar bowl in the breakfront, she would fetch down Sam's old shotgun and keep it loaded next to the door.

The man ambled slowly up toward the porch as the dust settled around him. Henrietta would not speak first. As he drew closer, Henrietta saw that he wore his hair long and had a full beard as well. *Lord, Lord,* she thought, fanning herself harder. She leaned forward in the rocking chair. This time her dress stuck to the chair back.

"Howdy," the man said, stopping just short of the porch. He put his hands on his hips and inclined his head. There was a metallic wink from his left earlobe. "Howdy," Henrietta replied in a firm voice. Could be he was lost and needing directions.

"Shore is hot, ain't it?" the man said.

"I reckon so," Henrietta said. "Whatcha wearin that jacket for anyway in this heat?" She recognized her mistake immediately. The question sounded like a challenge. Perhaps now the knife would flash and the mayhem begin. Henrietta was glad she had resisted the temptation to remove her corset.

"Well Ma'am," the man answered, "my onliest shirt got tore up last night in a fight over at that road house near Vining, and I didn't want to offend you by comin up here half naked."

"What were you fightin in a bar for anyway?"

"Wasn't no fight o' mine to start with," he said. "But a lady was bein mistreated—a tiny lady no moren a hundred pounds who was mindin her own business and not givin anybody cause for complaint. And I just can't stand to see a lady mistreated."

Henrietta declined to point out that no lady would be in the Vining road house in the first place. She shifted her weight in the rocking chair and resumed her fanning. She did not know what was expected of her. She didn't know if the crazy man was really crazy or telling the truth. He was staring at the ground and drawing a design in the dust with the toe of his boot.

Henrietta said, "Would you like a cool glass of water or some ice tea? My granddaughter drank up all the Coca Cola."

"Oh, yes Ma'am," the man replied looking up. "I'd sure be obliged. I worked up a thirst drivin out here."

Henrietta gestured toward the porch swing. "Have a seat." She snapped her fan shut and heaved herself out of the rocker. *I'm crazier'n he is,* she thought. *I oughta tell him to state his business.*

But something held her back. She opened the screen door and went through the dim parlor to the kitchen. She thought about it as she took down a glass, filled it with ice cubes and poured tea from the old flowered pitcher in the fridge. There was something about his eyes when he'd looked up at her the last time, after she'd offered him something to drink.

Henrietta started back through the parlor, but instead of continuing to the porch she turned abruptly and went into her bedroom. She set down the iced tea on her old marble-top dresser and went to the closet. Without turning on the light she pushed past her dresses and her winter coat to the back and felt among the hangers. When her fingers found what they were looking for, she released the collar button, tugged it off the hanger and carried it to the window. It was nothing special but it would do: one of Sam's old shirts, originally blue-and-white plaid but washed with lye soap so many times it was faded to a pale, muddled gray. She peered at it critically. It was clean. It would do.

When she emerged back onto the front porch, the man shot up off the swing seat like somebody had poked him with hot tongs. *Well, at least he's had some upbringin,* Henrietta reflected with satisfaction. She held out the shirt. "Put this on," she said. "It ain't much but it's clean."

The man went scarlet and started to demur. "Put it on," Henrietta insisted. "I don't want you droppin of heat stroke here on my porch."

He sputtered embarrassed thanks. She watched him with frank interest as he unzipped and removed the jacket. His chest was smooth and hairless but well-muscled and brown as an Indian's. *He must work some,* Henrietta concluded. She watched his arms disappear down the shirt sleeves. The sudden ripple of muscle at his shoulder and upper arm sent an unexpected pang through her vitals and she looked away. She saw Sam as he had been during the first years of their marriage, the same work-hardened muscles, the same lift of collar bone and that tender area where it joined his neck that was vulnerable as a child's. How she had loved the smell of him when he came in from the field for dinner, the male sweat-and-tobacco smell of him, and then again in the evening after his bath, all soapy-fragranced and clean, and the hardness of his shoulder under her head at night, the salt-sweet taste of him the night Braden was conceived.

The man finished buttoning the shirt and sat down. The swing joints creaked with his weight. He took a long swallow of iced tea. "Thank you, Ma'am," he said. "That's real tasty."

"I don't like that instant stuff from a jar," Henrietta said, commencing to rock again. "I make it with Lipton's tea bags, same as I always did. I set a big ole fruit jar in the sun and the tea comes up real nice, without no bitterness."

"It's real fine," the man repeated. He turned the glass in his hands, rubbing patterns in the frost.

"What's your name, son?" Henrietta asked.

"Paris," he said. "Paris Granger."

"Where your folks from?"

Paris Granger looked uncomfortable. The swing creaked and groaned, he drained the glass.

"I work over in St. Louis," he said. "Construction. I was born up at Marion but I come up mostly in Cairo and Shawneetown."

Henrietta nodded. "I was born in Jackson County, same as my husband. His name was Sam Harper. My name is Henrietta Harper but I was a Muhlhausen before we was married. My daddy farmed and worked some in the mines. I don't recall no Grangers though. What did your daddy do?"

"Nothin much. He got killed in Korea before I was born. He was just eighteen. Him and Mama got married right before he went overseas and then he got killed. Mama said he wanted to go up to Chicago and work in a steel mill but they never got to try it out."

"That's a shame," said Henrietta. "A boy growin up without no daddy. I'm grateful Sam and me got ours raised up before he went."

Paris Granger cleared his throat and rattled the ice in his glass. "How many children do you have, Miz Harper?"

"Five—three girls and two boys. One of my girls was stillborn, though, so only four growed up." Henrietta felt the ancient twinge in her chest almost without taking notice of it. It had been with her so long now that it was like an old friend, all she had left of the baby who never drew breath. More than thirty-five winters had passed since then and she was no longer certain where the baby's grave lay. It had been marked by a big gray rock Sam brought up from the creek bottom, but vandals had got into the little family plot one night shortly after the war, had smashed tombstones and rolled the rock down the hill where it came to rest once again in the creek. Sam was too stove up with arthritis by then to tote it back, so a series of wooden crosses had been substituted until these too had deteriorated. Henrietta had always meant to put up a real marker, but somehow there was never enough money. Outward signs of the little grave gradually disappeared. This made Henrietta sad, but then she thought of her mama and daddy in heaven too, and of Jesus who was so tender with the little children. Someday soon she would join them all: Sam, her mama and daddy, her brothers and sisters, her baby daughter.

She wondered sometimes if folks stayed the same age in heaven as they were when they passed over. Would her baby be a baby forever? Or would old folks get younger and younguns grow up? It bothered her so bad she asked Reverend Billy Sykes about it one Sunday after church. He'd looked at Henrietta thoughtfully and pressed the tips of his fingers together and rocked on his heels. Reverend Sykes had a habit of doing that, Henrietta noticed, whenever he didn't know the answer to something. Finally he'd said, "Sister Harper, we shall all be in glory. Scripture tells us we will be as angels, neither marrying nor being given in marriage, sitting at the right hand of our Lord Jesus Christ."

Henrietta knew that Jesus sat at the right hand of God Almighty and she envisioned a blinding column of celestial light with another bright light on its right, and lesser lights proceeding off into infinity like an endless string of Christmas tree bulbs.

"I reckon," Reverend Sykes continued, "that just as the angels are ageless we shall be ageless also. Does that answer your question?"

Henrietta stared off across the lawn and out over fields that had been plowed for the winter. "I can't rightly say it does," she answered frankly.

Reverend Sykes patted her shoulder. "Sister, the works of the Lord are mysterious and we can't always grasp the mind of the Almighty. We just need to keep our faith."

"Well, yes," Henrietta said, but she thought, *Why am I asking such of a man ain't but thirty-two years old anyway?* She drove home and baked a chocolate layer cake. That night when Rudolph Tilden came over to sit with her and watch Carol Burnett, they each had a big slab with ice cream.

"Miz Harper?"

Henrietta flinched out of her reverie. Paris Granger was eating the ice from his glass. "Your children all still here?"

Henrietta brushed a fly away from her brow. "Land, no. Braden—that's my oldest—went up to Detroit to work for Chrysler. Alex joined the Air Force. He's training pilots now for Vietnam, out in California. My youngest girl, Darla, lives over in Evansville, Indiana. Her husband's in Vietnam, got five more months to go and then he'll be home, Lord willing. Only my oldest daughter, Reenie, still lives here. She's got three children. One of them is Ruby Mae, who drank up all the Coca Cola. Reenie's husband got run over by a tractor two years ago come fall and he's on the disability now. Reenie's a checker at the A&P in Carlinville. How come you ain't in the Army? You want some more ice tea?"

"If it wouldn't be any trouble." Paris Granger held out the empty glass.

When Henrietta came back from the kitchen this time, the sun had dropped some and the shade from the big maple tree had begun to creep across the yard. She'd have to start thinking about supper pretty soon. Ruby Mae was coming over to help her with the garden. Henrietta thought about the pork chops in the fridge. There was a box of Kraft macaroni and cheese and plenty of fat red tomatoes in the garden. She turned to her guest.

"I got a high number," Paris Granger said, "you know, in the draft lottery. Still, I reckon I'll be called up one of these days. Don't look to me like Nixon's gonna get us outa Vietnam any time soon."

"Is your mama still in Marion?"

"No Ma'am, Mama died this spring. In April."

"I'm sorry. What ailed her? She couldn't of been very old."

"Thirty-nine," said Paris Granger. "But she was pretty wore out. She had high sugar. Was a stroke killed her."

"Lordy," Henrietta murmured, clucking softly. "You got brothers and sisters?"

"No. I ain't got nobody. Mama never married again. Daddy come from an orphanage. Mama's got cousins somewheres out in Oklahoma, but I don't rightly know where."

"So you ain't got no people left at all," Henrietta said. It was not a question. Paris Granger looked as nervous, she thought, as a long-tail cat in a room full of rocking chairs. She felt the tiniest stir of alarm.

"Well, Miz Harper," he said slowly, "I ain't entirely certain of that. An that's why I come out here today to call on you. It's taken me this long to get up the gumption to do it."

"What is it?" Henrietta asked.

"Well Ma'am," Paris Granger said, fumbling a pack of Pall Malls from the pocket of his motorcycle jacket which lay beside him on the swing, "I think I'm Mr. Sam Harper's grandson."

I'm too old for this, Henrietta repeated to herself, dropping pork chops into the hot grease. *I'm too old for this and it ain't fair.* The pork chops sizzled and spat; and on the back burner of the gas range, the water for the sweet corn was about to boil.

Ruby Mae had brought the sweet corn from Rudolph Tilden on the next farm, a dozen ears, fresh picked. Tomorrow Henrietta would take him homemade butter. Rudolph was widowed getting on for five years now, only a little longer than herself, and he and Henrietta traded. He plowed her garden spring and fall, did minor repairs around the house, kept her in sweet corn. Every fall he put half a fresh hog in her freezer. Henrietta cleaned his house twice a month and did his laundry, as well as supplying him with butter and cream from Junie, her old Jersey cow, who gave the sweetest milk Henrietta had ever tasted in a lifetime of living among cows.

"You're gonna have to do somethin about Junie one of these days," Rudolph had said over coffee just the other day. They'd sat right here at Henrietta's kitchen table with the yellow-and-white plastic cloth, and Rudolph stirred Junie's thick cream into his mug. Junie had failed to get pregnant only this spring.

"What do you want me to do, Rudolph?" Henrietta had spoken rather sharply because it hurt her to think about Junie. Only that morning, milking Junie at dawn, Henrietta had noticed how thin and loose her udders had hung, how her bag was never quite full anymore.

"Your old boobies is just about as useless as mine," Henrietta said. Her mother had taught her to talk to cows while she milked; it gentled them and the milk came faster. Henrietta finished milking and laid her cheek against Junie's warm flank. Junie lifted her head from the trough and turned to look at Henrietta. Her enormous, soft, long-lashed eyes were filmed with cataracts. *She's drying up,* Henrietta thought. She stood, her back and legs protesting, and kicked back the milking stool. She laid her arms across Junie's massive shoulders and wept.

"I ain't gonna send her to the slaughterhouse to end up in dog food," she told Rudolph across the table. Henrietta could not bear the thought of the electric prod, Junie bawling with terror, her eyes rolling back to show their whites as she was driven onto a truck.

"You can't afford to turn her out to graze. You'll need another milk cow."

"Maybe by that time I'll be dead myself," Henrietta said. "They can plant the both of us yonder in the graveyard next to Sam, us two old wore-out heifers together." Henrietta laughed, but Rudolph had been unamused.

"That's no way to talk," he said.

"I reckon we've both lived long enough to say what we mean," Henrietta replied, cutting Rudolph another slice of peach pie.

And I did mean it, Henrietta thought now, shucking corn onto the *St. Louis Post Dispatch* spread out on the yellow-and-white cloth. The ears were perfect from tip to stem. They would be the nearest a person could come to heaven in this life, boiled briefly and drenched with Junie's butter. Doc Stern had told Henrietta she should stop eating butter and cream because of her cholesterol. Henrietta did not believe in cholesterol.

She finished cleaning the corn and turned the pork chops. She looked out the kitchen window at the garden where Ruby Mae and Paris Granger were pulling weeds. An aluminum colander full of ripe tomatoes stood next to the border of marigolds. Henrietta lifted her apron and wiped the sweat off her face.

"I am too damn old for this," she said again, only this time she said it aloud.

Out on the porch, Paris Granger had talked through half a pack of Pall Malls and three more glasses of iced tea. His mama, he said, was the only child of Lettie Stark. She had been born out of wedlock. It was during the Depression, Paris Granger told her. Her family had wanted nothing to do with her. She'd gotten pregnant by an itinerant worker name of Sam Harper who'd farmed in Saline County.

Cash money was hard to come by in those days, Henrietta recalled, but Sam had gotten a few weeks of work one winter with the Civilian Conservation Corps down in the national forest. Henrietta remembered that winter vividly. It had been unusually cold and she'd gone through so much wood trying to keep the house warm for herself and the younguns. There were just Braden and Reenie then, and her pregnant. She'd had to chop half the morning most days just to keep from freezing. She'd been entirely alone for six weeks, just her and the children, and she worried that one of them would get sick and need a doctor. With no phone or close neighbors, she might not be able summon one. So she fed the stove constantly, and chopped firewood like a madwoman, her head wrapped in a shawl, her big pregnant belly getting in the way while cedar and oak and persimmon chips flew like startled birds, and her breath steamed like the breath of a plow horse. She'd chopped wood, fed the stove, read and sung to the children, took care of the stock, collected eggs, milked the cow and waited for the infrequent visits of the rural delivery man. Sam's letters always began, "My dearest wife, Henrietta."

Henrietta went to the screen door on the porch and peered out. Paris Granger was filling her watering can from the spigot at the side of the house. The spigot was rusted and Henrietta hadn't been able to turn it on all summer. She saw the muscles in Paris' shoulder flex as he opened it easily. He carried the can to her roses and began to water them carefully, avoiding the lush pink and red blooms. *He knows what he's doing,* Henrietta reflected, *at least about the roses.* She knew he had no idea what he was doing when it came to her own life.

They don't understand what it was like, she thought, as Paris bent over the roses. This world of theirs was too different, people having babies out of wedlock all the time, even movie stars. You saw it every week in *The National Enquirer* and on the TV, women having babies with no husband in sight and not making apologies for it either. But back in the old days it ruined your life. Period. A woman was shamed forever and unfit for the association of a Christian community. Like as not her family would turn her out— as Lettie Stark's had done—and her child would be marked. But they couldn't imagine, she mused, watching Paris, watching Ruby Mae fling a fistful of weeds into a peach basket. You couldn't imagine the calamity unless you'd lived through those times.

Henrietta turned back into the kitchen and began to set the table. The old flowered china was chipped, every piece of it. Darla had bought her a set of Melmac dinnerware three Christmases ago, but Henrietta couldn't bring herself to put it out. What was the use of things that would never show any wear, that couldn't match themselves to the pace of your own faltering days with their chips, cracks and cloudy stains? Henrietta liked the old things.

Her head was noisy with questions. Paris did not know how Sam met Letty. He did not know if Letty told Sam of her pregnancy. But now Henrietta was burdened with both too much knowledge and not enough. Her mind clamored like starlings at a grain spill. What could she do? She'd sat and listened in pole-axed silence as Paris Granger spun out his story on the front porch. Paris had not realized that Sam was married when Sam fathered Paris' mother.

"I'm sorry, Ma'am," he said after a hesitation. "Mama just figured he was a single man, not settled down yet, 'cause he was there just the one winter." Henrietta stared at Paris Granger's throat, remembering the familiar hollow above his collarbone.

Men, she thought now, banging knives and forks down next to the old chipped plates. The knives and forks couldn't properly be called silverware because they were made of heavy, solid stainless steel. Henrietta had saved Betty Crocker coupons for years and acquired them place setting by place setting. She looked at the fork in her hand. Tudor Rose, the pattern was called. It put her in mind of English castles.

She recalled the excitement and pleasure of finding the rectangular packages in the mail box, of unwrapping each gleaming piece. She had collected twelve place settings in all, and then the serving pieces: gravy ladle, solid and slotted serving spoons, sugar spoon, meat fork, cake and butter knives—even the little seafood forks, although she could never work out how you were supposed to eat fried catfish with such tiny implements. She sometimes worried that Betty Crocker would discontinue the pattern before she could complete her set. She remembered nights at the kitchen table after the children were asleep and her chores were completed. She would take out the tobacco tin where she kept the coupons and spread them all out on the oil cloth, counting them carefully, perhaps trimming the edges from the latest one from a box of Bis-Quik or cake mix and adding it to the collection. She refused to use a single piece until she had the entire set. Tudor Rose. How proud she had been the first time she put it out. Christmas dinner—or was it Thanksgiving? Sometime after the war. She figured the Queen of England wouldn't sit down to a prettier table, except her knives and forks would be made of real silver. Or maybe gold for all Henrietta knew.

She finished out the three places on the table cloth: knife, fork, spoon. "Men," she muttered out loud. "It's all so casual with them. Leave a pregnant woman and two younguns and sashay off for the winter. Get another girl pregnant while you're at it with no more thought than a tomcat."

Henrietta scooped the chops onto a plate and covered them. She spooned flour into the skillet and stirred it furiously. Had Sam loved Letty Stark? Henrietta browned the flour carefully, added salt and pepper, milk and water from the corn. The gravy began to bubble at the edges. She had to be careful now not to burn it. How many skillets of gravy had she made in her life, she wondered suddenly. It seemed sometimes that all her years had come to nothing but gravy and biscuits, raising kids and watching them go off into the world and forget where they came from. All she had in her moments of dark loneliness was the memory of Sam's love, which she had assumed was constant.

Henrietta turned off the stove, fished the corn out of the kettle and set the platter on the table. "Supper's ready," she called from the porch. Paris and Ruby were laughing, tossing a tomato between themselves like a softball. Henrietta stepped over a pile of cats dozing in the shade of the stoop.

"Ya'll come on in and wash up. Bring them tomatoes."

"Comin, Grandma," Ruby Mae called. She picked up the aluminum colander and began to run lightly across the yard. Her cheeks were flushed and her eyes shone with pleasure.

There is such a thing as living too long, Henrietta said to herself, watching her granddaughter. Paris joined her and took the colander of tomatoes, grinning down at her. Henrietta saw the spark strike between them and she felt the shock of rage press against her breast.

When they reached the porch, still giggling, they looked up at her. Ruby Mae's smile stopped. "What's wrong, Grandma?" They followed her into the kitchen. "Grandma, you look awful. You're not havin a spell, are you?"

Henrietta glared at the two young people, their hard, energetic bodies, faces fresh and unlined by responsibility, struggle and pain. She clenched her hands in her apron to stop them trembling. She watched Paris as he set the colander on the drainboard and leaned back against the sink. He drew a Pall Mall out of Sam's shirt pocket. As he struck the match and bent his head to the flame, he looked so much like Sam that Henrietta was astounded that she hadn't seen the truth the minute he set foot on her porch.

"What's wrong?" Ruby Mae repeated.

Henrietta regarded her granddaughter. Something shifted, shimmered out of focus, then resettled itself. Henrietta felt a surge, as though some current were flowing through her. She turned back toward Paris Granger. She was no longer trembling. "Put that damn thing out," she said. "Don't you dare light a cigarette in my kitchen without even the politeness to ask."

Paris looked at her in amazement, then stuck the tip of the cigarette into the dishwater. Henrietta heard its death hiss clean across the room. Ruby Mae had taken a glass from the cupboard and was reaching for the pitcher of iced tea. "Stop fussin and sit down in this chair. I want you to listen, Ruby Mae. I want you to pay attention, hear?"

Ruby Mae's head bobbed. "Yessum," she murmured. She sat down.

Henrietta watched her husband's grandson across the scarred old linoleum floor. She felt strong, calm. "You," she began softly. "You come up here like you're God or somebody, lookin for kinfolk now your mama's gone. Did you ever consider for a minute the damage you'd do? I was married to Sam Harper for forty-six years and I was faithful all them years. I always thought he was faithful to me. That winter he was startin up a baby with your grandma, I was alone here on this farm with two younguns and anothern on the way."

Paris was shifting his weight from foot to foot. "I'm sorry, "Miz Harper Ma'am," he stammered. "I didn't know, I mean, I didn't think—"

"You didn't think," Henrietta repeated. "You're damn right you didn't think—about anybody except yourself. But then that's your generation all over, ain't it?" Henrietta smoothed her apron carefully. She studied its dim pattern of red apples and green leaves. She'd sewed it up herself from sun-faded kitchen curtains which in turn came from old-time feed sacking. "That winter I'd lay awake nights, the children in bed with me so they wouldn't freeze to death in their sleep. And I had that baby alone."

She heard Ruby Mae suck in her breath. She looked at the girl's face, full of shock and confused horror. "Grandma, I didn't know that," she said. "What happened?"

"Never mind what happened." Henrietta braced herself as if for a blast of frigid January wind as she felt the uprush of the past: the locked door, her children crying on the other side, the smell of the duck-feather pillow as she tried to muffle her own screams, the hot cascade of water and blood and finally the small, slippery unfinished thing that emerged, still and lifeless, from between her thighs. Henrietta squeezed her eyes shut and gripped the back of a chair. She shook her head vigorously. It was done with all these years, and she would not allow it back in again. "Never mind!" she repeated. "Just you never mind." She lifted her eyes again to Paris Granger.

"I always thought Sam loved me," she said evenly. "That was the one thing I thought I could depend on. I'd ruther've ended my life with that notion intact."

"He did love you, Grandma," Ruby Mae said with sudden passion.

She gazed at Ruby Mae, moved suddenly by the earnest simplicity of her face, her need to believe in the immutability of love and family. "But I'll never be for certain again, will I, Honey?" she said gently.

Henrietta was aware of the ticking of the clock, something she hadn't heard in years because it had been with her so long. It was a dark wooden wall clock in the shape of an owl. The round owl eyes shifted from side to side with each tick. Henrietta had ordered it from the Sears Roebuck catalog in 1952 and it had never ceased ticking since.

The platter of corn on the table had stopped steaming, the ice cubes had melted in the tea glasses. She supposed the gravy had congealed and would have to be reheated. Henrietta looked round the kitchen. It hadn't changed much in forty-five years and more. There was new wallpaper and paint and a gas stove instead of the old wood-burning range, but water still came from a pump at the sink. Henrietta had arthritis in her right shoulder from decades of working the handle.

Ruby Mae was pale, and tears were getting ready to streak the black stuff around her eyes. Henrietta reached over and stroked her shoulder. She knew there was no way to shield her from the flowering of her woman's life. Henrietta said calmly, "I believe I'll go set a spell on the porch. Ya'll go ahead and eat your supper."

Henrietta sat up with a start. Her whole body ached as though she'd fallen out of a tree instead of merely asleep. An elderly barn cat, One-Eyed Agnes, was curled in her lap, blinking sleepily up at Henrietta with her single eye. Henrietta had been dreaming about Sam. She tried to gather in the wispy skeins of the dream, but they dissolved and floated away, leaving only a residue of unanswered accusations and something about being cold in a flimsy nightgown that she'd owned in the twenties, long since consigned to one of the many rag rugs she'd crocheted over the years.

The night wasn't cold at all. "Go on now, Agnes," she said, nudging the cat gently. Agnes flowed onto the porch boards, her paws making a soft thump. Henrietta grasped the arms of the rocker and rose, her joints stiff and uncooperative. She hadn't meant to fall asleep out here. She wondered what time it was, peering beyond the maple tree at the eastern sky. It was still pitch dark but over the peak of the roof, the crescent moon was low, rocking like a big golden boat on a filmy sea of cloud. She would take some aspirin and go to bed.

Once in the bathroom though, in her wrapper and slippers, washing down aspirin with cold water, Henrietta was wide awake. She put up a pot of coffee and rummaged in the fridge for something to eat. When she found the plate of leftover chops covered with plastic wrap, all the events of the previous afternoon and evening came roaring into her awareness like a freak cyclone out of a clear spring sky.

Henrietta closed the refrigerator door and leaned back against it. It was too much, it had taken her by surprise and she could not fend it off. She closed her eyes and let the storm engulf her. When she heard the coffee perking, she roused herself to lower the flame. Ignoring the pork chops, she made herself a ham sandwich.

She looked at the colander of tomatoes sitting on the kitchen counter. She wondered how many tons of tomatoes she had planted, weeded, picked, eaten and canned in her lifetime. She didn't care if she never tasted another tomato again.

Henrietta carried her snack out to the porch. She sat in the swing, nestling the coffee cup between faded throw pillows. One-Eyed Agnes was back, this time with a mouse, which she dropped courteously at Henrietta's feet. "Well ain't you somethin?" said Henrietta. She bent to scratch One-Eyed Agnes' ears. "I guess you can still earn your keep." Henrietta took a bite of her sandwich.

Paris Granger had left first, not long after Henrietta came outside. She didn't know whether he'd eaten his supper or not. He was wearing the motorcycle jacket again, Sam's shirt abandoned somewhere in the house.

"Miz Harper Ma'am," he'd said, his voice strained and embarrassed, "I 'pologize for the harm I done. You was right about me not thinkin about nobody but myself. I hope you can forgive me some day."

Henrietta stared straight ahead, not looking at him, but when he stepped off the porch, something about his hunched shoulders softened her.

"Son," she began.

Paris Granger turned. "Ma'am?"

Henrietta's hands worked in her apron. "What's done can't

be undone. Maybe it's for the best. Now you know where your kinfolk are, don't be a stranger. You've got plenty of family in these parts. I'm sure they'd be pleased to meet you. Ruby Mae can take you around some weekend before school starts up again if you ask her real nice."

Paris Granger had stood as if momentarily paralyzed. It was too dark for Henrietta to see his face. Finally he said, "Thank you, Miz Harper. You're a good Christian lady and I won't forget you."

Ruby Mae had come out a little later after washing up the dishes. "Grandma, are you all right?"

"I reckon so."

"Do you want somethin to eat?"

"No, I'm fine. You run along home now."

"Maybe I should stay all night."

"No, you go on, Honey. I'm okay. I've had a lot of shocks in this life. One more won't kill me."

When Ruby Mae came out again with her purse and car keys, she bent and kissed Henrietta. "I know Grandpa loved you," she said softly. "Anybody who ever saw the two of you together would know that."

She patted the girl's cheek. In her granddaughter's eyes, illuminated by the spill of light from the doorway, Henrietta saw her own young self.

The tail lights of Ruby Mae's car faded into the darkness and Henrietta was alone with the night music of crickets and the distant chant of frogs along the creek bottom. Bats swooped, gorging themselves on mosquitoes. Henrietta sat and rocked for a long time. *I ought to go to bed,* she told herself, but the weight of memory had pressed her against the chair.

The birds were starting to waken as Henrietta finished her

ham sandwich. She brushed crumbs off her lap, squinting at the east where the darkness was ebbing. She carried her dishes to the sink and looked around her kitchen. She saw it as she had never seen it before: faded, mildewed and tacky. A yellow water stain crept like a malignancy across the ceiling, the edges of the linoleum were ragged and curling. It was a miracle she hadn't tripped and broken a hip. Slowly, Henrietta walked through the other rooms, turning on all the lights, a tightness growing in her chest. But she had to look at the truth of it: the house where she'd lived her whole adult life and every object in it were worn out, musty, threadbare.

Her legs felt rubbery. She went back to the porch. *I been sittin in this house waitin to die,* she thought. *I been carryin flowers to that graveyard to them that's dead and gone and wastin whatever time I got left.*

The instant of crystallization bloomed within her like the flare of dawn, then exploded in a blaze of terror and elation that seemed to lift her from the chair and propel her out among the isolated majesty of the stars. Music filled her ears, angel voices, she thought, and the fire of galaxies streamed around her, pulling her higher and higher until she could see herself far below sitting in her rocker, a white-haired woman in a faded wrapper, old but still alive.

"Well, shoot!" Henrietta said in a loud, strong voice. She pounded the heel of her hand on the chair arm. "I haven't lived too long. I've just lived *in this house* too long."

Abruptly, Henrietta belched. From the swing seat, One-Eyed Agnes swiveled an ear in Henrietta's direction and regarded her with an expression of mild disapproval. "Excuse me," Henrietta apologized. Ham always gave her gas, but that never stopped her from eating it. She would mix some baking soda in a little water and drink it down before she tackled her desk.

The desk drawer seemed bottomless. Henrietta dragged out piles of gas bills, feed bills, medical bills, the infrequent letters of her children, an advertisement for cheap dentures, untried recipes for German potato salad, Polynesian chicken and something called Apricot Amazement, a broken fly swatter, thimbles and thumbtacks, an issue of *The Upper Room* from 1958 with a cover picture of a long-haired Jesus pointing somberly toward the sky. *Looks like he et ham,* Henrietta thought. *Surely a man with a life as hard as his would had some character in his face.* Who drew those Jesus pictures anyway? She tossed the magazine into the waste paper basket along with a child's navy blue sock and a free sample of breath mints, now crumbled to dust in their plastic packet. There were Christmas cards and postcards, birth and death announcements, balls of twine and fishing line, dried flower petals, worn-out emery boards, a violet hair ribbon, bobby pins and safety pins, broken pencils and ball point pens, seventy-three cents in small change, and of all things, an old button hook. She kept back the change and the button hook and tossed the rest onto the floor. At last she found the thing she was looking for.

It was a neat white business card. "Herman Weinberg," it said. "Rural Ventures, St. Louis, Missouri." At the bottom was a phone number. Why had she kept the card? She'd study that one later, she thought, tucking it into her pocket. She fetched a paper bag and began stuffing it with all the detritus from the desk.

Herman Weinberg had been to visit her three times over the last two years, and every time he'd offered her more money than the last. "You don't have to move," he'd said. "Keep five acres around the house. You won't even know you have neighbors." But she had refused each offer. The farm was for the children, and when she was gone, they could do with the land whatever they pleased.

Why? Henrietta asked herself now. *What for?* None of them had wanted to farm. They every last one had got as far away from it as fast as they could. Why, they hardly remembered her birthday. She had grandchildren out in California she'd never even *seen.* Only Ruby Mae was close, and she was growing up fast. She'd be out in the world before Henrietta knew it, going to nurse's training or airline stewardess school or the beauty culture academy or whatever.

Henrietta finished picking up the trash and started back to the kitchen. Junie needed milking, but Junie would wait, maybe all day, seeing how much she'd been slowing down lately. At the thought of Junie, Henrietta turned from the kitchen doorway and went into the bathroom where she had undressed earlier. Her clothes hung neatly on the back of a chair. She picked up her corset and dropped it into the bag along with the trash from the desk. She *would* put Junie out to graze and the hell with what anybody thought, Rudolph included. She could afford it once she finished selling off the land. Henrietta poured herself another cup of coffee and stirred a good dollop of Junie's cream into it. When she got back to the porch, One-Eyed Agnes was sprawled on the swing cushions washing her paws and ears. It was a beautiful morning. Meadow larks trilled, the sky was tender azure and a little breeze had sprung up.

Henrietta felt better than she had in years. Maybe she'd tell Reenie and her husband to move into the house. She, Henrietta, no longer wanted it. With the money from the land, perhaps she'd buy her a little mobile home and move into town. There was another thing, too.

She'd been at the John Deere dealership in Carbondale with Rudolph a few months back, and on the Chevy lot next door, new RVs were for sale. Henrietta had wandered around, waiting for Rudolph to conclude his business, and she'd marveled at the shiny vehicles with little kitchens and sleeping nooks—even bathrooms—inside. She knew they were popular with retired folks. On Sunday drives through the campgrounds of the surrounding national forest she had seen senior citizens outside their RVs stringing colored paper lanterns in the trees, grilling fish, playing cards, or simply sitting in the shade. They'd looked as contented as hogs in warm mud. Henrietta had heard tell that lots of them just drove from park to park all year round. In the winter they went south; in the summer they went north. Henrietta had never been west of the Mississippi River. Why, she'd hardly been outside the State of Illinois, she reminded herself. She'd always wanted to see the Rocky Mountains and the Grand Canyon and hear Frank Sinatra sing in Las Vegas.

Wouldn't her kids fling a pure fit? Likely they'd try to get her committed to a mental ward, but Henrietta would be well shut of this place by the time they got wind of what was going on. They could have the house and whatever was left of the money after she was gone.

She could see Sam's face at the Gates of Paradise where she'd pictured meeting him so often. "You done sold *what?*" he would say. "Well, I've got a few things to discuss with you too," she'd tell him.

Henrietta rocked, sipped her coffee and smiled at the new day.

MOON PATH

MY BOSS DOESN'T like surprises, so I always call him first thing whenever something unusual happens on a job site. I break a hydraulic line, find a septic tank where we didn't expect one, I'm on the phone pronto. So on the day when all the problems start, I don't waste any time tracking Bob down. He doesn't answer, so I call his wife.

"He's in a seminar," she says, "until five o'clock. Is this an emergency?"

"You tell me," I says. "I'm over here on the Cimarron Construction job, and I just dug up human bones. Site manager called the cops."

"Good God," she says. "They'll shut down the site, won't they?"

"Looks that way to me," I says.

"I'll see if I can get him out of that seminar," she says.

An hour later, we're all standing around staring into the

hole—me and the boss and the site manager and his boss and a bunch of cops. The cops have strung crime-scene tape around the perimeter. It looks like something straight out of *Law and Order*. In the hole are three people: a lady photographer and a couple of forensics types putting things into Ziploc bags. They're dressed in plastic suits that look hot as hell.

The bones are scattered around the hole. They look pitiful against the red clay. Right from the moment I realized what they were, as they fell from the bucket of the backhoe, I had a terrific urge to cover them up, like you'd lay a blanket over an accident victim while you waited for an ambulance.

"Well *damn*," my boss says for about the twenty-third time. "Damn, damn, damn." Sam is a born-again Christian and doesn't hardly cuss at all, so when he says *damn*, he's seriously upset. I couldn't blame him. Bush had just gotten re-elected, and business was starting to pick up again after the long slump following Nine-Eleven.

"How longer we gonna be down?" Bob asks the site manager.

The site manager is a Mexican named Ruben. Ruben takes off his cap and inspects the sweat stains on the inside band. Ruben is tall for a Mexican and real dark skinned, and he knows how to run a job better than anybody I ever worked with. "I don't know, man," he says. "Cops ain't tellin' me nothin'."

"Well, damn," Sam says again. There's nothing for us to do but shut down the equipment and go home.

A couple of days later we start a small job on the other side of town, a foundation for a new house. They call 'em starter mansions. The trend now is for these huge houses, thousands of square feet, and they cost about a million bucks a pop. The market is so inflated it's insane, but people keep getting the financing and these places are springing up all over town like poison mushrooms after a hard rain. What the hell—it keeps me working, so what do I care?

It's a hot morning to what is going to be an even hotter day, and the AC is busted in the cab of the backhoe, so I'm already in a bad mood when Bob shows up. He motions me to stop and comes up to the backhoe. I lower the bucket for the next load.

"What?" I says. I don't like to stop once I get going.

"The Cimarron job," Bob shouts. "I got a call from Ruben before I left the house this morning."

"The cops gonna let us get back to work?" I ask.

"Next couple of days," Bob says. "Seems like they I'd those bones you dug up."

"Already?" I says.

"Yeah," Bob says. "It was that high-school girl disappeared here a few years back, Solana Somebody-Or-Other."

I feel like I've been kicked in the nuts. I don't say a word to Bob as he goes on about clothing fragments and dental records and further DNA testing just to make sure, but as soon as he leaves, I climb down off the backhoe and throw up until I nearly pass out.

"A few years back" is actually twelve years. Solana and I went to high school together. I fell in love with her in the eighth grade at St. Alfonse, but she ran with a different crowd, all Mexicans, and she didn't know who I was. Her parents owned a popular restaurant, El Piñon, and Solana waited tables on weekends.

I started working on cars with my dad when I was ten. He was a skilled mechanic and he had his own garage. There wasn't anything he couldn't fix. He had an instinct, a talent, an ear—call it a special gift. He could listen to an engine for ten seconds and tell you exactly what was wrong with it. Didn't matter what kind of engine it was: automobile or motorcycle, tractor or dump truck, gas or diesel. And when he fixed it, it stayed fixed. He was a genius, I suppose, but his hands never looked clean no matter how much he scrubbed them, and my mother thought she'd married beneath herself. She was always pushing me toward college and some job where I would wear a suit every day and have a life "with some class," as she was fond of saying.

So Dad started teaching me the trade after school and on weekends. At first I think he was just trying to spite Mom, but then, after he saw I was good at it, he seemed to really enjoy teaching me. By the time I was sixteen, I was pretty good. I had my own car by then: a two-door '75 Chevy Chazelle. I fantasized about asking Solana to go to a movie with me, but my mom would've had fits. She didn't like Mexicans unless they were scrubbing her kitchen floor. Besides, Solana dated only Mexican guys who made good grades and were headed for college. She meant for her life to go somewhere. I was never much more than a C student.

So I was real surprised when she waited out in the hall for me one day after biology class. She was hugging her books and she looked so beautiful I got a huge boner just from her smile. She was wearing jeans and high heels and a sweater in a shade of vivid pink that set off her dark hair, which she wore shoulder-length and swept back from her face. There were little gold hoops in her ears and a gold cross at her throat.

"Hey, Gino," she said, stepping close to me. She smelled like flowers.

"Oh, hi," I said nonchalantly, like we talked every day.

"I hear you can fix cars," she said, getting right down to business.

"Yeah, sure," I said.

"I hear you're pretty good," she said.

I could feel my face go hot. "I'm not as good as my dad," I said, "but I'm learning."

She studied my face for a few seconds, which made me go even redder. "You're not egotistical about it," she said at last. "I like that."

I started walking up the hall to geometry class, just to have an excuse to turn my face away before it burst into flames. I hoped my shirt tail was long enough to cover up my hard-on.

"My dad wants to buy me a car for my birthday," Solana said, falling in next to me. "It's a Chevy Chazelle ."

"What year?"

"A seventy-five. It was my great aunt's, but she died last winter. It hasn't been driven in probably a year."

"That's the same car I got," I answered, kind of surprised.

"I know," Solana said, shifting her books to her hip. "I've seen you driving it. Yours is a two-door but my great aunt's is a four-door. That's why—well, I thought that since you probably know your own car so well, maybe you could take a look at my great aunt's. It may or may not be worth fixing."

My heart did an irregular little dance. "What's wrong with it?" I asked.

"Mateo—that's my brother—thinks it's the transmission. Maybe you could tell me for sure. I'd pay you for your trouble."

I waved my hand. "It won't cost you anything for me to look at it," I said. Mr. Magnanimous, that's me.

So the way it played out, I went over to her house that day after school. Mateo answered the door. He was a year older than Solana and me, and he was training to be an EMT. He was really buffed too; he got up at five a.m. six mornings a week to lift weights at a gym, and he liked to wear sleeveless T-shirts that showed off his muscles. He worked in the restaurant too, in the kitchen, and Solana told me he was nearly as good a cook as their dad. He totally checked me out, asked me a lot of questions about motors and transmissions. I answered him as best I could, and after driving Solana's car around the neighborhood, I agreed with his diagnosis that the tranny was toast. The valves would have to be replaced too. Me and Solana and Mateo spent a week after school going around to all the junkyards until we found what we needed, and then I did the work and Mateo helped. It took us three weekends. My dad even stopped by to check out the results. Solana was real happy.

The Monday we finished it, Mr. Pacheco offered me money, but I wouldn't take it.

"No thank you, Sir," I told him. "I'm not a professional, and besides, I learned a lot."

Mr. Pacheco threw his head back and laughed. "Well, at least come in and eat dinner before you go home," he said.

I didn't know any family who actually sat down and ate dinner together unless it was a holiday. But El Piñon was closed on Mondays, and the Pacheco's made a point of the whole family eating together on those nights. They had a big old-fashioned dining-room table set for eight people. Besides Solana and Mateo, there were two younger children, about ten and thirteen, Gabriela and Angelino, and Mr. Pacheco's mother. The younger Mrs. Pacheco was in her late thirties, and I could see where Solana got her looks. She welcomed me and showed me where to wash up.

When we all sat down at the table, everybody joined hands and Mr. Pacheco asked the blessing for the meal.

Nobody prayed at my house, so this seemed pretty exotic to me. I don't remember much about the food, except that there was a pot of pinto beans in the center of the table, a big green salad and another dish that was made with pork, plus bowls of red chili and a stack of tortillas about a yard high. I was suddenly very hungry. Mr. and Mrs. Pacheco kept urging me to eat more, and there were a lot of teasing and laughter around the table, another thing that never happened at my house. I wanted that meal never to end.

The next week at school, Solana would make it a point to say hi to me in the halls, and it wasn't long before I started walking her to her next class after biology. Some of the Mexican guys gave us strange looks, but nothing really hostile. That was until one morning a couple of weeks before Thanksgiving when Pablo Garcia made a remark under his breath to Solana as he walked past us.

"What did he say?" I demanded.

"Nothing worth repeating," she said, but I could tell she was angry.

"You dating him or something?" I asked.

"Are you kidding?" Solana said. "In his wildest dreams! He is such a creep. He keeps asking me out but he won't take no for an answer."

I didn't know what to say. I didn't want to fight with anybody. On the other hand, I didn't want to stop walking Solana to class either.

"You dating anybody?" I asked finally, swallowing hard.

"Not now," she said. "I went out with Mike Robles for a while, but he kept pressuring me to—" Solana blushed deeply, something I'd rarely seen a girl do. "Well, you know," she finished. "And I'm not ready for that. I want to go to college or maybe tech school before I get serious with anybody."

I didn't know what to say that wouldn't sound stupid, so I kept my mouth shut.

"What about you?" she asked.

I shrugged. "No, I don't have a girlfriend. My mom wants me to go to college but I don't know what to study." I could feel myself turning red again. I felt dumb because I didn't have any real picture of my future life like Solana did.

"What about your dad? What does he want for you?"

"I think he'd be happy to have me as a partner in his garage, but . . ."

"But what?"

"I don't know. That doesn't seem like much. Not like going to college, anyway. My mom thinks it's low-class."

We walked along a few more steps until we reached her classroom door. When I dared to look at Solana, she was frowning. "Well, I don't think it's low-class at all. My dad's a cook—one of the best in this state. That's what a lot of people say, anyway. The governor sends somebody to the restaurant once a month to buy four dozen tamales, made special just for the governor's table, did you know that?"

I shook my head. "No, I didn't."

"My point," Solana summarized, "is that the world needs cooks and plumbers and carpenters and mechanics. Just because you don't get a college degree doesn't mean you're stupid. On the other hand, if you go partners with your dad, maybe some business courses would be a good idea."

The bell rang then and Solana grinned up at me. "Think about it," she said and then disappeared through the door in a river of other students.

My life changed that day. I started looking at everything different after that. I realized that I could do something I liked, something I could be proud of, without having to wear a suit and sit in some damn cube farm all day. I even started making better grades. And I stopped caring about what my mom said about my dad's garage being low class. I even worked up the nerve to ask Solana out, and she surprised me by saying yes.

It was a birthday party for one of our classmates, and Mr. Pacheco had been asked to cater the food. He would be there himself, which is probably the only reason he let me take his daughter out.

I arrived at their house a little early and knocked on the door. My stomach was heaving. I studied the Mexican clay urns that flanked the entrance, blooming with big red flowers I couldn't name. Mr. Pacheco answered the door. "Come in," he said. Immediately I saw Solana behind him. She was chiding her father softly in Spanish. Mr. Pacheco was dead serious. He held up a forefinger and looked me straight in the eye. "No drinking," he said slowly, "and no fast driving, and no marijuana. And I want you to bring her home no later than eleven o'clock. ¿*Comprende?*"

"Yessir, Mr. Pacheco," I said. My knees were shaking. I didn't want to think about what would happen if we were late. A lot of kids in our school came and went as they pleased and stayed out all night drunk and stoned if they wanted to. But I knew the Pachecos were different, and it would never have crossed my mind to break their rules. I cared about Solana too much.

Looking back, I think that spring was the happiest time of my life. Solana and I were so much in love. We studied together, went to mass together, and I picked her up for school every morning. And we wanted each other so bad I can't understand how we avoided doing it. But it was important to Solana to be a virgin on our wedding night, and so we didn't.

She was going to New Mexico State after graduation, and I was going to live at home and take classes at the community college and work part-time for my dad. Even my mom liked Solana and started opening up her heart a little bit to the rest of the world. It all spun out before us, a gilded and happy and productive future, like the path the rising moon makes across the dark desert.

Fall passed into winter and winter into spring. All of a sudden we were ordering graduation gowns, class rings and making plans for the senior prom. Solana decided to make her own dress, and she and her mother went to Santa Fe to shop for the fabric. They showed it to me on a Monday evening just before dinner. Solana had made the dress pattern herself from a picture in *Vogue* magazine, that's how smart she was. And the cloth was very beautiful—a deep, rich red, like the color of rubies. In fact, Solana's *abuela* had a pair of fine ruby earrings that had belonged to her own grandmother in Old Mexico. She had given them to Solana to wear with the dress.

The day I went to rent my tux I was so nervous I couldn't eat. I hadn't worn a suit since my first communion and I felt nerdy and awkward. Old Mr. Goldblum at the rental place knew all this, but I didn't realize it until years later. He helped me with the shirt buttons, the tie and the cummerbund, which I thought was totally faggy. Finally I was completely dressed, including shoes, and Mr. Goldblum was satisfied that everything fit. I couldn't wait to get back into my Levis and T-shirt and get the hell out of there. But the old guy took me by the arm and led me out of the dressing room. "Take a good look at yourself," he ordered. "You need to be confident of yourself when you go to pick up your girl."

I was red with embarrassment as I stumbled toward the

three-way mirror. I raised my eyes to consider my reflection. For a moment, I didn't know who I was looking at. Behind me, Mr. Goldblum said, "Yes . . . Stand up straight. Pull your shoulders back . . . There, yes. Get a haircut tomorrow, but just a trim. You don't want that new-haircut look for the prom."

I gaped at the mirror, stood a little straighter, pushed my hair back off my forehead.

Mr. Goldblum, staring over my shoulder, nodded with satisfaction. "You are a very handsome young man," he announced. "You didn't know that until now, did you?"

Next day, driving to school, I told Solana about the tux, everything but what Mr. Goldblum said about me being handsome. Since I'd been procrastinating, I thought she'd be pleased, but she hardly paid attention. This was so unlike her that I said, "Hey, what's wrong? You got your period?"

"I'm sorry, no, I haven't got my period. It's Pablo Garcia."

Something small jolted my gut. "What about him?" I asked carefully. "Is he bothering you again?"

"He keeps asking me to the prom."

"Didn't you tell him you're with me?"

"Of course I did!" Solana snapped. "He keeps saying stuff like, 'You need to stay away from that *gringo*,' and 'You belong to me,' and shit like that."

I had the distinct impression there was more that Pablo Garcia had said but that Solana wasn't going to tell me. "I'll beat the hell out of him," I said reflexively, although I didn't exactly know how I was going to do that, since I hadn't been in a fight since third grade.

"Oh, right," Solana said angrily. "That solves everything doesn't it? *Machismo* is the answer to all problems—even for you

Anglos!"

"Hey," I said, "What the hell is the matter with you anyway?" I eased into a spot in the parking lot. "I'm just trying to protect you, that's all."

Solana's eyes flashed furiously as she threw open the car door. "I don't need anybody's protection," she said, and ran across the parking lot to her first class.

I sat there for awhile, stunned. We had never had a fight before and I didn't know why we'd had one now. To my shock and shame, tears gushed down my cheeks. Angrily I dragged my shirt sleeve across my face.

"Hey, Bro," a voice said, and I jumped like I'd been jabbed with a soldering iron. My buddy Josh leaned down to look at me through the window. "Christ, dude, what's happening?"

"Nothing," I said tightly. "Just fucking allergies, okay?" I got out of the car and Josh and I walked silently into the building. The prom was two days away. Solana and I had just had our first fight and I didn't even know what it had been about. I had absolutely no idea what to do about Pablo Garcia or anything else. As it turned out, I never had the chance to figure it out.

Solana and I made up on the way home from school. She insisted that she could handle Pablo Garcia and that I shouldn't interfere. I told her that if he kept being a pain in the ass that Mateo and Josh and I would have a conversation with him.

That night I went to bed with a bellyache. My mom gave me some Pepto Bismol. "Prom jitters," she said by way of diagnosis. "Don't worry, it's normal. I was so nervous about my prom that I broke out in hives. You should've seen me!

Grandma and I spent two hours applying makeup to all my red spots before I could even put on my dress. You'll be fine in the morning."

But I wasn't fine. I woke up at 4:00 AM and vomited. The pain in my gut was worse. Dad found me at the kitchen table when he got up to go to work, and Mom felt my forehead. "You've got a fever," she pronounced. "I'm going to call the doctor."

I felt too sick to argue. By the time Mom got hold of the doctor's nurse, I was moaning with pain, and the nurse told us to get to the emergency room right away. I was admitted quickly and an hour later, they removed my appendix.

When I woke up, both my parents were there. "Hey, kid," my old man said. There were white lines around his mouth and dark circles under his eyes that I'd never noticed before.

"Your appendix burst," Mom said, taking my hand. "You've got to have lots of antibiotics and stay here in the hospital for a few days."

"The prom—" I started.

"Sorry, son," said my dad. "You and Solana will have to make your own prom after you get well."

Even my hair hurt and I was in no shape to argue. My mom went to the nurse's station and demanded pain medication. While she was gone, Solana and Mateo arrived. Solana's eyes were puffy.

I thought she was crying from disappointment about the prom. "I'm sorry," I apologized. "I'm really sorry about the prom, Baby. I'll make it up to you."

"*Idioto*," she said, bending to kiss me. "I don't care about the stupid prom. I was afraid you were going to die."

Mom came back, followed almost immediately by a nurse with a syringe. The relief was nearly instantaneous. "I want you to go to the prom anyway," I told Solana. She opened her mouth to protest, but I stopped her. "Mateo, I bet my tux will fit you just fine. The tickets and the dinner are already paid for. Promise me you'll take your sister to the prom."

"What a wonderful idea!" Mom said. "And then when he's well, you kids can dress up in your prom outfits and Dad and I will take you to Santa Fe for dinner and dancing, someplace fancy like La Fonda." She looked meaningfully at my father.

"Yeah, sure," he agreed. He even sounded like he meant it.

Mom and Dad stayed through the night and Solana held my hand until I went to sleep.

So that's the way it all fell out. Solana's parents took pictures and my folks were invited to the Pacheco's house to see Mateo and Solana out the door. Mom took photos too, although I saw them only once. Even after Mom died and Dad and I went through the family picture albums, we never did find those pictures of Solana and Mateo. I have often wondered what she did with them.

Here's the rest of it: Mateo and Solana went to the dinner and then to the prom, and when Solana went outside with her girlfriends during the dancing, Pablo Garcia was waiting for her. According to the other girls, Pablo came out of nowhere, called her a whore and grabbed her wrist. Solana fought with him and he punched her in the face with his fist, then kicked her twice as she went down. The screams of the other girls brought people running, but by that time, Pablo had thrown Solana into his car and driven away.

That was the last time anybody ever saw Solana until my backhoe uncovered her grave. Pablo was arrested the next morning at his own house. According to the cops, he never said a single word, never told them where Solana was or if she was dead or alive. That night he hanged himself in his jail cell.

Right about now you're saying to yourself, that was a terrible thing to happen, but you were young and resilient. You grieve and then life goes on. But I'm telling you right now, sometimes it doesn't. Oh, I got up in the morning and went to work and tried college classes for a while. But I couldn't concentrate on anything and then I couldn't stand living in the same town anymore. I joined the Navy and drank my way through those years until my discharge. Then I moved to Chicago, and that's where I learned to operate heavy equipment. I dated a lot of girls but I never fell in love with any of them. I kept drinking. I went back to New Mexico when my mom died. By that time, my dad was on disability from a back injury, and he'd sold the garage.

I never saw the Pachecos again either. Mateo could never forgive himself for not protecting his sister. He got into drugs, using and then selling, and right now he's in New Mexico State Prison, doing twenty-five to life for murder. After Mateo went to jail, Mr. Pacheco dropped dead in the kitchen of El Piñon. Mrs. Pacheco runs the restaurant now, and I hear that her hair has turned completely white, although she's barely fifty. I also hear that the ruby earrings were recovered by the forensics people and returned to the family. I know I have to go see Mrs. Pacheco now, and I have no idea what I'll say.

I finally stopped drinking after I developed a bleeding ulcer. I joined AA and got clean and sober. A counselor suggested that I go back home and deal with the past. So I did, and for a while, things seemed to go pretty well. I got into therapy, and then one Saturday, shopping for food at Safeway, I ran into Patty, an old classmate. I asked her out and she accepted, and six months later we got married. She got pregnant right away, but in the third month, she miscarried. I knew then that I couldn't stay with her. I had tried hard to love her the way she deserved to be loved, but it didn't work. We got an amicable divorce and she's married to some lawyer now and has two kids.

I live way out in the desert. I like it that way. I've got a couple of dogs and they're good company. My dad and I have dinner every Sunday afternoon. He's dating a widow, a friend of my mom, whose husband died around the same time Mom passed. She's a good woman and I'm happy my dad has found someone to salve his loneliness. Funny about him and Mom. They never seemed to like each other much, but he misses her all the same.

Last night I went back to the Cimarron job site. It was a clear evening with a light wind, and the crime-scene tape still fluttered raggedly around the perimeter of the hole. I listened to the yips and howls of coyotes, and it seemed to me that their voices carried the lonely sorrow of the whole wounded world. I need to go back to AA, because if I don't, I may start drinking again and never stop.

There's been plenty of speculation, of course, about how and why Pablo Garcia hid Solana's body way out there where nobody ever thought to look. There were no houses then, just miles and miles of empty desert whose only inhabitants were snakes and lizards and coyotes. How did Pablo choose this spot? Solana was only about three feet down, but digging that deep in the hard-packed desert earth is nearly impossible without equipment. Maybe Pablo had help. Maybe the hole was a natural declivity and he just filled it in. No one will ever know.

Tomorrow another backhoe operator will continue where I left off and dig a septic system for a new house. The owners will move into their dream home and never know what happened here twelve years ago.

I sit next to the hole and smoke cigarettes and weep and wait. I watch the eastern sky as golden light comes over the mountains, followed by the disk of the nearly full moon. Perhaps now, I can finally let Solana go, say goodbye, take the next step. I watch the moon until its silver path stretches to the edge of her grave.

THREES

THE FIRST MURDER happened in June.

Mr. Smalley was a railroad man. He lived across the street with his pale pudgy wife and four pale pudgy children. They kept to themselves. The only time he ever spoke to me was the spring I turned twelve. "Get off the grass," he said.

Mr. Smalley was shot to death as he sat in the cab of his engine in the Pennsylvania Railroad yard in Hammond, Indiana, awaiting the signal to leave on his regular run. There had been union troubles, but Mr. Smalley was not thought to have been involved.

The news hit our little town like a seismic tremor. People clustered on street corners, leaning into one another. They reminded me of shocks of corn in the late-summer fields. They spoke in subdued tones, shook their heads and began locking their doors. Mrs. Smalley abandoned their house, including a notch-eared tomcat named Elroy, who came to live with us, and moved herself and her children to Nebraska where her parents owned a hardware store.

I had just started waiting tables at the Airport Café. It was, with the exception of babysitting, my first job. I collected a few bucks a day in tips and watched toylike single-engine planes land and take off on the grassy field that passed for a landing strip. At first I felt ghoulish curiosity as my customers, mostly airplane mechanics and pilots in greasy coveralls who ferried people between our town and nearby Chicago or Milwaukee, speculated about the murder over cups of rancid coffee. But I was in love with Bobby Whitlow and spent most of my time with my eyes glazed over in fantasy. I was twenty pounds thinner and had hair like Lauren Bacall.

Bobby and I are onto the union thugs who killed Mr. Smalley. They kidnap Bobby and hold him, bound and gagged, in the basement of a Calumet City strip joint. I burst in on them with a loaded thirty-eight as Big Al—"The Cruncher"—Sloan, who has a three-day beard and smokes vile cigars, is about to dip Bobby in concrete and drop him into Calumet Harbor. "Look out!" Bobby cries, as Big Al's moll, Cherry DeLite, the star stripper who works upstairs, comes at me from behind. She brandishes a switchblade. Deftly, I incapacitate her with a judo throw, never taking my gaze off Big Al. "Now," I order Big Al in a cool voice, my gun hand unwavering, "pick up that telephone and call the cops before I blow your head off." Later, of course, I will weep fetchingly in the arms of Bobby Whitlow, but only after the reporters have left.

Lola Sue picked me up from work one muggy night as the murder had receded into second place on the gossip agenda. I was peeling off my pink-and-white apron. That was the thing I hated about my job. I had to wear white uniforms and white nurse's shoes that made my legs look like dock pilings. I used to break out in a cold sweat at the thought of Bobby Whitlow coming into the café, but I needn't have worried. That fall, he was to leave school for a hastily arranged wedding with Sheila Travis, captain of the cheerleading squad. (At our ten-year class reunion, Bobby had lost his hair and was working on a third chin. Sheila looked as though she ate anabolic steroids for breakfast.) But on that July evening after the first murder and before the second, I didn't know that, and when the screen door of the café banged open at closing time, I had my moment of panic followed by acute disappointment. Lola Sue walked in, a big grin on her face.

"Oh, it's you," I said.

Lola Sue's grin dissolved. "Gee thanks," she said. "I thought you'd be glad to see me."

"I am," I lied. "I'm just tired, that's all."

"We have to plan our new diet," Lola Sue said. We were always losing the same five pounds over and over. "Let's go to Szado's."

Szado's Bar and Grill was on Ridge Road, the main drag through town. The bar contained a warped pool table and a half-dozen scarred booths where people played matchstick poker and pinochle. There were usually a few children in the bar in the early evenings, accompanied by fathers who stopped in for a beer while wives cooked supper at home. Older children sat on bar stools, their feet far above the floor, sucking at cherry cokes while younger brothers and sisters played on the ruined pool table with wooden blocks supplied by Old Man Szado. The place smelled, not unpleasantly, of hot grease and cigarets and beer.

Off to the side was a tiny dining room where you could eat fried perch or smelt in season and hamburgers all year round. They were grilled and served by Old Man Szado's son, Carl, who had been a Chicago cop. After the birth of their fourth child, his wife begged him to take a safe job. So they had moved back home and Carl went into partnership with his father. Carl had black Mediterranean eyes and hair, and when he smiled, which was often, his teeth looked like a row of fluorescent Chiclets. Lola Sue had a crush on him. After Carl put down the plates of hamburgers and the double order of french fries and Lola Sue had stared wistfully at his back, she turned to me with an announcement. "Pearl Krugenhoffer is coming to spend the rest of the summer."

I was busy pounding the end of a Heinz bottle over the french fries and I stopped as ketchup began to flow like red magma onto the plate. I looked at Lola Sue and considered the pleased expression on her face.

Lola Sue was a farm girl from Southern Illinois. She lived with the pastor of our church as nanny to his four children and general household drudge. She thought she had a cushy spot, and considering what she had come from, maybe she did. What she really wanted was to marry and have children of her own. At present, however, neither of us had boyfriends, so we had formed an alliance. We went to see beach-party movies on Saturday night at the Moonlight Drive-In and envy all the couples necking in their cars behind steamed-up windows. She ate dinner frequently at our house and we talked of moving into the city when I got out of high school, where our lives would begin and marvelous things would happen to us. We wore each other's clothes, borrowed each other's trashy novels and consoled one another when the absence of male companionship became overwhelming. On the whole, it was a satisfactory arrangement, and now it was going to be sabotaged by Pearl Krugenhoffer, a girl whom I had met one time and to whom I had taken an instant aversion.

"Lucky you," I said to Lola Sue.

"Look," Lola Sue said earnestly. "I know you don't like Pearl, but you've never given her a chance. She's very nice, and a dedicated Christian. I'm meeting her bus on Saturday. Will you come with me?"

I worked a full shift on Saturday, and Lola Sue picked me up at the end of the day. In silence, we drove to the Greyhound station in Hammond, just across the state line. As we left the village limits, I saw that what had been a cabbage field last fall now sprouted a crop of ugly prefabricated houses. There had been a lot of that in the past few years. Only a decade earlier, when I started first grade, we had kept chickens on our property. Our neighbors grazed a pair of sheep in their back yard, and the prairie stretched behind us unvexed all the way to 170th Street. Surrounding the village were immaculate farms owned by first-and second-generation descendants of the original Dutch settlers. They had names like Huizinga and Jabaay and Van Der Hoek. They took their shoes off at the back door, and they did not drink, lie, dance, shirk, attend movies nor fail to worship every Sunday in the prim red-brick church that was the abode of their austere Dutch Reform god. They made our village prosperous. Then after World War II, Chicago, which had always seemed remote as the moon and stars, began reaching south toward us. Farms started to disappear and tract housing popped up like poison sumac after a hard rain. We found ourselves turning inexorably from farm town into suburb.

The bus was late and Pearl was the last person to step off. She wore a print sundress with huge half-circles of sweat under the arms and cheap white sandals without stockings. Pearl had the strangest distribution of body hair that I had ever seen. Most of it was on her arms, legs and face. What little grew on her scalp was thin and lank and devoid of color, but she had a moustache that Clark Gable would have envied. Her downstate accent was filtered through a nasal, whiny voice, and when she laughed, she made snorting sounds in the back of her throat.

It wasn't true that I didn't like Pearl. The fact was that she filled me with a vague sense of horror. As I watched her and Lola Sue clutching and kissing each other, I was sorry that I had come. I clenched my teeth, greeted Pearl as courteously as I could and wrote off the rest of the summer.

Lola Sue had decided that Pearl's introduction to town life should begin with dinner at Szado's. As we parked the car and started up the sidewalk toward the front door under the lighted sign that proclaimed FINE FOOD AND DRINKS, Pearl acted as though she were entering a house of ill repute. The biggest town she had ever seen, she confided too loudly, was Evansville, Indiana, and she hadn't ever been in a bar. She pursed her pale little mouth into a white line and said she didn't know if this was a proper place for a lady. Lola Sue looked hurt. I wanted to slap Pearl. We settled into a booth in the corner of the dining room.

In the bar, I could see Joe Scarletti playing cards with three other men. Mr. Scarletti owned the barbershop, and his son, Gino, was my friend. Mr. Scarletti made dago red in his basement from grapes he grew along the back-yard fence, and often customers left his shop clutching brown paper bags. I liked Mr. Scarletti. He smoked panatelas and looked like Gilbert Roland.

There were several other people sitting at the bar and in the booths. Both old man Szado and Carl were behind the counter. Carl came to take our order, flashing his neon smile. Lola Sue introduced Pearl and he said a couple of polite sentences of welcome. I wanted to slide under the table.

I studied the scars in the wooden table top as Lola Sue and Pearl caught up on back-home gossip and family news. Pearl was only twenty, but already she had the sour pinched look of an old maid. She lived with her parents and a retarded sister on a hog farm. There was another sister who was married with children, and a brother who had spent most of the years since Korea in the Looney-Tunes ward of a VA hospital. I could see the sterile featureless plane of Pearl's future stretching in front of her. She would inherit the hogs, the retarded sister and all decisions regarding the wigged-out brother. I felt a spasm of pity and resolved to try to be nice to Pearl.

Carl came back with our burgers and Cokes. As he was putting the plates on the table, a loud boozy voice floated back from the bar. "Hey, barkeep, we wanna 'nother round."

I saw Lola Sue's eyebrows lift and I leaned back to see who had uttered the rude statement. Nobody ever called Carl or his father *barkeep* or raised his voice in anything but laughter or friendly argument. I saw the muscle in Carl's jaw flicker. He was not smiling. He looked at us with a silent apology in his eyes. "Some people got no manners," he said softly.

A man and woman sat at the end of the bar, hunched over empty glasses. I had never seen either of them before. Carl walked back to the bar, scooped up the mugs and began drawing fresh beer. The woman leaned over onto the man and whispered.

"Aw, fuck off!" the man said, just loud enough for everybody to hear. The word resonated through the room like the crack of doom. Heads flew up. I saw Mr. Scarletti take his panatela from between his teeth and narrow his eyes at the bar. Across from me, Pearl's face was turning fuchsia.

Carl set the mugs down. "Hey," he said in an easy voice,

"keep it down, Mister. We got ladies present."

"Who are these people?" Lola Sue hissed at me.

"How would I know?" I snapped.

"I don't give a shit who's present," the man said. This time the other customers turned toward the couple with undisguised hostility.

"Take it easy," Carl said in the same low-key way. "Why don't you and the lady—"

"Why don't you mind your own goddamn business, asshole?" the man said. I couldn't see his face, but his shoulders were thrust forward and his chin stuck out in a suggestive way.

Carl reached out with both hands and took back the brimming mugs. "I'm sorry," he said curtly. "This is a family place and we don't like that kind of language in front of women and kids. I'll have to ask you to leave. No charge for the drinks."

The man made a lunging movement but the woman clutched his sleeve. "C'mon," she whined, "Let's get outa here. Let's go somewheres else." The man looked around, saw the faces of the other customers and lurched off the stool toward the exit.

At the door, he turned suddenly and bellowed, "Nobody talks to me that way, you sonofa—" The woman pushed him outside and the door clunked shut. There was a loud collective sigh, and card games and conversation resumed.

Carl came over to the table drying his hands on his apron. "I'm sorry," he said. "Once in a while we get people passin' through town into the city. They act like they never been around decent folks before. Cokes all around, compliments of the house."

Lola Sue and I mumbled our thanks as three fresh Cokes were brought to the table by Old Man Szado, but Pearl continued to stare at her lap, her face red. Lola Sue and I exchanged uncomfortable glances. We felt as though we had been the ones who had uttered the obscenities. In silence we finished the burgers and Cokes, paid our bill and left. It wasn't all that late, but I wanted to go home. I said goodnight to Lola Sue and Pearl and walked the six short blocks alone.

To my relief, everyone was asleep. I showered, put on my pajamas and watched a Bela Lugosi flick on *Shock Theater*. I loved Marvin and Dear, host and hostess of the show, and the music of the Deadbeats, a little band dressed like vampires who played surprisingly good jazz during breaks in the movie. They made me forget the disappointment and embarrassment of the earlier evening. Around one-thirty, as I floated in the drowsy region between consciousness and sleep, I thought I heard the moan of a siren.

When I stumbled into the kitchen next morning, the whole family was gathered at the table, even my brother, Arnie, who worked the night shift at Inland Steel. My grandmother was dunking biscuits in her coffee and expounding on the end of the world.

"Yessiree," she said. "It says right there in Matthew Twenny-Four that there'll be signs in heaven an' earth an' brother agin brother. Armageddon can't be far away. It says that generation will not pass away afore it happens."

I poured myself a cup of coffee and sat down. Mama was staring at her untouched eggs, sunnyside up, as though they were an answering pair of eyes. Dad slurped sullenly at his coffee, ignoring everyone. Arnie paved a biscuit with margarine and Mom's homemade cherry jam. "What's wrong?" I asked. "You all look like you just came from a funeral."

"Carl Szado is dead," Arnie said.

For a moment, I just stared stupidly. "What?" I asked

finally.

Arnie flushed, and I saw that he was enjoying himself on some level I couldn't grasp. "Somebody shot him last night in the bar with a sawed-off shotgun."

"*What?*" I cried. Suddenly, without being aware that I'd knocked over my chair, I was standing. My coffee spread a brown stain over the tablecloth. I looked at it, saw biscuit crumbs in the margarine. "That's impossible," I said. "I was there last night."

"I'll have to Clorox that," Mama sighed.

"Sit down!" Dad snarled.

Mama began to flutter around me like a worried bird, dabbing at the coffee with a towel and shushing me. "Not so loud, Honey," she soothed.

"I'll sit down if somebody'll tell me what happened."

"A man with a fam'ly orter have no truck with a saloon," Gran announced. "It's gittin' to be jest like Sodom and Gomorrah, people drinkin an actin' up an never givin' a thought to the Lord."

"Is he dead? Are you sure he's dead?"

"That Smalley feller asked fer it too, foolin' around with them strikebreakers," Gran continued. "The Bible says they're all gonna be swept away, jest like in Noah's time, only He won't do it with water next time. Next time, it'll be by fahr, and when them Russians start droppin' their atom bombs, we'll know the end is nigh."

This time I screamed. *"What happened?"*

"Shut your mouth!" Dad roared, and Gran stood up from the table.

"You jest wait 'n' see if it ain't," she said. "Is anybody goin' to church?"

Lola Sue took it even harder than I did. As Lola Sue, Pearl and I sat on the early-American sofa in Reverend Gibson's living room, her nose was geranium red and her eyes were inflamed. We had just come from the police station, where we had all three given statements to Chief Van Weldon, who seemed as upset and confused as we were. He was fat and he wheezed, and I couldn't picture him apprehending a jaywalker, much less a murderer. We weren't much help. The light in the bar had been dim, and none of us could describe the man or woman beyond the generalities of sex and approximate age.

Now Pearl was alternately grim and elated. This was undoubtedly the largest event of her life, and after Lola Sue and I had filled her in on Mr. Smalley's murder, nothing could convince her that homicide was not an everyday occurrence in the shadow of The Big City.

I was numb with the effort of trying to absorb what had happened. Until this summer, there had not been a violent crime in our town in anyone's memory, although Lydia Gibson said that old Mrs. Snyder recalled a wife who had dispatched her husband with a giant butternut squash when she caught him with another woman, then made soup with the squash. But that was before the village was incorporated, so perhaps it didn't count.

"Two murders!" Pearl kept chiming until I wanted to smack her. "Lord o' mercy, wait'll Ma and Pa hear this. And it may not be over yet."

"What might not be over?" Lola Sue asked, dabbing at her eyes with a kleenex.

Pearl sat up smartly and pressed her mouth into the familiar tight little line. "Trouble comes in threes," she intoned mysteriously. "Trouble always comes in threes. It's true. I could tell you lots of stories to prove it, like the time we lost seventeen sows—"

"I don't want to hear it," I said rudely, thinking that all Lola Sue needed was some redneck superstition to really set her off. Pearls' face blazed but she shut up.

The next night we went to the wake. It was ghastly. The four Szado children, ages three through eight, sat lined up on chairs like dolls on exhibit. Mrs. Szado accepted condolences with a kind of blank uncomprehending stare, as though people were speaking to her in Swahili. Old Man Szado kept sobbing, "That's my boy in there. That's my Carl." He said he was glad his wife was dead so she didn't have to endure the sight of her only son laid out for burial.

The Szados were Roman Catholics, members of St. Ann's Parish, and the funeral home was full of priests and nuns. Next to Old Man Szado sat Sister Mary Grace, the principal of St. Ann's School, who had been Carl's fist-grade teacher. She wept silently, twisting her rosary in arthritis-crippled fingers.

Lola Sue and I stepped up to the casket, propelled by Carl's aunts, to view the body. "Doesn't he look natural?" purred one of the aunts. She looked like Carl, except that her neck was covered with tiny brown moles that looked like toast crumbs until you saw them close up. "I told Mr. Hoekstra myself, I said to him, 'Mr. Hoekstra, you did a wonderful job on poor Carl. He looks just like he's asleep.'"

He looked just like he was dead to me, in his wedding suit with a silk handkerchief in the breast pocket and a heart-shaped arrangement of pink roses at his shoulder that said, "We love you, Daddy." His frozen hands clutched a prayer book, and his face was orange with pancake makeup. His mouth, closed forever over those matchless accordion-key teeth, looked waxy and hard.

I stepped back and bumped into Gino Scarletti. His parents stood next to him. Mr. Scarletti, who had witnessed the shooting, was white and grim and smelled distinctly of dago red. Mrs. Scarletti cried noisily.

Gino and I went outside into the fragrant summer night. People stood in tight groups, smoking and whispering. "They say there's a hole in his chest big enough to drive a truck through," Gino said with a shudder. "Pop says the guy just walked right up to the bar and put the barrel to Carl's chest and fired point-blank before anybody had any notion what he was up to."

"Oh my God," I breathed.

"He brought down that mirror in back of the bar when he fell," Gino continued. "My pop and Old Man Szado saw the whole thing. There wasn't anything anybody could do. He died real fast."

"Don't," I implored. "I'll start crying again."

"Did you see him?" Gino asked. "Pop says you and Lola Sue were there with some other chick when Carl threw the guy out."

Bobby Whitlow and I had been discussing elopement in the dining room of Szado's that fateful night, and are the only ones who can positively identify the killer. Now he stalks us as a hunter stalks a deer, and we will narrowly escape death before capturing him and turning him over to the authorities. Our pictures will appear on the front pages of The Chicago Tribune *and* The Daily News.

"We didn't see their faces," I said.

"Well," Gino said.

"Well what?"

"This sure has been a helluva summer. First, Mr. Smalley

and now Carl. I wonder who's next?"

"Nobody's next," I said. Conversation around us stopped, and people turned in our direction. "I'm sorry," I apologized in a softer voice. "I guess I'm just upset."

"I'm sorry too," Gino said, patting my shoulder awkwardly. "It was a dumb thing to say. It'll be all right."

But it wasn't all right. My chest felt as though it were full of stones and broken glass, and a few days after the funeral, when Lola Sue called and said that Pearl was cutting her visit short, I couldn't even gloat. I went over to Reverend Gibson's house to console Lola Sue. She was still crying over Carl Szado, and now her so-called *friend* was abandoning her.

I sat on Lola Sue's bed as Pearl arranged piles of ugly white-cotton underwear in her suitcase. Lola Sue sat on a straight-back chair, sniffling. I watched Pearl's nail-bitten fingers as she folded a pair of panties. The panties reeked of chlorine bleach and there was a hard crease on one side that could have come only from an iron. Good heavens, I thought. I tried to imagine ironing my underwear.

The nurse, searching frantically for an uncollapsed vein, slits Pearl's dress up the center and pulls it open. She recoils, eyes widening in disgust, and looks up at the doctor. "My god!" she gasps. "Wrinkled panties!" The doctor shakes his head, his lip curling with contempt. He yanks off his stethoscope. "We can't spare time for people with tacky underwear," he snaps, turning to another patient.

"I just don't know how you can live up here," Pearl said, as though I were invisible. "I went with Mrs. Gibson yesterday to the supermarket and there was a woman who couldn't even talk American. They ought to give them a test or something before they let them in."

We drove to the bus station in silence. I sat in the back seat with Pearl's cardboard suitcase and stared out the window. I watched carpenters moving around the prefabs in the old cabbage field. Violets had grown along the perimeter of that field, and in the spring, Mama and I always stopped to pick bouquets. The blossoms were big with long stems and a cunning, subtle fragrance. I supposed they had all been bulldozed.

"I can't wait to get home," Pearl said to no one in particular as we bumped across some of Hammond's endless railroad tracks. She turned her head to glare at an old man emerging from a liquor store. "I haven't had a good night's sleep since I arrived. At home, we don't even have to lock our doors."

The bus was mercifully on time. We stood with Pearl as luggage was loaded and the passengers climbed aboard. "I wish you were coming back with me, Lola Sue," Pearl said. "I wish you'd come back home where it's safe. You're just too close to Chicago here, and all the trouble that goes along with—"

At that moment, a Negro couple with a little girl stopped at the door of the bus. The man was wearing an army uniform. He swung the little girl up and kissed and hugged her, and then, still holding the child, he pulled the woman into his embrace. I could see tears in his eyes. Pearl glanced meaningfully at the couple and then back at Lola Sue. "You see what I mean," she said.

I turned away, exhaling slowly through puffed cheeks. Later, when I'd had time to digest the events of that summer, I was glad that I'd made the trip to the bus station with Lola Sue. I watched as the Negro soldier got onto the bus and then I handed Pearl the sweater I'd been carrying for her. It was the color of Pepto-Bismol. "Better hurry," I said sweetly. "We wouldn't want the bus to leave without you."

Lola Sue and I resumed our routine of drive-in movies, clothes-borrowing and novel-trading. We even found a new place for hamburgers. But it wasn't the same. I was still carrying rocks around in my chest and I even lost the faculty of fantasizing about Bobby Whitlow. A new foundry opened on the edge of town, and there was a lot of excitement because of the jobs it provided. But I noticed walking home from work at the Airport Café that the sweetness had gone out of the night air, and on clear evenings, you could see in the eastern sky the red glow from the steel mills in Gary, Indiana.

The days dragged on toward September, and I almost looked forward to going back to school. Then one day Jeanette Renfrew, our next-door neighbor, came running across the yard and onto the back porch. Mama and I were canning tomatoes in the steamy kitchen.

"Did you hear?" Jeanette asked breathlessly. "Aggie Haskell just called me. They arrested the man they think killed Carl Szado."

Mama made a sound like air rushing out of a balloon. She went to the refrigerator and poured out glasses of iced tea while Jeanette recited the details. I stood at the tomato-splattered stove, stirring the muttering kettle. I watched sunlight glinting off the ranks of Mason jars lining the counter top next to the sink. After Jeanette left, Mama asked if I were all right. "Sure," I said. I kept stirring the tomatoes.

School started. I was a junior. I took shorthand and typing, subjects that were to prepare me to fill the time usefully until I married and began producing babies. I kept my job at the café, working evenings and weekends. Lola Sue began dating Dale Van Der Leit, who sold butter and eggs from the back of his pickup truck. Lola Sue was embarrassed to be seen in the pickup truck, but better offers were not forthcoming. That left me alone on Friday and Saturday nights, so I took to reading the novels of Leo Tolstoy, counting my savings and planning my ultimate escape.

Then one day, another Sunday as a matter of fact, I sat reading the *Tribune,* and a small headline on page three caught my eye: DOWNSTATE FAMILY DIES IN MURDER-SUICIDE RAMPAGE. I felt a small prick on the back of my neck. I began to read the accompanying article.

"Oh my god," I murmured a few seconds later. I was sitting in the living room and Mama and Gran were in the kitchen preparing Sunday dinner. Arnie and Dad stared at a baseball game on TV, Cubs versus the Yankees. Roger Maris had just hit a homerun and the crowd in Yankee Stadium was throwing things in the air.

"I wish you wouldn't use the Lord's name in vain," Mama said irritably from the kitchen.

I paid no attention whatever, because now words were leaping at me, emblazoned in red neon, off the page of newsprint, and I kept chanting over and over as if it were some magical formula, "Ohmygod . . . Ohmygod . . . Ohmygod . . ."

Mama appeared in doorway. She wore a blue calico apron with a huge starched ruffle and she was holding a wooden spoon. "I. Told. You. I. Don't. Want—" The telephone interrupted her, and I knew instantly who it was. I pushed past Mama and grabbed the receiver before it could ring a third time.

"What's the matter with her?" Arnie asked. His attention was diverted from the slaughter in Yankee Stadium and he reached over to where I had flung the newspaper and began scanning the page.

"Lola Sue," I said, answering.

"Holy Christ!" Arnie said.

Lola Sue was shrieking, incoherent.

"Yes," I told her with great calm. "I just now saw it. Just this very minute."

"Holy Christ!" Arnie repeated.

"I can't stand it!" Mama yelled suddenly, throwing her wooden spoon against the kitchen wall. It struck with a *thwok*, splattering chicken gravy. "You kids have mouths like garbage pails, like *sewers!*"

"The paper says it happened on Sunday, is that right? Nobody found them until yesterday?" I asked Lola Sue. I tried to decipher the words she was delivering between great wet sobs. "Pearl Krugenhoffer," Arnie said meditatively, ignoring Mama. "Hey, wasn't that the broad with the moustache that was here in July? Hey, Sis—"

I covered the receiver with my hand. "Will you *please* shut up?" I said. For once, they did. "I thought he lived at the VA hospital," I said to Lola Sue.

"He did," she wailed, "but he used to come home for visits, and this time he didn't want to go back." Lola Sue lapsed into chokes and sobs. Finally she blew her nose and recited what she had heard from her mother on the phone only a few minutes before. I stood listening, saying nothing, watching chicken gravy run down the little clocks and tea kettles on the wallpaper. My brother, father, grandmother and mother formed a cluster in the doorway. They looked like crows waiting for a combine to exit a sorghum field.

Pearl had been right after all.

"Give me half an hour," I told Lola Sue. "I'll be over." I

hung up.

"Holy Christ," Arnie repeated, looking at the *Tribune* and then at me. Mama was silent.

"What's goin' on?" Gran demanded. As Arnie started to read the newspaper account out loud, I opened the screen door and stepped into the yard. It was a lovely late-summer afternoon. "What were they doin' home of a Sunday mornin' anyway?" I heard Gran say. "If they'da been in church where they orter been..."

The garden was crowded with marigolds, dahlias, chrysanthemums and asters, and the trees were beginning to acquire a golden cast. In a patch of sunlight on the patio snoozed old Elroy, orphaned by the first murder. I wondered what it was like to look down a shotgun barrel and see it explode in your face, down there on the hog farm where everything was nice and safe and folks never had to lock their doors. I probed the soft spaces of my psyche, trying to find a vulnerable spot so that I could somehow reconstruct the horror and connect with it. But it was useless. All I could think of was that compressed, judgmental mouth, the hard smug eyes as she had sneered at the Negro soldier, the way she had spoken as though I didn't exist. I stared at the dahlias. A big black-and-yellow spider was making its way fastidiously up the stem of one of the blooms. I grinned.

I am dressed completely in black, a slim, mysterious silhouette against the green background of the country churchyard. Bobby Whitlow and I stand at the foot of the graves as one by one, the mourners file past, their sobs muffled by handkerchiefs. No one knows, except for me and Bobby and, of course, the real murderers, that the deaths of the Krugenhoffer family were a Soviet plot to cover up Pearl's identity as a double agent. The breeze lifts a corner of my veil as Bobby's voice murmurs in my ear softly so that no one else can hear, "You got the microfilm?" "Yes," I whisper. "Now we must get it to the CIA before the Soviets suspect that we found it." "There may be danger," Bobby says. "We may be followed." Almost imperceptibly I straighten my back and lift my chin. "As long as we're together," I tell him. "I'm not afraid."

"Meearrrh," said Elroy, rubbing against my legs. Slowly, the back yard reassembled itself. I bent down to scratch Elroy's ears as he squinched his eyes shut and leaned into my hand. I plucked a dry leaf out of his fur. I liked the new Bobby Whitlow fantasy. It had real possibilities, but first I would have to see to Lola Sue. I couldn't stop grinning. I was sure that Pearl had gone to meet the Lord in clean underwear.

HAZEL'S LIGHTS

HAZEL SITS IN HER great-grandmother's rocker next to the window and stares out at the sky. It's 12:20 AM and the lights woke her about ten minutes ago. It's the fifth time this month.

Hazel is sixty-nine years old and has never in her life seen the beat of them. The lights don't have much form—they're blobs, really, and put Hazel in mind of the flying saucers in that movie Harlan took her to see at the old Starlight Drive-In, *The Day the Earth Stood Still*. It was their third date. She'd pretended to be scared so that Harlan would put his arm around her. They'd brought along a big paper sack full of popcorn and a Mason jar of lemonade from home, because Harlan had only enough money for gas and the movie tickets. After the popcorn, they'd necked, and six months later, right after graduation, they'd gotten married. Hazel was already pregnant with Greg.

Harlan has been dead for over thirty years now. She wonders what he would make of the lights. Harlan shot himself with his twelve-gauge out in the barn one dark December morning just before Christmas and only a few days shy of his fortieth birthday. Hazel has always thought that if he'd just put it off until after the winter solstice, the longer days might have given him hope. But he hadn't. He'd been weak and he'd ruined Jesus' birthday for her forever, and Hazel has been mad about it ever since.

Hazel has lived alone all these years, although she stopped raising sheep and leased her acreage to another rancher several years ago. But Hazel is no frail will-o'-the-wisp. She's a big woman, strong and solidly built. She drives a 1986 Ford pickup, which she tunes up herself. She has also replaced the clutch three times and put in new brakes twice without any help. Engine work she leaves to Diego at the repair shop in town.

Her daughter, Lucy, wants Hazel to move to Los Angeles and live with her, but Hazel is more likely to sprout wings and fly to the moon than move to LA. Hazel despises LA. All those emaciated women (Lucy is one of them) with their identical cascades of blinding-blond hair, cosmetic orthodonture, breast implants and liposuctioned thighs make Hazel twitch with irritation. From her observations on her one visit to the West Coast back in 1998, they've got no more depth than a mud puddle and all they can talk about are money and each other. They get on the scales every morning of their lives and if they gain so much as a pound, they yark up their Beverly Hills lunches for the next week.

No, Hazel likes it just fine where she is and she aims to die right here in Colorado. The house is solid, she has a TV and a computer and her cat, a fearsome mouser called Mad Max, and a new lab puppy she's christened Marigold. She also keeps a few chickens and a retired barrel pony named Octavia, whom she rides a couple of times a week in the arroyos and when she hunts antelope and birds in the fall.

Marigold sleeps in her lap right now. Hazel strokes the puppy's silky fur, knowing that the dog will soon be too big for her lap. *She's growing fast, just like kids do*, Hazel thinks. *One minute they're at your breast, and the next minute they're gone.* Lucy had gone off to the West Coast where she'd gotten bit parts here and there in the movies and had landed a featured role in a TV series that lasted exactly three weeks before it was canceled. Then she'd gotten a job with some lawyer who'd dumped his wife for her, and their marriage had lasted about as long as the TV series. Lucy is married currently to a Japanese landscape contractor named Something-or-Other Hirayama and has taken up wildflower painting.

Whatever, Hazel thinks, watching the blobs of light dip and weave across her corral. To be surrounded by fools and weaklings has been her cross to bear in this life. It has been a hot day and the night is still warm. Hazel wears only a much-laundered sleeveless cotton nightgown. Her left breast fills one side of it, but the right side lies deflated against her chest. She will never admit it to a soul, but she misses her breast. She'd gotten cancer the year after Greg was killed in Vietnam.

He'd had a high number and was in no danger of being drafted, but then he'd gone and *volunteered* for the army. Hazel had been opposed to the war by then and was one of the few people in their part of the state to attend a big antiwar rally in Denver. When Greg came home from the recruiting office and made his announcement, Hazel was nearly insane with anger. "What are you *thinking*?" she had shouted, hurling a china plate against the kitchen wall. "It's something I've gotta do, Mama," was all Greg had ever offered by way of explanation.

All through his basic training, Hazel had wept and ranted, and then Greg went overseas. Hazel never mentioned his decision again. She wrote to him twice a week, always signing her letters, "Your loving Mama." Two weeks before he was scheduled to come home, he stepped on a land mine.

When the government car pulled into their driveway early one morning and two uniformed men got out, Hazel fell down on the kitchen floor and vomited. Harlan was in the barn, and Hazel pulled herself to her feet just as the uniformed men knocked at the side door. She remembers thinking crazily that at least one of the men had to have been a farm boy and knew that in the country, nobody ever uses the front door. As she pushed open the screen, she saw Harlan emerge from the barn. He stopped in midstep at the sight of the car, then dropped the tools in his hands and began to run toward the house, screaming, "Oh Jesus! Oh Jesus!" But instead of coming to the porch, he'd jumped inside the government car, where apparently the keys had been left in the ignition. Before any of them could react, Harlan had turned the car around and gone speeding up the county road in a fury of dust and gravel. A patrolman found him an hour or so later twenty miles away, sitting on the roadside with a blown-out tire, just staring out through the windshield, his eyes as flat and dead as two stones from a creek bottom.

Ten months later, a lump appeared in Hazel's breast, clinging tenaciously to her chest wall, and she knew immediately what it was. Only rage sustained her. Eventually the chemo and radiation worked, and she got better and cared for Harlan, who was like a child after Greg's death.

Hazel has told no one about the visitations of the lights. And not one of her neighbors has said a word to her about them, so Hazel doesn't know if anyone else has seen them or not. Greg would have loved the blobs, Hazel reflects with a sigh. Greg had a telescope and he would gaze at the sky on clear nights, learning the names of the constellations and the planets and the stars. He wanted to be an astronomer when he grew up. She remembers a summer night when he was about ten. He'd been talking for weeks about a meteor shower in the Pleiades, and he wanted his parents to watch it with him. Greg spread a blanket in the front yard, well away from the trees, and as soon as it became dark, the four of them lay on their backs and watched the heavens. Hazel remembers how shocked she was at the richness of the night sky. How long had it been since she'd had time to gaze at stars? Lucy went to sleep almost immediately, but Hazel and Harlan and Greg watched for hours as the meteors flashed across the sky, so ephemeral that if they blinked their eyes, they missed them. Greg had been mesmerized, and Hazel remembers the wonder in his eyes as he lay beside her, his dark curls scattered across his forehead, the strong curve of his jaw, so like his father's, and the way he silently sought out her hand. She knew then that her kids' childhoods were like those meteoric flashes, gone so quickly that it took your breath away.

Tears gather at the corners of Hazel's eyes. Angrily she scrubs them away with her knuckles and refocuses her attention on the blobs. They had alarmed her at first, but since they don't seem to do much but float and weave, Hazel reckons that they are harmless. *Perhaps they are some rare natural phenomenon,* she speculates. *Or perhaps not. Maybe they're from outer space. Or maybe they're angels or demons.* She wishes there were someone she could ask, but there isn't. Nobody whose opinion she would respect anyway, thinking of the young pastor at St. John's Lutheran who looks like he's about fifteen years old and gives sermons with the damnedest titles, like "How Would Mary and Martha

Feed Jesus Today?"

Personally, Hazel thinks they would send out for KFC, since nobody seems to cook anymore. The whole nation lives on junk food, Hazel observes furiously as she studies the contents of other shoppers' grocery carts on her visits to the Safeway. No wonder everybody's so fat and sickly.

Hazel takes vitamins and rolls out her own whole-grain tortillas, and every spring she fasts on organic juices for a slap month to rejuvenate her liver. She intends to live to be 103 like her own mother did—maybe longer, since her mother never knew about liver rejuvenation.

Along about 1:30, Hazel gets too sleepy to keep up with the comings and goings of the lights. She lifts Marigold carefully off her thighs and places her on the foot of the bed, then lies down and draws up the sheet. She switches on the radio and tunes in *Coast to Coast AM*. George Noory is interviewing a man from some UFO reporting outfit. Hazel wonders fleetingly if she should call in and ask if they know anything about her lights, but in fifteen seconds, she is deeply asleep.

Hazel sleeps late—at least for Hazel, 6:00 is late. She wakens to the molten sun pouring heat into her bedroom already at this hour. As she makes breakfast, she recalls the lights floating over the corral. Maybe she ought to speak to the sheriff. God knows, Bobby Santiago of all people would take her seriously. But then again, maybe not. *Nobody takes old people seriously,* she reflects irritably, and although Hazel regards herself as middleaged, she knows that other folks don't.

After a quick shower, Hazel waters her garden and feeds Octavia and Marigold and the chickens. Mad Max heads off into the brush to hunt prairie dogs. By then it's time to drive into town for her volunteer shift at the nursing home. Out on the county road, Hazel notes a pile of darkish clouds spilling over the western mountains, and she flips on the radio to the NOAA weather band. "Thank God," she whispers out loud as she listens to a forecast of rain.

Hazel's first job at the nursing home is to feed patients who need help eating. She gets Rupert Sunderson's tray. Rupert is younger than Hazel, but he had a bad stroke last year and with no kinfolks he ended up here. The old people are object lessons for Hazel. They are living proof of what happens when you give up, refuse to take care of yourself, eat junk food and watch TV and drink and smoke. First it's those little electric carts at Wal-Mart—complete with a compartment to carry your oxygen—when you get too fat to walk. Then you're only a small stroke or heart attack away from the county home, watching TV in the day room with other people who slobber and drool and talk nonsense. The other indignities hardly bear thinking about: enemas and Attends, and pretty young CNAs wiping your butt and talking baby talk while they mop cream-of-wheat off your chin.

Rupert is a huge man, both tall and fat, and getting him into a wheelchair is out of the question. He spends his time in bed, waiting for death. Nevertheless, he is unaccountably cheerful. Hazel wonders if his good mood is from brain damage brought on by the stroke. Hazel intends to shoot herself if such a thing happens to her.

Hazel washes Rupert's face and hands and sets up his breakfast on the tray table. Rupert gives Hazel his most angelic smile—a half-smile, that is, since the right side of his face is paralyzed. Feeding Rupert takes a long time. Hazel arranges a napkin under his chin and sticks a straw in a carton of apple juice. Rupert takes a long sip and smiles again. Apple juice runs down his chin and throat and onto his napkin. Hazel looks at her half-day each week at the nursing home as her Christian duty. Since Rupert doesn't speak much, Hazel tells him stories while she feeds him. Usually, she talks about things she reads in *The Denver Post* or on Bill O'Reilly's website, but this morning all Hazel can think about are the lights.

What the heck? she figures. Rupert is safe. If he thinks she's crazy, that's okay. It's not like he'll summon the charge nurse and have Hazel committed to some loony bin. So she tells Rupert about the lights as she spoons stewed prunes, scrambled eggs and oatmeal into his mouth. Rupert looks Hazel straight in the eye as she speaks, and when he is finished eating, he makes a coughing sound. "What?" Hazel asks.

Rupert leans toward her with some effort and clears his throat. "I saw 'em too, back in ninety-seven," he whispers.

Hazel is momentarily speechless. "Where?" she demands finally. Rupert coughs and wheezes some more and Hazel gives him a handful of Kleenex. "Please tell me," she says.

Rupert clears his nose noisily and wipes awkwardly at his eyes. "My Caroline," he begins in his halting way.

"Yes," Hazel answers. Rupert's wife had died in a highway accident—when was it? Nine, ten years ago? Her lover, someone everyone in the county knew about except Rupert, had died with her. Hazel leans forward in her chair and listens for the next twenty minutes as Rupert tells her about his lights.

Hazel drives home slowly. Heavy curtains of rain have shrouded the foothills, and they are beginning to sweep out over the plain where giant drops send up cloudlets of dust as they strike the road. Then it begins to pour, but Hazel hardly notices. She switches on the windshield wipers and her windshield is clean for the first time in weeks. When she finally pulls up next to the house, she turns off the ignition and sits until the rain stops. Hazel is deeply afraid.

Nothing has frightened Hazel since her son was blasted to shreds by the land mine and her husband blew his head off. Five years ago, Hazel wakened in the night to the snickers of burglars pillaging her house. She calmly got out of bed, walked halfway downstairs and confronted two kids in their twenties. They had cut the throat of her elderly German shepherd, Fritz, who lay at the bottom of the stairs in a small pond of congealing blood. When the kids saw her, they grinned at each other and rubbed their hands together like movie caricatures. "We gonna have us some fun, ain't we?" the first one told the second. "C'mere, old bitch," said the second one. "Whatcha got behind your back?"

The kid started toward Hazel, stepping over Fritz and putting his foot on the first step. Hazel shot him twice in the chest just as the look of surprise began to claim his face, then immediately shot the second one before he could turn his back. After that, she reloaded, called the Chipita County Sheriff's office, got dressed and made a pot of coffee. It was ready to drink by the time Bobby Santiago and his deputy arrived.

Hazel waits for the lights to return. She finds herself waking at odd hours and going to the window to look out over the corral. The nights are clear and the moon is waxing, rendering the landscape black and silver. Coyotes howl, crickets sing, raccoons scrabble and owls hoot, but the glowing blobs do not appear.

Nevertheless, after the full moon passes and the weather begins to cool toward fall, she is awakened once again by the glare of light through the window. Hazel sits up, a chill making gooseflesh of her arms. She steps into her jeans, pulls on a shirt.

She tries to tie her Reeboks but she is shivering so violently that she can't. Without turning on a light, she creeps down the stairs and out the back door. The tubs of yellow day lilies that flank the stoop look almost black in the dark as Hazel leaves the shelter of the house and moves toward the corral. It's very quiet. There are no sounds of insects or small creatures rustling in the chamisa, no wind.

Over the corral, two blobs of light hover expectantly, maybe thirty feet overhead. Hazel has not brought her forty-five. She goes to the corral fence and places her hands on the top rail to stop their trembling.

"What do you want?" she asks aloud.

The lights quiver, as if contemplating her question, and Hazel hears the crunch of boots on gravel behind her. She whirls around, her heart slamming. "My God!" she exclaims, putting her hand to her throat. "You like to scared me to death!"

Standing a few yards off are her husband and her son. It seems the most natural thing in the world to see them there in their Levi jackets and jeans and broad-brim hats, grinning at her like they've just come back from a long and particularly successful hunting trip. Harlan approaches, removing his hat. She sees that he looks as he did in his early thirties, before he lost his hair, before Greg went to Vietnam.

"I'll make coffee," Hazel says. "I'll cook us some breakfast."

Harlan smiles and kisses her on the lips. "No, Honey," he says. "We can't stay that long. I love you, Hazel. I always loved you, ever since that drive-in movie."

And then Greg is beside her too. "Mama," he says, embracing her, "remember that lamb we saved in the spring blizzard when I was fourteen?"

"Of course I do," Hazel replies. "Rosie." They had found the lamb huddled under its frozen mother. She and Greg had taken it into the house and fed it from a bottle, and Greg had warmed the lamb with his own body. Rosie followed Greg around like a puppy until he went off to basic training.

"I never thanked you for that."

"You didn't have to, Son," Hazel says, her eyes streaming.

"Hazel, we've got to go now," Harlan says.

"It's all right, Mama," Greg smiles. "Everything's good." And before Hazel can say another word, the two men dissolve like smoke. Hazel has forgotten the lights, and when she turns back to the corral, they are gone.

From her rocking chair by the window, Hazel watches the sun come up. First the sky goes deep blue as one by one the stars dull and fade out. Then come bands of purple and fuchsia and orange intersected by fanning rays of crimson and gold. The colors are so intense that Hazel thinks her heart might break. Mad Max is stretched out at her feet on the Mexican rug, all four paws in the air, and his head is twisted at an angle only a cat could tolerate. In her lap, Marigold half snoozes, waking occasionally to lick salt from Hazel's cheeks.

Hazel has been weeping nonstop for four-and-a-half hours, ever since she came back into the house. At first, the tears were bitter as gall, but as she continued to cry, hour after hour, the bitterness passed into something else, something to which she will have to devote a great deal of thought.

Hazel is all cried out for now. Crumpled tissues are piled in a drift next to the rocker as though she had opened her window to a winter storm. Maybe she should sleep for awhile. Or maybe she should eat something. She thinks about the pot of pinto beans on the back of the stove, the *ristra* of red chilies drying in the kitchen window and fresh eggs from her hens. Yes, surely food is what she needs. And strong coffee. Perhaps she will call Lucy after breakfast. Hazel eases the puppy off her lap, then rises stiffly from the chair. Every muscle and bone in her body aches as though she's been in a bar fight.

Even so, Hazel notices, she feels lighter than she has in years.

ABOUT THE AUTHOR

JANE LAWLESS, a Chicago native, has worked as a script writer for an Emmy Award-winning children's television show, senior editor of *Chicago Quarterly Review*, freelance editor, and writer-producer of educational materials, including an audio tour-guide program for Chicago's Field Museum of Natural History. Her short stories have appeared in *Absolutes!*, *Bellowing Ark*, *Big Muddy*, *Chicago Quarterly Review*, *The Clothesline Review*, *descant*, *Rosebud* and *Zahir*. She has been a resident of Colorado Springs, Colorado, since 2000. Jane and her husband, Rick, are the managers and vintners of a private wine co-op, Lingering Deer Winery, where they live with two cats and assorted wild creatures on the edge of the Pike National Forest.

Made in the USA
Charleston, SC
16 February 2017